For Snowy.
In fond memory of a good friend
Doreen Wells.
Jan 1937–July 2017

THE
FOURTH
FRIEND

DI Jackman & DS Evans Book 3

JOY ELLIS

Published in paperback 2020
by Joffe Books, London
www.joffebooks.com

ISBN- 978-1-78931-176-1

Printed and bound in Great Britain by

Clays Ltd, Elcograf S.p.A.

PROLOGUE

Carter McLean stared out of the plane's tiny window at a vast cumulonimbus. The pilot had assured them they would make it through the storm, and Carter trusted him. He had flown with him before.

The plane dropped suddenly, making his stomach lurch, and then there was nothing but grey cloud, and rain lashing the window. They were in.

Carter enjoyed an adrenalin rush. Throughout his life, he'd never taken the easy route. And now his job as a CID drugs squad detective kept him where he liked to be — on the front line. So with a grim smile, he pulled his safety belt a little tighter and braced himself for a bumpy ride.

In retrospect, maybe he would not have been so cavalier if he had known that the plane was approximately thirty seconds from going down.

The engine noise changed, the steady thrum seemed to break up, cough. Carter peered through the sheets of rain slashing across the cockpit windows. He frowned, not understanding what he was seeing. Trees? He put his hands over his ears, the aircraft lurched drunkenly to one side and it seemed to scream. Carter's mouth was dry as sandpaper. He looked at his four best friends. Just moments ago they had been discussing Ray's stag weekend and his forthcoming wedding. Now their faces were masks of horror and disbelief. They knew what was coming.

Carter felt no panic. Instead, he felt cheated. He was thirty-six, fit and healthy. He had all his teeth, a full head of hair. It was too soon.

Sounds inside the cabin became hollow, slow and echoing. When it happened, the impact was not sudden. The six-seater Piper Seneca jerked and slewed, ricocheting across the uneven ground. Then with a scream of tearing metal, one wing ripped away and the plane's nose dug into the earth, throwing the tail section high into the air and flinging its occupants forward towards the cockpit.

* * *

Carter couldn't move. He had no idea why, and no inclination to find out. For a while he seemed to float in the eerie silence. It was a cold, disturbing quiet. The only thing he could hear was a ringing in his ears.

He lay, suspended. It could have been hours, days even. Then, from the remains of the cockpit, a tangle of exposed wiring suddenly fizzed and spat. Carter needed to act.

He moaned. He tried to move and found that something was pinning him to the back of the pilot's seat. It took a while to realise that it was Jack's weighty torso, crushing him and forcing the air from his lungs.

He tried to slide from under his friend's motionless body and cried out at the pain that tore through his chest. The safety belt, before it tore free, must have broken his ribs. He thought of the wire, fizzing like a lit fuse, and knew he had to get out, fast. Groaning, he managed to ease out from beneath Jack.

'Guys . . . ?' Was that his voice? He sounded like an eight-year-old. 'Hey, guys? Are you okay?' He waited.

'Oh, sweet Jesus!' Tom's Scouse accent filtered across the cabin's gloom. 'Carter? Is that you?'

He closed his eyes in relief. Tom was his best mate. Tall, dark, and far from handsome, but all heart. 'Yeah, it's me. Are you injured, mate?'

'I dunno, but my head bloody well hurts.' There was a pause. 'Oh my God! The others?'

Carter stared across at Jack's lifeless body. He had seen many dead bodies. It was his job. But those bodies, although often terribly harmed, were strangers. This was one of his closest friends.

Jack's throat was split open. His shirt was dark with blood. Something had sliced through his windpipe, severing it, and the creamy white bones of his spinal column were visible through foamy blood. Carter stifled a sob and began to cast around for the others. There was little or no hope for the pilot. He hung, half in, half out of the torn cockpit section of the plane, his head at an impossible angle to his limp body.

At least Matt was still breathing. Thank God! Carter could hear his uneven gasps and see the erratic rise and fall of his chest. One of the seats had ripped from the bulkhead and pinned both his legs to the floor.

Ray. 'I can't see Ray,' said Carter.

'He's here. Still trapped in his seat.' Tom's heavily accented voice came back quickly. 'He's out cold and his arm's a mess, but he has a pulse and it's pretty strong.'

The wiring spat and crackled again. Carter fought to quell his rising panic. 'We have to get out of here. Tom, I think I'm close to the door. If I can open it, we can drag the others out.'

'The pilot's dead, isn't he?' whispered Tom. 'And you haven't mentioned Jack or Matt.' His voice shook.

'Matt's alive, but we can't deal with their injuries now. We have to get them out and away from this wreck! It could go up at any moment.' Carter crawled towards the door and struggled with the lock.

'Ahh! Shit!' Pain tore through his neck, arm and shoulder. The door remained jammed shut. 'You have to help me, Tom! The sodding thing is buckled. I can't budge it.' He groaned again. 'I've bust some ribs and I think my arm is knackered too. I can't grip the damn thing!'

Carter heard muffled swearing and then Tom was crawling into the tiny space between Jack, bits of wreckage, and the door.

'Jack? Oh no!' Tom looked at his friend and crossed himself.

'The door!' breathed Carter. 'Concentrate on the door! We have to get them out of here!'

Tom drew in a noisy breath and knelt beside him. 'Okay, okay, you're right. Look, you free the handle and get ready to push. I'll brace myself and kick forward with both feet. Ready?' He sat down and put his feet to the door.

Carter nodded, twisted the handle and screamed. The door flew open, catapulting him from the plane, a human projectile.

He hit the sodden ground painfully. The Piper had come to rest at an acute angle. The wing had torn off, and this had lifted the right side of the fuselage high into the air. To his horror, the door, now flapping open, was some ten feet above him. He shrieked into the wind. 'Tom! I can't get back in! Just push them out and I'll try to drag them to safety!'

Tom's face appeared in the doorway. 'I'll get Ray and Matt first. Maybe they have a chance.'

The face disappeared. Then Tom was back at the door, 'I've got Ray,' he gasped. 'He's still unconscious. Are you ready down there?'

'Just get him out!' wheezed Carter, and stared up at the dark hole above him.

Tom moved back into the plane and began to drag Ray forward.

A sudden squall of rain and wind blasted against the wreckage, and slammed the door closed. Carter froze.

'Tom?'

4

Carter could see the dark shape of his friend desperately throwing himself against the jammed door. He staggered to his feet and stared up, aghast. Carter could see Tom clearly, silhouetted against the bright light coming from the interior of the cabin. He stepped back, his jaw slack and his eyes unblinking. It wasn't just light, it was flames. Tom's gentle face was now twisted in anguish.

With a cry, Carter started forward and tried to claw his way back up to the closed door. He forgot his pain in his struggle to get back to his friends.

The blast denied him even that.

* * *

At dawn the next morning, Carter McLean awoke and tried to ease himself up in the uncomfortable hospital bed. With each movement, the pain in his ribs tore the breath from his lungs and left him gasping. When at last the pain subsided, Carter saw Tom sitting at the bottom of the bed, staring in silence at his burnt and blistered hands.

It wasn't just Tom. On the other side of the room Matt, Ray and Jack leaned against the wall and argued noisily about whether Man U could win the Europa League or finish in the top four.

Carter tried not to look at them. Something was terribly wrong. Why had he received immediate treatment while his friends were left untended? He looked closer. They hadn't even cleaned up Jack's neck. His head wobbled unnaturally each time he spoke. If the doctors don't do something soon, thought Carter, it will fall off.

And poor Matt! His legs looked like raw meat. Worried about infection, Carter rang the bell for the nurse.

'No point, mate,' said Tom quietly. 'Why don't you just try to get some rest and forget about us for a while?'

'But I don't understand,' whispered Carter.

'No, I know, I know. But just try to sleep, yeah?'

Carter stared at his best friend, and tears coursed down his face. He only knew it was Tom because of his accent. Half of his face was gone, and most of his flesh. He smelt awful. The acrid stench clung to Carter like a second skin. 'Why don't they *do* something?' Carter whined. He barely recognised his own voice.

'Because it's too late. So you just rest, huh? We've got to go now, but we'll talk later. Try to make things better, alright?' Tom stood up, beckoned to the others, and they followed him out of the room.

Must be their turn for treatment. He hoped so. He bit his lip. He knew the health service was in a bad way, but their treatment of his friends was appalling. With a sigh, he pushed the button on the morphine pump, slid down under the sheets and waited for oblivion.

CHAPTER ONE

Eighteen Months Later

DI Rowan Jackman handed DS Marie Evans a memo. 'Have you seen this?'

Marie skimmed through it, and handed it back. 'Carter McLean? Yes, he's been returned to full duties as from next week.'

Jackman raised his eyebrows. 'You don't look exactly delighted.'

Marie shrugged. 'I'm not sure how I feel, sir.'

'He's been riding a desk for almost six months now, and doing a damned good job too. I'm sure he's ready. I heard that he steamrollered through his medical assessment.' Jackman smiled at her.

'Mmm.'

His smiled faded. 'What's that supposed to mean, Marie? What's the problem?'

Marie sank down into a chair and sighed. 'I've been friends with Carter for a very long time, sir, and I'm sorry but I don't think the force medical officer and those in charge are seeing the whole picture.' She paused. 'Well, I think Laura Archer has her reservations, but she's just one voice against many.'

'Surely, as the consultant for the psychological assessment, she would have the greatest say?'

Marie nodded. 'I think she doesn't want to stand in Carter's way. If he believes that he is ready, she is prepared to go along with the FMO, at least for a trial period.'

'He'll be monitored carefully, I'm sure.' But Marie still looked worried. Jackman stood up and went to the door, closed it and returned to his seat. 'If you are really concerned, my friend, perhaps we should talk about it.'

Marie sighed. 'Yes. Especially since he'll be working with us, and we are in the middle of investigating the disappearance of Suzanne Holland.'

Jackman nodded. 'Ah, I see. The wife of one of Carter McLean's dead friends.'

'Carter says that obviously he knew her. After all, she was the wife of his oldest mate. But they were never great pals or anything. Even so . . .' Marie shook her head.

'Mmm, but it's a connection to the past, isn't it? Something Carter does not need.'

'Exactly," she said. "I think he wants to prove that he's fit for whatever the job throws at him, even if it's painful.'

'Painful *and* dangerous,' added Jackman. 'I've seen coppers and soldiers suffer from flashbacks, and it isn't pleasant.'

'I get the feeling the upper echelons have decided that as long as he can pass muster as a police officer, they don't give a shit if his world falls apart as soon as he gets inside his own front door,' Marie said angrily.

Jackman looked at her. 'You think that's what's happening? On the surface, he seems to be coping remarkably well. The chief constable thinks his conduct is pretty amazing, considering what he's been through.'

'God! He makes it sound like a stiff upper lip is all you require to recover! And you too, sir. Talk about *Carry on Regardless!* Marie was almost shouting.

8

Jackman looked at her in surprise. Such an outburst was most uncharacteristic. Then he laughed. 'That's not what I meant, and you know it. Carter McLean has just put a really high-profile case to the Crown Prosecution Service. Complex stuff, but he's nailed it. *And* without moving out of the CID office.'

'Yes, *exactly*. You said it yourself, sir, he did it from the office. He's *safe* there. He's in control. Unless the Good Lord was unkind enough to crash a plane directly on top of the nick, he's unlikely to have to confront his worst fears in the CID room, is he?' Marie frowned. 'It's when he's alone in his bed that I suspect things get really bad.'

'He's still having nightmares?'

Marie nodded. 'Carter McLean will probably be having nightmares for a very long time, along with disturbed sleep patterns, increased anxiety, panic attacks, clinical depression, oh yes, and those flashbacks you mentioned.'

Jackman stared at her. 'You seem to know a lot about this.'

'I know very little, other than what Carter has told me himself. We've talked a lot.' She gave him a sad smile. 'He was my Bill's crewmate when they were in uniform, and they were very close. I saw a lot of Carter before Bill was killed, and I guess I feel I owe it to Bill to try to be there for his old friend.' She paused. 'Someone has to look out for him. After that bloody crash, he has no one else left.'

Jackman nodded slowly. 'I see. Well, I do understand what you are saying about him, but he really is keeping it together remarkably well at work.'

'As I said before, it's a safe place to be, and what else has he got, sir? He needs the stability of the job he loves. He was always so damned good at the paperwork side that he probably put that whole last case together simply by working through the records. I'm just not so sure how he will react out in the great wide world.'

'We need to let him try, Marie. You know what they say, *The one who falls and gets up is so much stronger than the one who never fell.*'

'Oh Lord, you sound like one of those ghastly life coaches.'

'You think maybe I should stick to detective work?'

'A very good idea, sir.' Marie grinned.

'Well, before we get stuck in to some proper police work, have you read the new directive from the chief superintendent?'

'Oh yes, but I'm not paying too much attention to it.' She grimaced. 'Nor will most of the other officers here.'

'Personally, I can't see a problem with it.' Jackman sat back. 'We obviously can't take it too far, but we are all working together in a very demanding job, and we become a pretty tightknit unit. I think relaxing some of the "sirs" and "ma'ams" is a good thing. I'm more than happy for my colleagues to address me as Jackman. They are closer to me than most of my family! Sometimes I think they *are* my family.' He grinned. 'We'll just need to make sure Max doesn't call the super, "Me old cock sparra!"'

'Perish the thought!' Marie laughed. DC Max Cohen was one person who would have no trouble with relaxing the rules. The young detective came from the East End of London, and he had never lost his distinctive Cockney accent. 'Still, it wouldn't come easy to most of us and frankly, I think there should be boundaries. Some of the rookies really need them.'

'Surely those of us with rank should win the young-sters' respect by the way we behave and work? Most forces dropped the formalities years ago. We in the Fens are just behind the times.'

'Nothing new there, then.' Marie still looked unconvinced. 'And we aren't "most other forces." I can't see it working here, sir.'

'Oh well, ask the others what they think, and I'll report back to the super.'

Marie nodded absently. 'I was going to ask if the super has given Carter the go-ahead to work here, considering we have the Holland case running.'

'She's tight-lipped where Carter is concerned. You know they've never been the best of friends.' Jackman raised an eyebrow. 'She says that as far as she's concerned there is no conflict of interest. She can see no problem with Carter being part of our investigation, unless he finds it difficult, then naturally she would have to relocate him.'

'So we play it by ear?'

'One day at a time.' Jackman looked serious. 'Marie, you know Carter McLean better than any of us, so watch him like a hawk, okay?'

Marie nodded solemnly, though she really did not need to be told this. She was worried sick about Carter, and she was not about to take her eyes off him. Not for one minute.

* * *

Jackman and Marie were not the only people reflecting on the case of Carter McLean. Laura Archer stared gloomily at her computer screen and wondered if her thesis would ever see the light of day.

Muttering a curse, she stood up and began to pace her office. Who would have thought *A Study into Psychosocial Transitions* could be so bloody draining? But then it wasn't the thesis that was really bothering her.

She saved the document and reluctantly closed the program.

Her first meeting with Carter McLean had caused her heart to leap, for no other reason than that he was the perfect case study for her paper. He was complex, one of the most interesting clients she had ever dealt with. Now she was reconsidering her decision to use him as her key study. In fact, she was on the verge of abandoning the whole thing and starting again. With a sigh, she headed to the kitchen. Time for yet another coffee.

She spooned coffee into the jug, thinking about her meeting with Barry Richards, the force medical officer. The conversation had left her with an uneasy feeling, and his words reverberated in her head. Six months ago, a medical panel had decided that Carter McLean was physically fit to return to work. The only person to disagree was Superintendent Ruth Crooke, who in any case had nothing to do with the final decision. Laura and Richards had agreed that Carter ticked all the right boxes and was good to go. He would start with desk work, and if he showed no deterioration, he would be allowed to return to full duties.

Now Laura was perturbed, but she had no idea why. Her gut instinct told her something was very wrong, and her gut never let her down. She was still seeing Carter once a month for counselling, and on the face of it, he was doing very well. Or rather, Carter was doing very well *at work*. She had a deep suspicion that away from the office, things were very different. For Carter McLean was a very good actor. Sometimes he even fooled her, and she was a psychologist. His work colleagues would be a pushover.

She took a mug from the cupboard, threw in two lumps of sugar and waited for the coffee to brew. It wasn't Carter, but Richards who was bugging her. The conversation had gone like this:

'Absolutely incredible, the way he's coped. If you saw him in his working environment, Laura, you'd be pretty astounded too. He's a real trooper to come back from all that. Top Brass are very impressed with him. You should know that they are talking about moving him up the ladder if he carries on the way he is now,' Richards said.

Laura inhaled slowly. She raised her eyebrows. 'Well, that's certainly not something I'd recommend just yet. In fact, if you want my opinion, I strongly oppose any such suggestion. Out of his comfort zone, you might find that Carter McLean doesn't act the way your Gold Braid expect him to.'

'Well, as far as his commanding officers are concerned, if we've signed him fit for duty, he's fit for duty, along with everything that

involves, including possible promotion. But okay, I respect your assessment and I'll take it on board. Nothing's concrete as yet, although I'd hate to be the one to stand in the way of someone's promotion.'

'And I'd hate to be the one to light the blue touch paper.'

The FMO shrugged. 'All right, you win. I'll monitor him for a while. At least that will please Superintendent Crooke. She was the only one to oppose the suggestion.'

'Well, that's par for the course, I guess. Carter told me that Crooke has never liked him, and it's common knowledge that Carter only got his last promotion because she was away helping with the hunt for the Golf Course Killer.'

'I hadn't realised that old feud was still going on. Hey, did you know Carter's running the marathon?'

She grinned. 'Yes. He made quite sure that I put my name on his sponsor sheet beside an exorbitant sum of money! He's running on behalf of Matthew Blake.'

'Ah, one of his deceased friends.'

'Mmm. Nice lad, by all accounts. He was a master carpenter. Carter wanted his friend to have what he called a "meaningful memorial."'

'But actually he's done it out of a sense of guilt?'

'Almost certainly. He blames himself for the whole thing. In his mind, he owes all of them, big time.'

'Well, it wasn't exactly his fault that the pilot tried to take on a storm force gale that had suddenly changed direction. I saw the accident report. He should have asked to be vectored away from the worst of the storm, but they believe he took a "push through" decision and, well, he misjudged it and paid with his life.'

'And that of four young men. And Carter believes it is entirely his fault. He organised the stag do in Amsterdam. He chartered the plane. Ergo, he is to blame. If it had been down to the other lads, they'd have had too many beers in a club in town, ripped Ray's pants off and tied him to a lamp post. Everyone goes home and has a monster hangover. End of story.'

'But instead, they all died, except Carter.'

'Exactly. With the exception of Carter.'

'So how on earth does he cope so well with work?'

'As I said, he's in an environment he understands. He's in command of what happens. Luckily his friends weren't coppers, so there's no connection there either. He's not immediately reminded of a dead friend every time he sees a uniform.'

'How come they were such a close group? From what the papers said about them it seemed that they were all as different as chalk and cheese.'

'Carter knew Tom Holland from school. Apparently they teamed up with the others doing voluntary work with disabled and disadvantaged kids. Some kind of outward bound holiday thing? They just gelled. Then they found an old lifeboat rotting away in a boatyard down on the estuary. They'd spent the last five years restoring it, using Carter's money, their joint expertise and hard work. I understand it was almost finished.'

'The best laid plans, and all that. Let's just hope McLean gets rid of the damn thing. He'd never be able to set foot on board without thinking of his mates.'

Laura smiled. 'I don't think that's quite how Carter sees it. It's very precious to him, but for now, he's rather sensibly making no decisions about it.'

'Well, in conclusion, I'm very happy with his progress, and as we still have two more cases to discuss, perhaps we should move on . . . ?'

Laura pressed the plunger on the cafetiere down hard. So that was that. Carter was fine. End of story. We can all move on.

She poured her coffee and stirred it, slopping some onto the table. Carter McLean was far from fine. She knew it. Maybe she was closer to him than most — well, she should be, it was her job to be. She would hate to see the force put pressure on him simply through sheer ignorance. He needed stability and order in his life, not the stress of a new position — the responsibility, the administrative garbage, and the interminable senior management team sessions it would involve. It seemed the only thing that the powers that be had listened to was her suggestion that he take a step back from the drugs squad. It would have had

14

him racing all over the place on dawn raids and the like. She gave a small laugh. Like so many other specialist units, the drugs squad had been disbanded, so her suggestion had amounted to nothing in the end.

For some reason she felt unusually protective of Carter McLean. She was no fool. She knew what disasters befell therapists who became personally involved with their clients. It was just that she *liked* Carter. Nothing more. Some people you just liked, and he was one of them.

She took the coffee back to her office and opened up her paper again. Sadly, she thought, this was the problem. Carter McLean was interwoven with her thesis as tightly as an Axminster carpet. A sudden, serious accident, like his, was one of the most stressful of life changes, and one of the most dangerous to mental health. And that was what her paper dealt with — life events, their impact and finding appropriate coping mechanisms.

For the fifth time she re-read what she had written, and wondered if it would be prudent to shelve it for a while. Every time she began working on it, those niggling worries about Carter crept back into her head, and her concentration flew out the window. Better to leave it for a while, until Carter McLean no longer occupied such a large part of her thoughts.

With a sigh, Laura closed the document and checked her diary. She looked through her games, selected Mahjong and began to play.

CHAPTER TWO

Carter threw himself across the finish line, pushed the timer button on his watch, and collapsed onto the tarmac. His lungs felt as though they were full of hot coals and his legs were like jelly.

The atmosphere, the camaraderie that came from running with thousands of others had not been the thing that spurred him on. He had run the twenty-six miles and three hundred and eighty-five yards alone, in a big private bubble of pain.

He accepted the thermal blanket that a steward wrapped around him, and as he tried to thank the man, he found he had no voice. Tears were streaming down his face.

He'd done it! He'd actually done it. But not for himself. No, he'd done it for Matt. Well, for Matt's dad to be precise.

After his dad had died, Matt had felt the need to do something in his father's name, something special. Tom had suggested the East Coast Marathon and Matt was well up for it. But no matter how hard he tried, he never quite built up the fitness level or the stamina for the long, gruelling race. Now that Matt was gone, Carter was running it for him. It was the least he could do.

On the back of his vest there was a picture of Matt Blake Senior, and the legend, "I'm running for Matt and supporting the Macmillan Fund."

Carter staggered to his feet, and saw two of his fellow police officers jogging over the line. He must have overtaken them somewhere, but he hadn't even seen them.

'Blimey! Talk about focus!' gasped DC Max Cohen. 'I was sure we'd beat you by a mile at least.' The two young coppers sank to the ground beside him.

'Yeah, that's what they call *in the zone*. You were in a world of your own, sir,' gasped DC Charlie Button.

Carter managed a painful grin. 'It's the only way I could do it,' he gasped.

He'd been training for six months. Not just running, but studying the science behind it too. He'd worked out his food and training regime like a pro. And it had worked. He'd made a hell of a lot of money from his sponsors, and he had promised Matt that whatever he made, he'd match it from his own pocket.

He slowly moved off after his two colleagues to collect his medal. Matt's medal. He touched the shiny metal almost reverently.

It was done.

* * *

A couple of other officers from their station collected them up in a 4 x 4 and drove them home. Most of the lads were meeting later for a celebratory drink in the social club, but Carter declined. The last thing he wanted was to share his evening with a raucous bunch of coppers, all getting rat-arsed. Anyway, he was expecting guests.

He showered, pulled on some loose pants and a sweater, and went down the wide, open-plan stairs to his lounge. He unlocked the big patio doors and slid them open. Then he leaned on the rail of his wide balcony and stared out. The vista stretched for miles across the landscaped gardens, to the town and the acres of fields beyond.

He should be grateful. He was the owner of an apartment that most people only ever saw in magazines. He could furnish it with the best of everything and not even need to check his bank balance. It meant nothing to him. How was it that he felt so empty, so detached, so cut adrift from life?

He walked back inside and poured himself a drink. There was no point trying to find answers, and anyway, they'd be here soon. He glanced at his watch, flopped down onto the couch and picked up the TV remote. For a while he flicked through the channels, then pressed the off button. He wondered why he'd bothered with the best TV money could buy when he couldn't concentrate on anything.

Carter threw the remote onto the soft leather of the couch and looked around. As always the apartment was meticulously tidy. Nothing out of place, no mess, no clutter, everything just so. Carter smiled bitterly. His mother would have been proud of him. He remembered Laura carefully explaining it to him. "Your whole life had broken down, Carter. It was chaos. It's quite natural that you now choose to live in a carefully structured environment. You have control over your world when everything is in its correct place."

She was right, of course. Laura Archer was a damned good shrink. Sometimes he wondered what she was doing working for the police. With her ability and endless patience, she could have made a fortune in private practice. And she was good-looking too.

Carter yawned. He ached all over, as though he had been play-fighting with a polar bear. He closed his eyes. Matt's charity stood to receive a pretty impressive cheque. He had raised nearly three grand today, plus his own contribution. Carter sighed. It was a small gesture, but it was the best he could do. He hoped it would make his friend happy.

His eyes were still closed, but now he knew they were there. A sickly smell of burning flesh was slowly filling the room. Deep down, Carter knew that it was his mind playing tricks — insidious, nasty tricks. He knew there was no such thing as ghosts. Like most policemen he was a staunch sceptic, but nevertheless, he saw them.

'So, you actually did it then?' Tom's voice held a touch of admiration. 'That's champion, mate.'

'Yeah, well done,' said Jack. 'I bet it hurt like hell. How many blisters have you got?'

'Enough, thanks,' replied Carter dryly.

'Well, respect! I take my hat off to you, man. I'm damn sure I couldn't have done it.' Ray was always generous.

Carter opened his eyes. 'Where's Matt?'

'He said to say thank you.' Tom's voice was soft.

Carter looked at them. His friends visited him all the time, and this was the first time that one had failed to turn up. 'Is he okay? Is something wrong?'

'Nothing's wrong,' answered Ray. 'In fact he's good, he's really good.'

So why wasn't he here? Carter frowned. 'But the race, I . . . I wanted to tell him . . . it was for him, and his dad.'

'No need, mate. He knows.'

Carter closed his eyes and the smell began to dissipate. When he opened them again, he was alone.

* * *

Marie sat on her sofa. Her lodger sprawled opposite in a comfortable armchair.

PC Gary Pritchard had transferred from the neighbouring division of Harlan Marsh, and was currently occupying Marie's guest room. The arrangement was intended to last until Gary made up his mind whether he wanted to commute each day across miles of fenland, or sell his Harlan Marsh home and move to Saltern-le-Fen. Several months had now passed, and neither of them was tired of their new domestic situation. Gary was an excellent cook, and Marie had put on weight, but chose to ignore it. She hated cooking. She was tall and athletic-looking, especially in her motorcycle leathers. She could cope with a few extra pounds if it meant having more of Gary's "this'll set you up for the day" breakfasts. In return, she was the perfect landlady. She kept a clean, warm home and imposed no restrictions on her guest, besides feeding the cat if she was on a back-to-back shift. Two lonely people, both bereaved, were no longer quite so lonely. What was to lose?

Marie grinned at him over the rim of her wine glass. 'I hear Carter made it to the finish line ahead of Max and Charlie.'

'I know.' Gary shook his head. 'Between the three of them, I've spent a small fortune in sponsorship money.'

'You and me both. Carter was very persuasive, wasn't he?'

'He's going to double whatever he receives.' Gary stared into his glass. 'I though DI Jackman was well off, but Carter is something else. He's a very rich man, isn't he?'

Marie grimaced. 'In some ways. But even before the accident, he'd had a really tough life. No loving family, no siblings, just a cold, distant, workaholic father. His mother died when he was quite young. He was a very sad little boy.' She looked at Gary. 'My Bill was his best friend when he was in uniform. Another loss he's suffered.'

'He has something of a reputation, hasn't he? Bit of a risk taker? Not much he wouldn't do to bring the criminals to justice?' Gary shrugged. 'Whatever. I've not known him very long, but I like him.'

'Me too, and I've known him for years. I just don't like what is happening to him.'

'I don't think I could come back to work if something like that happened to me.' Gary shuddered. 'But he's younger than me. I suppose work will help to ease the pain. You can only hope that as time passes, he will find a way to live with the terrible memories.'

Marie wanted to agree with Gary, but in her heart of hearts, she could only see Carter's future as dark.

* * *

Jackman stared across the flat fields towards the marshes and the distant Wash. It was a beautiful summer evening and the setting sun was putting on one of its spectacular light shows. The darkening sky was shot through with bands of fiery orange and scarlet, and purple grey clouds gathered in great mountainous drifts. He never tired of the sunsets.

With a contented sigh, he walked to the door of his mill house and turned the key in the lock. He was hoping for an early night. He needed to make some kind of headway with the Suzanne Holland case, and he wouldn't do that if he was overtired. He thought of the blood at her house, the body gone and no witnesses to what happened. His contentment disappeared.

He sat down at the kitchen table. On the top of a pile of manila files lay the forensic report, giving details of the blood spatter analysis. He was certain that this evidence in particular pointed to foul play, and not an accident, as had been suggested at the time. Although it had happened some eighteen months before, the case had never been closed. Now Superintendent Ruth Crooke had received a request from the ACC to bring it to a conclusion. It seemed that an online group had taken it up and were running with all kinds of weird speculation. It was now the subject of some considerable comment on the Internet. It had become known that the missing woman, Suzanne, had been the wife of Tom Holland, who had died in a light aircraft crash shortly after she went missing. People were suddenly calling for answers and demanding that the authorities do more. It was Jackman's unhappy lot to take up the case again before it went viral.

Jackman heaved an irritated sigh and stared at the thick file in front of him. Bloody media! On top of all that, it seemed that Suzanne Holland might have led some sort of double life. She'd certainly had a chequered past. Every avenue the detectives explored produced more questions than answers.

Jackman closed the report and yawned loudly. He badly needed sleep. Suzanne Holland would have to wait until tomorrow.

His brain, however, had other ideas. At three in the morning, Jackman found himself pacing the bedroom floor. He hated investigations that had no structure. Was the woman dead? Had she wandered off after having some awful accident? Had she been abducted? Apparently she'd been something of a good-time girl but their investigations had unearthed no vengeful wife or jealous lover lurking in the shadows. She had been briefly married before, and her ex was now living a mostly intoxicated life as a holiday rep in Spain. Reading the old case files, Jackman found that no one had actually spoken to this man. He made a mental note to get someone to double check this first thing.

Jackman flopped back down on the bed.

Then there was another problem.

Marie was a positive, energetic person, but right now she looked eaten up with concern over McLean's imminent return to full duties. Jackman trusted Marie's judgement, and if she was worried, then he was worried too. Perhaps he should pull a few strings and keep Carter away from the Holland case. If Ruth Crooke had her way, Carter would stay behind a desk for all eternity. He had no idea why the two officers disliked each other so much, and did not intend to ask them. The feud had been running forever, and he really did not want to get involved.

For the first time in years they were fully staffed. CID had undergone a major overhaul over the past few months, but finally things seemed to be calming down. The Saltern-le-Fen detectives now worked together, allocating jobs to whoever had the smallest backlog on their desk. At last Jackman and Marie had several good officers to call on, and Ruth Crooke had told him to use whoever he needed.

His long-serving detectives, Max and Charlie, would work on the Holland disappearance, plus DC Robbie Melton, a new and very welcome transfer from a neighbouring division. Robbie's previous partner had been seriously injured on duty and after she left, he had been lost, unable to settle back into his old job. The change of scenery had worked wonders for him. Robbie had developed a real affinity for Marie Evans, and she liked him. He was slightly built and often wore jeans and a hoodie, but he was actually well into his thirties, despite looking almost like a teenager. His forte was blending in on the streets. He prided himself on the fact that no one ever gave him a second glance. In fact, Robbie was a very astute and intelligent detective.

Then there was DC Rosie McElderry. She was pretty bogged down in a drugs case at present, but could still lend a hand. And of course, they had good old PC Gary Pritchard.

Now for the downside — DS Carter McLean.

Jackman crawled back into bed and pulled the duvet over himself.

No, he would *not* put Carter on the Holland case. There were other investigations running that Carter could work on. Looking into the seedier side of his dead friend's missing wife was a definite no-no. He closed his eyes. At least that should make Marie slightly happier. He hoped so, because he didn't like the preoccupied, anxious expression he saw on his trusted sergeant's face these days. He needed the old Marie back.

CHAPTER THREE

'Marie?' It was three in the morning.

She recognised Carter's voice immediately. 'Are you okay?'

'Apart from being unable to sleep and worried sick, I'm fine.'

'That's not surprising, now, is it? Big day tomorrow, my man. Back on the front line.' She fought off sleep and spoke as casually as she could. But she was worried.

'I guess. But that's not why I phoned.' He sighed. 'Oh hell, Marie, this could have waited until tomorrow, I know, but I wanted to you to know how much I appreciate what a good mate you have been to me since . . . the accident. You've been my rock. To be honest, I don't know what I would have done without you.'

'Rubbish! You'd have done fine, and what have I done anyway? It's Laura you should be thanking.'

'We both know that's not true. You've listened to my inane ramblings and never criticised me once. Laura has been amazing, but it's her job. She's paid to worry about me. You're different. You've been a real friend.'

'I am your friend, Carter, and you were my Bill's closest mate. Would I leave you to suffer alone? Besides, if you'd ranted like that to anyone else, they'd have locked you up, and you are far too good a copper for that.'

Carter gave a low laugh. 'You are not wrong about locking me up!'

'Are you really *that* worried about tomorrow?' she asked softly. 'Three in the morning is a bit extreme, even for you.'

'I'll cope. I'm well on the mend. It's not that.'

There was a very long silence.

'I see them.'

Marie took a moment to realise what he meant. 'I'm sure you do. I saw Bill for months after he died — at the station, here in the garden, in shops . . .'

'No, I *see* them.'

'But that's natural, Carter. Denial is one of the stages of grief. *You* know that.'

'But I'm not denying anything. Jesus! I *know* they are dead. I watched them burn, didn't I? What I'm saying is that . . .' Carter stumbled over his words, then whispered hopelessly, 'I see them, really I do. And I smell them burning.'

Marie exhaled. She was just not prepared for this. Carter should be talking to Laura Archer. But apart from Laura, she was the only one Carter could speak to about what had happened. It was a heavy weight on her shoulders. Wise words were sometimes hard to come by, and she was never quite sure how to answer his questions. All she wanted to do was say something that would really help him, but every time she opened her mouth, the tired old clichés emerged.

She knew Laura Archer had warned him that he might "see" his friends, especially in crowded places or walking along the street. He would see them in his mind's eye in all the places where they had been together. After he was killed, Marie had seen her lovely husband everywhere. Laura had told Carter that because his trauma had been so extreme, he might even hallucinate in the early days. But these were no longer early days. Marie wondered what he was getting at. Was he thinking of spirits? Ghosts? Surely not! Not the down to earth DS Carter McLean. 'So how do you see them?' she asked quietly.

'Just like anyone else. They are as real as you and I.' Carter's tone was unnervingly matter-of-fact. 'I've been seeing them since day one. They mainly visit me at home in the evenings, but it can be anytime, anywhere.'

Marie shivered. They'd talked about his friends for hours, days. Sometimes it seemed like they talked about nothing else. But he'd never mentioned this. 'What do they do?' she asked tentatively.

Carter inhaled. 'We just hang out really. Try to make sense of things.'

Well, this made very little sense to her. She found it spooky. A group of dead guys "hanging out" at Carter's place. She surmised that it was Carter trying to make sense of everything. Imagining that his friends were there helped him sort out his screwed-up head.

'You do know they would never blame you, don't you?'

'Yeah, I know. They tell me that themselves. It's just that there's so much unfinished business. They never should have died, Marie. They all had things that they really needed to do. Things that were desperately important to them.'

Marie tried to massage her aching neck with her free hand. Surely, no one, whatever the circumstances, was ever prepared to die? We all leave unfinished business.

'The weird part is,' Carter paused, 'I believe it's down to me to finish what they started.'

Marie stopped rubbing her neck. The penny was dropping. 'Ah. Like the marathon?'

'Exactly. I didn't know it then. I just did it because it was Matt's dream. But he's gone, Marie. From the moment I crossed that line. The others still come, but Matt isn't with them anymore.'

26

'And you think that you've somehow freed him by doing this for him?'

'I do.'

Marie said nothing. She wondered what Laura Archer would make of it. Survivor's guilt, she supposed. Carter was trying to make amends. When she thought about it, it actually made a lot of sense. Carter had freed himself of his guilt about Matt. It was actually bloody great!

'So who is next?' she said.

Carter answered swiftly. 'I think it should be Ray. After all, it was all about him, wasn't it? The best stag do ever?' There was a catch in his voice.

Marie felt a rush of intense sadness. She cared for Carter in a way that was almost impossible to explain. There was something intensely vulnerable and sad about him that evoked the deepest emotions. Marie knew that she would lay down her life for Carter McLean, just as she would for Jackman. Carter would do the same for her. He had already stopped a wicked blade that might have ended Bill's life even sooner than it had been. In his turn, Bill had defended Carter against a crackhead with a gun. Not that Carter had ever been an angel. Gary had said that Carter was a risk taker. He was right. Carter bent rules and pushed boundaries to get a good collar, and thought nothing of it. He believed that the bad guys should always go down, one way or another. Yes, Carter was a chancer, but Marie had seen the lonely little boy inside, one with something to prove.

What could she do to help him right now, other than support him? His wounds had healed and he was physically fit. On the surface he was the same as ever, apart from a few small signs, like claustrophobia. Carter's most damaged part was hidden from the outside world. Only she and Laura Archer knew.

'So, about Ray?' Do you know what you can do to help him?'

Carter grunted. 'Hmm. I'm not sure yet, but I'll ask him when I see him next.'

* * *

Images of Carter shooting the breeze with dead men banished sleep completely. By four thirty, Marie had raided the fridge twice. She was on the verge of waking Gary and telling him everything, but stopped herself. Carter was her problem and hers alone.

And what had he meant by smelling them burn? Carter was outside the plane when it caught fire. He was unconscious when he was rescued. He could not have smelled their flesh burning, so what was that all about?

Marie took a loaf from the bread bin, hacked off a thick slice and slathered on a thick dollop of peanut butter.

She took her snack out to the conservatory and flopped into one of the rattan chairs. Rover, her elderly tabby cat, joined her. Rover was a great listener, never complained and rarely interrupted. She told him of her decision. She wasn't going to shoulder Carter's revelation alone. She wouldn't burden Jackman, though. He was in the middle of a high-profile inquiry. Tomorrow she would book an appointment to see Laura Archer.

Marie swallowed the last of her third pre-dawn snack, and returned to bed . . . to an hour's restless sleep and indigestion.

* * *

Carter was having an even worse night. At four fifteen, he pulled on his running clothes and left the apartment.

He ran towards the estuary along a narrow towpath. In the fleeting light of the moon breaking through cloud, the river snaked across the landscape like a great slick of oil. His feet pounded the riverbank in darkness, but he knew the route well. On nights like this, with the moon to guide him, he liked to take the longer circuit along the sea bank and the fen lanes, and back to his home via an alley-way that skirted the fishing boats. It was a gruelling run, but it was better than lying in bed waiting for some new nightmare.

He thought about Marie. She was looking tired these days, and he feared he was the cause. He had never set out to use her this way, but she was the best listener he'd ever met, and endlessly patient. Best of all, Marie didn't judge him. He wondered what he would do without her. How did she put up with him? Carter knew he had changed. He hated his new impatient, volatile self, but he couldn't control it. He prayed that she wouldn't give up on him. After Bill had died, he and Marie had become close confi-dantes. After all, Bill had been very special to both of them. But now he was putting too much strain on her, and he hated himself for doing it.

Carter slowed his pace and looked around. He had arrived at the junction of the sea bank and Back Lane. That meant stopping to negotiate a big, heavy old gate and an ancient cattle grid. You had to be careful here. An awkward step, a slip on the wide metal bars of the grid could bring about a broken ankle, and there was no way of getting an ambulance down to this stretch of the marsh.

The acrid stench of burning flesh filled his nostrils. He drew in a breath and looked around for his friends.

'If you keep exercising like this and get no rest, you'll keel over one of these days,' murmured Tom in his ear.

'Yeah, not good, mate. You're living on your nerves,' added Ray.

Their three dark figures were standing close to his shoulder.

'*You* don't want to crash and burn, do you?' whispered Jack.

Carter swallowed. For the first time, their presence frightened him. He took a step back. He'd never felt like this before. 'Guys? Are you mad at me?'

Tom sighed. 'Of course not, mate. We just get kind of homesick sometimes.'

'Yeah,' added Jack. 'We're all over the place right now.'

'And Matt?' asked Carter.

No one answered him. His friends seemed to drift a little further away.

Carter drew in a deep breath. It looked like he was right. It really was down to him to do something for them. 'Okay, tell me what I can do. Ray? You first. How can I help you?'

Ray moved closer and the stench made Carter almost gag. 'I had a nest egg, Carter. No one knew about it. It's not in my name. You know why, don't you?'

He did. Ray's younger brothers were known as the evil twins. They spent more time in the young offenders' unit than they did at home. In fact, Carter wouldn't have trusted any of Ray's family. His mate had definitely been a foundling. It had been one of the reasons why he, as best man, had decided to hold the stag party well away from home. He didn't want to risk Ray's celebration being wrecked by his dodgy siblings.

'Yeah, I know why,' he said.

'Well, I want Joanne to have it.' Ray's voice faltered. 'She's going to need it. Sort it for me, Carter? Give it to her. Tell her I was never very good at saying it, but I really loved her.'

'Of course I'll do that, Ray. Just tell me where it is, and I'll get onto it first thing tomorrow.' Carter looked at Ray eagerly. This was something that meant a great deal to his friend.

'Ray?' Carter gazed around. The night smelt only of salty ozone. The moon shone down onto an empty lane.

'Shit!' Now what? His friend had told him what he really needed, but not how to go about it. Carter gave a deep sigh and began the run home.

CHAPTER FOUR

Charlie Button hurried into Jackman's office, where Carter was sitting. 'Super wants to see you, sir. And she said you too, Sergeant McLean.'

Carter glanced at Jackman and pulled a face. Together they stood up and headed for her room.

Superintendent Crooke looked distinctly uncomfortable. Her thin lips were tightly pressed together. She seemed to be wrestling with her words. After a while, she took a deep breath and said, 'My youngest niece is in trouble.'

Couldn't happen to a better woman, thought Carter, recalling all the snide remarks he'd had to put up with from her. He kept his face impassive.

Jackman raised an eyebrow.

'The thing is, she thinks someone is watching her.'

Carter sucked in air. 'Oh?'

'How can we help?' asked Jackman.

'I know that you have the missing woman to contend with, but I would like you to allow DS McLean here, and possibly DS Marie Evans, to make a few discreet enquiries.' She sat back in her chair and stared at Carter. 'Look, I know we don't always see eye to eye . . .'

Too bloody right, thought Carter. And after all the hell you've put me through over the years, I have no intention of becoming your best buddy just because you suddenly need my help. And why me? You hate me. Ask Jackman to help you, not me.

'. . . and I can't expect you to know how I feel. My niece is the child of the sister I lost last year, and I've rather taken her under my wing.'

Carter bit down hard on the inside of his cheek and said nothing.

'But I *do* know that you and Marie can be trusted to act, er, tactfully, especially considering that this is a personal matter.'

'Oh good, so it's nothing to do with the fact that DI Jackman here has a priority case, there's a major drugs case to tie up for the CPS, and everyone else is up to their necks in paperwork from the money-laundering scam that they've just put to bed?' Carter couldn't help himself, it just came out.

He felt Jackman grow tense beside him, but Ruth Crooke got in first.

'I knew that would be your attitude, McLean.' Her face tightened, then she sighed. 'Look, we both know that you've always worked on the edge. You treat the Police and Criminal Evidence Act like a vague set of guidelines to be disregarded at will, you bend the rules, and—'

'And I get results,' said Carter calmly.

'You get results, and I hate to say it, but that's why I want you to help my niece.'

Carter wanted to laugh. Suddenly his methods were acceptable, were they? Just because the crime was close to home. He took a deep breath. *Careful, Carter.* He needed to keep this job. It was all he had left. He would have to treat this unwanted request professionally, just like any other case. He must forget all the shit the woman had dumped on him. With a huge effort, he straightened up. 'Okay, ma'am. If it's alright with DI Jackman, we'll go and see her straightaway. What can you tell me, and where can I find your niece? We'll obviously need to talk to her.'

Ruth Crooke nodded. 'Thank you. Is that alright with you, Jackman?'

'It's fine by me, ma'am.'

'McLean?' She handed him a sheet of paper bearing names, mobile numbers and addresses. 'You get on. I need a few words with Rowan.'

Carter left, unsure of how he felt. His dislike of her clouded rational thought, but he supposed it was a compliment of sorts. But why had she asked *him* in particular? He sighed. He hadn't seen this coming, but he'd show willing. A few enquiries wouldn't take him long anyway.

* * *

Robbie Melton scanned through the notes he had made at the morning meeting. Suzanne Holland was beginning to occupy his every waking thought. His method of working an enquiry like this was to get inside the victim's head. He was certain that the solution was to be found in the woman herself. Someone, a person as yet unknown to them, was responsible for her disappearance. Robbie just needed to find her, dead or alive.

He had read all the reports. The main thing that emerged from them was the lack of forensic evidence. Apart from the quantities of blood at the house, whoever attacked Suzanne had been very careful. Robbie knew what the old adage said. Wherever you go and whatever you touch, you leave a trace. Well, Suzanne's assailant seemed to have blown that hypothesis out of the window.

Marie was smiling down at him. 'You look pensive.'

He held up a photograph of Suzanne Holland. 'This woman fascinates me. It seems that despite being married, she had an awful lot of men friends. But there are so many different sides to her that it's hard to get a clear picture of what she was like.'

'Have you managed to contact the ex-husband in Spain?'

Robbie grinned. 'Kind of. I'll try again when he's sober.'

'Any idea of why they got divorced?'

'No idea. He was too pissed to string a coherent sentence together.' Robbie laughed.

Marie sat down opposite him. 'Robbie, I'd like you to look deeper into her marriage to Tom Holland. And if you could do it rather quietly? I need to know if there's any skeletons in the cupboard that the initial interviews missed.' She frowned. 'As you know, Carter is back today on full duties, but Jackman and I don't want him getting involved with this case. Best he doesn't hear the name Tom Holland too often. He reckons he's fine with it, but we don't think so, okay?'

Robbie nodded. 'I totally agree. Don't worry, Sarge, I'll come to you directly if I find anything of interest.'

She nodded. 'Oh, by the way, have you read the memo about dropping the formalities? First names and all that?'

'Sure have, Sarge. But I'd never be able to manage it. If there's a choice, I'd rather keep the status quo.'

'Good man! You and me both.'

Marie walked off, leaving Robbie staring at the photograph.

Suzanne Holland had rich auburn hair just a shade or two away from red. She stared out of the picture from beautifully made-up hazel eyes. Her smile was seductive, full-lipped. Robbie shook his head. 'Not my type. But I can see what her admirers saw in her.'

'Me too.' Max Cohen leaned over his shoulder. 'That's one hot lady.' He slumped down in the chair Marie had just vacated. 'I'm beginning to think this was a random wrong place, wrong time thing. I've spent days interviewing her acquaintances and friends, and all I've got is a big fat nothing. No one wanted her dead.' He grunted. 'And for once, I bloody well believe them. Maybe it was a bungled burglary, or she just met someone with a grudge against red heads.'

'No, I'm certain she was the target.' Robbie looked at her hazel eyes. What secrets did they hold? 'She is a mystery woman.'

Max stood up. 'Well, I hope she bleedin' well hurries up and spills the beans, mate, 'cause this case is becoming a right pain in the arse.'

'Indeed, it is.' Robbie nibbled on a thumbnail. 'But we'll get there in the end. We'll find out what happened.'

'You reckon she's brown bread?'

'Oh yes. Don't you?'

'S'pose so.'

'We'll find her, Max. She'll talk to us, when she's ready.'

'Typical woman. Gotta be on *her* terms.' Max strolled back to his desk. 'Even if she is bleedin' dead.'

* * *

Marie sat in front of her computer, staring into space.

'Penny for them?' Carter said.

She jumped a little, but then looked up hopefully. 'Hey! Scrap the financial negotiations, how did you get on in there? What did the super want?'

Carter screwed his face up. 'Mmm, that was sincerely weird! She actually showed a human side.' He gave a shrug. 'This is most likely just a time-waster, but she wants you and I to check something out for her.'

Marie frowned. 'So what about the case I'm already working on?'

'This is no big deal, just a few inquiries. Jackman's okay with it, and we'll be back here in no time.'

'So what is all the urgency about?'

'Because, believe it or not, she wanted you and I *specifically* to deal with it.' He lowered his voice. 'Apparently it needs tact and diplomacy and she thinks we're the right people to do it.'

'She said that? About *you*?'

'As good as. In fact, yes, she did. And I think Jackman was as shocked as I was.' He gave a rueful grin. 'Although Jackman wasn't quite as rude to her as I was.'

Marie gave an incredulous laugh. 'Jackman is *never* rude. You on the other hand . . . Still, that's a first, isn't it? You and Ruth Crooke are like Sherlock and Moriarty. There has to be a catch, doesn't there?'

'Oddly enough, I don't think there is.' He lowered his voice to a whisper. 'It concerns the super's niece. Now, let's go somewhere more private and I'll bring you up to speed.'

Carter led the way downstairs and out of the building. They could talk freely in the car.

'You've seen the girl here once or twice, haven't you? Visiting her aunt?' Carter turned on the ignition and let the windows down.

Marie nodded. 'Leah, isn't it? Tall, skinny, long dark hair in a ponytail and teeth white enough to spook horses?'

'That's the one. She's nineteen and studying psychology at the Fenland Uni.'

'And?'

'She thinks she's being stalked.'

'What? With those teeth?'

Carter grinned. 'Naughty! Apparently the kid is pretty upset.'

'Sorry. Ignore me. I'm probably just denture envious. Being stalked is horrendous, actually.' Marie's face darkened. She had once been in a bad situation with a man who was obsessed with her, and knew the fear it generated.

'Yeah, so let's go talk to her, shall we?' He started the car. 'Oh, and when we've finished tonight, do you fancy a beer on the boat?' His tone was light, but Marie could tell that something was worrying him.

'Now that sounds more like it.' She smiled brightly, but her heart sank. Going to the boat meant he wanted to talk, and that meant going over it all again. Yet another

36

harrowing evening listening to a dear friend hating himself for simply being alive.

Marie tried to concentrate on Leah's stalker. It was far less draining.

* * *

'It first started when I found a bunch of flowers on my doorstep.' Leah Kingfield looked from Carter to Marie. 'I didn't think too much of it at the time, but now . . .' She shrugged.

'Was there a card with them?' Carter asked.

She nodded. 'It had a single X on it, and sorry, but I threw it away.' She looked down. 'I have a boyfriend, you see.'

'You're certain they weren't from him?' said Marie.

'Flowers? No. Definitely not his thing. A book on parapsychological phenomena maybe, but twenty-four red roses? No way.'

Marie raised her eyebrows. 'Two dozen! Wow. He's no cheapskate, that's for sure.'

Carter frowned at her. 'When was that exactly?'

Leah picked up a sheet of paper from the coffee table in front of them. 'Auntie Ruth told me to list everything that had happened — times, dates and places.'

'I should have known.' Carter smiled wryly, taking the list from her slender hand. 'Very professional.'

Marie glanced around the flat. It was a far cry from the usual student's grotty pad. It wasn't quite as antiseptic as Carter's place, but it was dusted and tidy. Marie suspected that Leah's allowance was subsidised by her auntie, and probably stretched to a cleaner. 'Do you live here alone?'

'No. I have a flatmate, but she's on holiday in the Algarve with her parents.'

'So, you *are* on your own at present?'

'Sounds pretty feeble, but actually I'm staying with Auntie Ruth until she gets back. I've only come here now to meet you and to grab some more clothes and things. I'm afraid all this has freaked me out a bit.'

'It's not feeble at all,' said Carter. 'It's very sensible.'

Marie was still taking in the surroundings. Not cheap. Nice area. 'How about CCTV?'

'Yes, that's weird, isn't it? Somehow he avoided the cameras, although I have no idea how. They seem to be everywhere.' She stood up abruptly. 'Sorry, where are my manners? Can I get you a drink? Police officers thrive on tea, don't they?'

They both nodded. 'White, no sugar for both of us, thank you,' added Carter.

Leah disappeared into the kitchen. Carter passed Marie the list and she scanned it quickly. It began with notes under her car windscreen wipers. Then amorous notes through the door, followed by a sense of being watched, then actual sightings of a shadowy lone male staring at her flat. More recently she thought that a dark van was following her every time she drove away from the apartment block. She had never been able to get close enough to see the number plate and she couldn't identify the make and model. Now it was telephone calls. The caller never spoke but Leah was certain she could hear soft, rapid breathing down the line. The calls often came at dead of night, and it was these that scared her most of all.

Marie took her mug of tea and placed it on the coffee table. 'Have you any idea who it could be? A jilted ex? Someone from uni? Maybe some guy who's too shy to actually talk to you?'

Leah sat down on the sofa and drew up her long legs beneath her. 'I've gone over it again and again, Detective. Auntie Ruth asked the same questions. But no, I really have no clue, and I find that very disturbing.'

Marie found it disturbing too. There was nothing normal about a stalker. It was a perverse and creepy way to approach someone. She glanced out of the big picture window and saw dense woods, close to the block of flats.

Oh, great! The perfect spot for a peeping Tom. She caught Carter's eye and nodded towards the window. He returned the nod. He'd seen it too.

Carter looked at the girl. 'Okay, Leah. We are going to take this very seriously. I would suggest you continue to stay at your aunt's house until we get a fix on this guy, and make sure that wherever you go, you always have someone with you. I'll organise an officer to keep an eye on you, and we'll both give you our direct mobile numbers. Anything scares you, don't hesitate, call us straightaway. If he persists, we'll see about getting your phone tapped as well. Are you happy with that?'

Leah nodded. 'What do you think he wants?'

You really don't want to know, thought Marie.

Carter said, 'Probably nothing, Leah. It's most likely just some love-struck kid with a crush on you. If you met him in the street he'd probably run a mile, too scared to even speak to you.'

A love-struck kid with enough spare cash for two dozen best red roses? He's a pervert, and if he goes according to pattern, he won't stop at a bit of heavy breathing down the phone. Marie gathered up a reassuring smile. 'I'm sure Sergeant McLean here is quite right. We'll catch the little sod, give him a blistering ear-bashing and you'll never hear from him again.'

Carter stood up. 'So, if you'd like to grab your things, we'll follow you back to your aunt's place. Okay?'

Marie wondered just how much of their crap Leah had actually believed. Very little, probably. She looked like a smart kid. She was studying psychology, after all. No, she would know the score as well as they did. They'd sounded so patronising! Marie opened the door, wishing they'd told Leah the truth. At least she would know exactly where she stood. Even if it was a horrible place to be.

* * *

Jackman spent the rest of the day trying to understand how Suzanne Holland's life fitted together. It wasn't easy.

39

Robbie Melton was by far the most committed officer on this particular case. He seemed to have taken it up as a personal crusade. Well, Jackman wasn't complaining. Max and Charlie both disliked old cases. They wanted the adrenalin charge of fresh evidence, witnesses that actually remembered something.

Unsolved cases were tedious to begin with, until the moment when you uncovered something new, and then everything changed.

So far they had found nothing, apart from a dipso-maniac ex-husband, who was always too drunk to speak to them.

Jackman looked at the clock. End of play. Maybe tomorrow something new would come to light.

* * *

Stone Quay was a lonely spot, and rarely visited. It sat on a wide stretch of the Westland River, miles from anywhere. Years ago there had been a small boatyard here. Now it was deserted, and the only building left standing was tumbledown and windowless.

And the only remaining boat was an ancient lifeboat called the Eva May. She was a Liverpool Class vessel, built in the 1930s and had been a fine rescue boat. In her day, she had braved mountainous seas and terrifying storms to bring both survivors and her brave crew home to safety.

Not that she was actually in the river. She stood raised up on heavy wooden support trestles, waiting for the summons to set off back into the water.

Carter and Marie sat together on the smooth, sanded wood of the aft deck with bottles of craft beer. The sun was setting in the western sky, staining it with dazzling streaks of lilac, pink and flame orange.

'If I were the super, I'd be well worried about my niece,' said Marie.

'Even more worrying because she's a police officer's niece, isn't it?'

40

'Sure is. Threats to families aren't common, but there are some nasty bastards out there, and I'll bet Ruth Crooke has thrown an awful lot of them in the slammer in her time.'

Carter nodded. 'Yeah. She may not be my favourite person — in fact I wouldn't piss on her if she was on fire — but she's made her fair share of good arrests. If I had kids, I'd be shit-scared for their welfare. I must say I was surprised by Leah. She's nice, isn't she? Nothing like her aunt.'

'I know the super can be a battle-axe, Carter, but I find her fair enough. I always feel she's on my side in a crisis.'

'Good, and that's how it should be. It's an old grudge, Marie, and it's to do with me, no one else. Let's not go there, huh?'

Marie nodded and sipped her beer.

For a while they sat in companionable silence, and Marie began to hope that all Carter wanted was to enjoy the peace of a summer's evening out on the river.

'I know what Ray wants me to do,' Carter broke the silence.

Ah, here it comes, she thought.

'He has a nest egg, and he wants me to find it and give it to his fiancée, Joanne.'

'Sounds simple enough. Why the long face?'

'Because I don't know where it is.'

'Mmm, I see the problem.'

'He said it wasn't in his own name, so that indicates a bank or a savings account of some kind. So how could an ordinary, honest bloke like Ray get himself another name?'

Marie shrugged. 'Simple enough, if it was really important to him.'

'It might have been *very* important to him. His whole family were trash, and his twin brothers were the worst of the lot. They'd have had his money away in a flash.'

'Did you know Joanne?'

41

'Yes, she's a lovely girl. She was totally devoted to Ray, and all she wanted was to make his life comfortable. Her favourite day out would probably be a trip to Ikea, and her spare time seemed to be filled with cooking for the freezer and scanning women's magazines for ideas on decor.'

'Oh dear.' Marie couldn't imagine a life like that.

Carter sighed. 'I know, but Ray thrived on it. And given his background, who could blame him? Ray and Joanne were a perfect match. The grafter and the home-maker. Now Joanne is cooking dinners for one, and Ray is sitting in an urn on top of the mantelpiece. Thanks to me.'

Marie frowned at him, but said nothing.

Carter sighed again. 'Okay, so let's imagine I'm Ray and I want somewhere to stash some cash for my wedding. I'm not too keen on banks, but they should give me a few bob in interest at least.'

'Yes, and these days a few bob is probably all you will get! Since your wedding is coming up, you might need to get your hands on some readies at short notice. That puts a high interest account out of the running. Perhaps you would just find a safe place and hide it.'

Carter frowned. 'I suppose Ray *could* have meant it wasn't in a savings account or in a bank at all. Do you really think he might just have hidden it?'

Marie thought about it. 'But that means it has stayed hidden for over eighteen months. Surely someone would have found it when they sorted out his things?'

'Mmm. So where would be safe? One thing's for sure, it wouldn't have been at his parents' place. That leaves his flat, and Joanne regularly cleans it from top to bottom. She moves the furniture around as often as she brushes her teeth.' He paused. 'Not only that, I'm sure Joanne knows nothing about the nest egg. She's naïve — not a fool, but deception never enters her mind. If you ask her a question, she will answer you honestly. Even if it's the evil twins who are doing the asking. No. Ray would have kept his mouth shut.'

'How about where he worked?'

'No way. Ray worked as an engine fitter at that big tractor company out near Swineshead. He might have trusted his mates, but the place was full of strangers. He couldn't stash any cash there.'

'So where?' Marie had run out of ideas.

Carter sat up straight, almost overturning his beer.

'Of course! The Eva May! Right here! When Ray wasn't with Joanne, he was always here on the boat. Sometimes with me, or with the others, but often on his own. He slept here for three nights once, when Joanne was off on some course. Where better to hide it?'

'But surely this boat is a prime target for vandals or dossers? Would you leave a load of wonga unattended in the middle of nowhere?'

Carter gave her an enigmatic smile. 'Ah. But the boat is not unattended.'

'Explain, please.'

'My dad owned Stone Quay. Years ago he owned the boatyard. He damn well owned half the county.' He coughed. 'Anyway, you wouldn't notice it, but the Eva May has a neighbour. Ever heard of Silas Breeze?'

'Crazy Silas?'

'The same. Only he's not as crazy as he makes out. Sure, he's a bit odd, but he's loyal, and he likes me.'

'Hang on. You saved his brother from drowning, didn't you? When you were still doing your training?'

'Something like that. Wasn't exactly a dramatic rescue. I hauled him out on the end of a boathook, actually. Pissed as a newt he was, but Silas was grateful to me.'

'And?'

'Silas worked on my father's boatyard. He taught me to shoot and to fish, and he used to take me poaching on Dad's land. Happy days!'

'Get to the point, Carter. Where is he now?'

'In a tiny cottage about five hundred yards from here. You can't see it from the lane or from the quay. It nestles in a tiny inlet of the river, surrounded by reeds and stubby windblown trees.' He smiled and pointed. 'Over there.'

Marie shook her head. She could see nothing.

'I doubt if more than a handful of people know it's there, and that's just how he likes it.'

'Is his brother with him?' asked Marie.

'Eli died some years ago now. Silas is alone, with his dog. That's another reason no one comes looking for him. Klink, his dog, isn't exactly friendly.'

'Funny name.'

Carter grinned at her. 'Haven't you learnt anything since they threw you out of Wales? It's local dialect for marvellous.'

'Well, you learn something new every day. And my dad came from here, I'll have you know. He was a pure yellowbelly, just like you.'

'Aye, true Lincolnshire, born and bred.' Carter smiled proudly. 'Well, ya takin' a long whiles learnin', me duck.'

'So Silas and his pooch keep an eye on this boat for you? Nice one.'

'After his brother died, he couldn't stand his old home. I gave him the cottage and a small allowance when we brought the Eva May down here. We put a petrol generator into the one remaining storeroom and kept some of our equipment and tools there. We couldn't have done it without having someone close by to keep an eye on it. As you said, a deserted boat is a prime target for vandals or bored kids.'

'And did Ray know Silas?'

'He met him a few times. Ray was a bit of a bird-watcher, especially water fowl. That made him acceptable to Silas. He wasn't too keen on the others, but he seemed to like Ray well enough.'

Marie could sense Carter's growing excitement.

'If I can get this right, I'll know for certain that I'll be able to let my friends move on.'

Marie nodded. Carter needed closure. If he had to live the rest of his life waiting for that smell of burning, she wasn't sure how long he would last. Marie stood up. 'Okay, let's start the treasure hunt.'

For thirty minutes they searched the boat, but they found nothing.

Carter rubbed a sweaty forearm across his brow. 'Damn! I was so sure it was here.'

'I thought so too,' said Marie. 'I hate to say this, but it's getting dark.'

Carter nodded. 'Back to the bloody drawing board.'

He stared back up at the old vessel.

Marie had a feeling he would come back after he'd dropped her off, and dark or not, he'd tear the Eva May apart if he had to.

Carter picked up a stone and flung it far out into the river. They watched the rings spread out from where it had struck the water.

'Let's sleep on it,' said Marie softly. 'I think we are on the right track, don't you?'

'I guess.'

* * *

Carter took a deep breath and set off after Marie. She was leaning on the side of his car. Suddenly he stopped and sniffed the air. Oh no! Not here. Not with Marie just a few steps away.

'Not now,' he hissed. 'Go away!'

'Carter?' Marie was moving towards him. 'What's wrong?'

'No, no,' he mumbled, looking around him.

'Carter, you're scaring me.' She, too, looked around. Then she stopped. He saw her look up and wrinkle her nose.

My God! She could smell it too!

Carter froze. Did that mean she would see them as well?

'Get into the car, Carter. I'll drive. Just get in, close the windows and take some deep breaths.' Marie held out her hand for the keys.

You won't keep them out by shutting the windows, he thought, almost giggling at the notion.

'The car, Carter! Bloody get in!'

He did as he was told and they set off, hurtling down the lane and over the fields. Suddenly she braked and pulled over.

'Look.'

She pointed. Across a vast field he saw a bright orange glow spreading across the old corn stooks.

'The farmer is burning off his field, getting rid of the old stubble. It's supposed to be illegal, but they still do it. That's all it is. Just a farmer at work. Okay?'

Carter closed his eyes and sank down in the seat. How could he be so stupid?

'It's okay, honestly. You're safe. The smoke was a trigger, that's all. It caused a flashback, a panic attack.' She smiled at him gently.

'Yes, I suppose it did.' He bit his lip. Let her believe that. It was certainly better than the truth. He remembered her reaction when he first mentioned seeing the guys. How could Marie be expected to understand, when he certainly did not?

'I'll get you back home and we'll have a cup of strong coffee, yeah?'

He put on a weak smile and nodded.

This couldn't go on. He had to find that damn money, sort out whatever Jack and Tom needed, and kiss them goodbye. Otherwise he would go mad.

CHAPTER FIVE

The following morning, Marie arrived at the station early. The CID office was empty, which allowed for a private call to Laura Archer. The psychologist wouldn't be at work yet, but she could leave a short message on her answerphone asking for an appointment.

She didn't feel that she was being disloyal to Carter. In the early days, she had accompanied him on so many of his visits that, in the absence of a next of kin, it had been agreed that she would speak for him if things got difficult. It meant she had his blessing to consult with Laura if she felt the need.

She left a message and switched on her computer.

'Is McLean in yet, Marie?'

Marie jumped. She hadn't noticed Superintendent Crooke come into the office. She hurriedly stood up. 'I haven't seen him, ma'am.' She noticed the deep, worried creases in the super's forehead, and the dark shadows beneath her eyes. Marie suspected that Carter was not the only one suffering from lack of sleep. 'Nothing's happened, has it, ma'am? With your niece, I mean.'

'Nothing *she* is aware of, Marie, but *I* was up at three in the morning chasing round the garden like a madwoman. I'm certain someone was out there, watching the house. Well, watching Leah's bedroom window to be precise.'

'Who was on duty, ma'am? They did show, didn't they?' She had heard Carter put in the request to uniform to keep an eye on the place while on patrol.

'Oh yes, I saw your crew on several occasions. I'm not complaining about that. Whoever it was just seemed to pick the time when there was no one here. If I hadn't got up for a call of nature, I'd never have seen him.'

Marie wondered how he knew which window was the girl's. Or even know that she was there, and not in her own flat? 'Want me to check out the garden, ma'am? See if the intruder left any traces?'

Ruth Crooke shook her head. 'Did it myself, at first light. Fine tooth-comb and all that. There's nothing.' She massaged her temples for a moment. 'I'm not even a hundred per cent sure there really was someone. I may be a police officer, but I was half asleep, had a bursting bladder and was deeply worried about Leah.' She shrugged. 'Doesn't make me the most reliable witness, does it?'

Marie shook her head. It was weird. Crooke loathed Carter and vice versa, but the super didn't seem to have it in for her or anyone else. She positively *liked* Jackman, and he in turn was quite happy to let Ruth Crooke call him by his first name. No one else did that.

Ruth Crooke was shrewd, and very aware of what went on in her division. She was also straight-laced, and everything had to be done by the book. She had been an awesome and very active copper in her early years, and then when she finally made superintendent, she found that the post suited her. Although she would never admit it, she revelled in the bureaucracy. She understood all about service performance indicators, information cascades and the rest of that rubbish. Somehow, despite the red tape, the budgets, targets and flow charts she managed to keep the division ticking over.

Marie just could not understand why Ruth Crooke persisted in holding Carter back. Whatever, right now she felt genuinely sorry for the super. 'Pound to a penny, ma'am, if you think someone was there, he *was* there.'

'I appreciate your confidence, Sergeant. I just wish I felt as sure myself.' She turned away. 'Tell McLean to come to my office when he gets in, if you would.'

'Yes, of course.'

Marie felt decidedly unsettled.

* * *

Danny Hurley looked out of place. Under the watchful eye of the shop assistant, he wandered around the upmarket handmade chocolate shop looking for the right gift. He took a while to decide on the right box and the gift wrapping, and then he paid the uneasy girl with a fifty pound note. She made sure to test it under the light box.

'She must be very special,' she said.

Danny's eyes lit up. 'Believe me, darling, she is.'

He left the shop and sauntered over to the bridge. He stood for a while at the bottom of the ramp, listening to a busker playing a guitar. Danny clicked his fingers and swayed to the beat. When the song ended, Danny threw a tenner into the open guitar case. 'Sweet, man. Really sweet.' He nodded appreciatively and walked off. The amazed musician grabbed the note and stared after him.

Another man joined Danny on the bridge and they walked together in silence until they reached the far bank. They strolled a little way along the riverside path until they came to a wooden bench where they sat in silence, staring at the slow moving water. The other man looked thin, unhealthy, with lank hair and skin like unbaked dough.

Danny glanced around briefly, reached into his trouser pocket and took out an envelope. Wordlessly, he passed it to the man, who put it in his pocket without looking at it. 'Same as before?' he muttered.

'No.' Danny nodded towards the university buildings, further along the towpath. 'Her car this time. Red Citroen Saxo.' In a whisper, he gave him the registration number and handed over a pass card and a key. 'The card will get you in to the Emerson House car park, west side. She parks along the back row. Their CCTV is rubbish, just two cameras for the whole area. Go in at one forty exactly and you are clear for one minute fifty-five seconds. Plus, if she's being watched by the Old Bill, they are coming up to shift change, so you're safe as houses. Got it?'

'Understood.'

Danny handed him the gift. 'Place this in the passenger footwell, and be careful, they cost a bloody arm and a leg.'

The man gave a lecherous gap-toothed grin. 'This bird really must be the dog's bollocks.'

Danny glared at him. 'You have no idea what she means to me. Now shut the fuck up and go earn your money.'

Danny made his way back down the path, seething with anger. His next job would be to find himself a different runner. No one made comments like that about his girl. No one.

* * *

Carter fought hard to concentrate, but lack of sleep and Ray's final request were playing havoc with his brain. If it weren't for the super's "problem," he might have thrown a sickie and tried to get his head down for a couple of hours. But after his earlier terse meeting with Crooke, it was clear that taking time off to sleep would not do much for his career. This was not how he had planned his return to full duties. He should be on the Holland case.

He finished his second black coffee and forced himself to focus on Leah Kingfield. Marie was busy scanning through a box of CCTV tapes of Leah's home address. She trusted no one else to do the job properly, and was ploughing through the whole lot herself.

His mind wandered again. He'd had to dump poor Rosie because of Leah's problem, and now the young detective was up to her armpits in statements and reports that he should be helping her with. They concerned a complicated drugs case involving a family of villains called Cannon. They were all vermin, especially the eldest son, Louis, who had an encyclopaedic knowledge of the law, and especially how to evade it. Rosie would need to sew everything up tighter than a duck's backside if she wanted to make the charges stick.

Carter was very good at paperwork. It came naturally to him. His head for figures and his easy grasp of everything from spreadsheets to police law was about the only thing he had to thank his father for.

He scribbled down some points to discuss with Rosie as soon as he was free again, and then his mind wandered back to Ray and his missing money.

Maybe someone had found it already and pocketed it. Nothing would surprise him about the Barratt family. He had been so certain that Ray had concealed the money on the Eva May. Maybe he was on the wrong track altogether, and his mate had done the sensible thing and put it safely away in a bank.

He sighed, picked up the sheet of paper with all his ideas of places to hide money and stared at it morosely. Then he screwed it up and threw it into the waste bin.

Oh, sod it! Come on, Ray. Help me out here, for Joanne's sake, and for mine. I want to find that bloody money!

* * *

Marie found nothing on the CCTV footage. She had just received a text from Laura Archer asking her to be at her office at noon. She hated keeping things from Jackman, but didn't know how to explain to him about

51

Carter and his "hallucinations," and that she was visiting his shrink.

Laura Archer's consulting room was in the basement of an old three-storey terraced house that soared majestically above a quiet stretch of the river. Marie stepped inside and immediately a feeling of calm washed over her. It happened every time. Was it the room or the woman inside it? It was weird when you thought about it. The place must have heard a thousand cries for help. Sadness, fear and pain must have washed around this room in torrents, but you could feel none of it.

'Thanks for fitting me in.' Marie looked around at the shelves weighted down with books, the soft grey walls, the restful watercolours and the two comfortable recliners. Uplighters diffused a warm glow. Nothing jarred the senses. All that was missing was a cold bottle of Chablis and two glasses. 'I do appreciate it.'

'No problem.' Laura indicated one of the chairs. 'I always keep an hour free, just in case someone needs a chat.' She smiled and sat down opposite. 'How have you been? I haven't seen you for over six weeks.'

'Oh, I'm fine. I wanted to talk about Carter.'

'I thought that would be the case. But first, let's try again, and this time the truth. How are *you*?'

Marie didn't answer immediately. She wished she had that glass of wine in her hand. 'I feel like I'm breaking up, from the inside. Someone I care about has stuck me in a pressure cooker and is tightening the weights over my head.' She listened to her own words, and felt mildly surprised. Laura was nodding. 'I'm lost. I used to know all about priorities. I had very clear views. I could listen to my heart and my head, and know that morally I could nearly always get it right, but now . . .?' She bit her bottom lip to stop it trembling.

'That's perfectly understandable. Someone close to you is in turmoil and you feel the need to be there for him, but you are also a committed police officer. You never shirk your duties, and you resent Carter because he has interposed himself between you and your hundred per cent loyalty to your job and your colleagues. And it hurts, because you want to do the right thing by Carter *and* the force.' She paused. 'Marie, you have to do the right thing by *you*. You are not responsible for everyone else.'

'It feels like I am.'

Laura leaned back in the chair and stared at her. 'You are a strong woman, Marie, but you must not become a crutch. People who rely on crutches never learn to walk properly on their own two feet. It's alright to be there for them, but to fully support another person you have to have almost superhuman strength, both inside and out.' She sighed. 'Forgive me for saying this, but you look exhausted.'

'I just wish I could stand back from the situation, and get a better perspective.'

'And that is exactly what you should do.'

'I'd like to know how, when we have a major missing person investigation running, and now another high priority case,' murmured Marie, hating the accusatory tone.

Laura laughed softly. 'I know you can't distance yourself physically, but you can look at the situation differently.' She leant forward. 'Look, I know some very useful techniques that could help you. Want to try one?'

Marie shrugged. What did she have to lose except for a few minutes of her precious time? 'Not sure about all that New Age stuff, but, hey, whatever, I'm game.'

'Okay. Well, you were talking about gaining perspective. Do you ever use Google Earth?'

Marie nodded. What an odd question. 'All the time. To find specific locations.'

'Right. Close your eyes and think of that program, but we'll run it backwards. Don't zoom in. Zoom out from where we are sitting right now.'

Marie put her head back and closed her eyes. Laura's voice was almost hypnotic.

'So here you are, Marie Evans, with all her worries, sitting in this chair, in this room, in this house, on this road. Now, imagine yourself floating effortlessly upwards, away from your body and towards that satellite spinning around the earth. Keep looking down at yourself, but allow yourself to pass through the ceiling, through the floors above, through the roof and up into the sky. Go up through the clouds, higher and higher into space. See the town become little more than a spot on the map, the countryside a hazy tapestry of green and brown, until you see the clear outline of the island we live on. Are you with me?'

Marie gazed down from above the clouds. She nodded.

'Can you see yourself? Can you see your problems?'

'No. I'm too far away. They are too small.'

'Exactly. Every house in every street has people with problems, and they all seem insurmountable, but seen from where you are now, those problems are very small indeed.'

Marie exhaled and reluctantly floated back down to earth.

'It's a way to escape your pressure cooker, if only for a short while.'

'Mmm! Do you have any more of those?' Marie drew in a long breath. 'Just for a moment there, I felt really good, so *apart* from all the crap.'

Laura nodded. 'Sure. I've got a few relaxation exercises that might help. And by the way, you may not think so, but you're very receptive to this sort of thing.'

'Comes from having a Welsh Witch for a mother, I guess.'

'Have you ever been hypnotised?'

'No.'

'You'd be a brilliant subject.' Laura smiled. 'Unlike Carter.'

Marie understood at once why that would be.

'But I'm digressing. I want to know what your particular worry is.'

Marie stretched, and took a deep breath. She told Laura about Carter and his evening soirees with his dead friends.

'Don't get me wrong, I could completely understand his believing that he sees their faces in a crowd. I can even imagine him holding conversations with them. It's natural. I did that when my Bill died. I still do sometimes, but I'm fully aware that I'm talking to myself, or to a mental image. And I don't get answers. Ever.'

'And Carter does?'

'Oh yes. And I don't know how to handle it, Laura. He talks about them so casually, as if he were going down to the pub for a drink with them. Next thing, he's telling me he watched them fry.' She gave a long shaky sigh. 'If I didn't know him better, I'd think he was either psychotic, or messing with my mind.'

'But you *do* know him, don't you? And you know it's not his fault,' said Laura gently. 'The shock and the grief have changed everything for him. It's a bit like someone doing a really bad job of rewiring the circuit board in his head. He's working his way through the components of his grief, but they are all getting jumbled up. I think he's trying desperately to move on to resolution, to acceptance, but he gets sidetracked by his denial and guilt.'

'Will he ever get his life back?' Marie blurted out. 'Okay, he's working, and doing a damn good job, but I'm afraid that it's all an elaborate facade.'

'His life was not ruined, you know, just terribly altered. He will get through this, I'm certain of it. He is very much like you. You are both strong-willed, comfortable in your own bodies, aware of who you are. He'll survive, Marie, but when I said *get through*, that is exactly what he has to do, go *through* the whole horrible process. There are no short cuts and no slipping around the outside. He has to walk across those hot coals until he reaches the other side.'

'So I just go along with these bizarre ideas?'

'The idea of doing a good turn for each of them is actually not so bizarre. And if at the completion of each goal he "releases" that particular friend, then I'd say he's found a mechanism for moving out of his nightmare and back into the real world. Wouldn't you?'

'Maybe. Well, that's what I hope. And the things he's doing, these targets, as you call them? They are things he already knows about? Things his friends talked about when they were alive, and now Carter is remembering them subconsciously and using them to try to make amends?'

'Oh yes, most definitely. Carter is recalling old conversations that he had with his friends, and transposing them into new ones. It's possible that after the accident he really did forget, and now it's all coming back to him.'

'So these "chats" with his dead friends are simply memories. It all sounds very plausible sitting here. It's just so damned spooky when it's Carter talking.' Marie shivered.

'Just listen to him, Marie, and don't argue with him, but do try to be the voice of reason. Help him keep his feet on the ground.' Laura looked at her intently. 'But not at your expense, okay?'

'I'll try. I hope you didn't mind me off-loading on you like this, but his last call at three in the morning and then that panic attack when he smelt burning really freaked me out.' She shook her head. 'I've been terrified of doing the wrong thing. You know, like feeding his delusions.'

'I honestly think he has hit on a very good way of cutting the ties that bind him to his dead friends. And the sooner he can complete his targets, the sooner he will be able to move forward.'

Marie stood up and held out her hand. 'Thanks, Laura. I really appreciate this.'

'Any time.' Laura Archer looked at her shrewdly. 'And I mean that, Marie. Don't let yourself be pulled back and forth. Be there for your friend, do the job that you love, but do both on your own terms. Don't be bullied by your own emotions, or by guilt. Okay?'

Marie nodded. Easier said than done.

'And don't forget Google Earth.'

* * *

Back in the office, Carter looked at Marie quizzically. 'Get everything done?'

'More or less, thanks.' She hung her jacket over the back of her chair. 'Anything helpful turn up regarding Leah?'

Carter shook his head. 'Sorry, nothing definite yet. Max found you a street CCTV camera though, just a little way from her home. He's taken a quick run through it and he's isolated someone he described as looking "dead shifty." He's sent it to IT to get it cleaned up a bit. It's pretty grainy, so don't hang by your eyelashes on it.' He grimaced. 'To be honest, I'm finding it hard to get my thoughts off Ray and his money.'

'Then try harder, Carter. The super is getting greyer with every moment that passes.'

'Maybe I don't have the same bad feeling about Leah Kingfield that you do. Blokes get the hots for girls all the time. Just because they are total arseholes in the way they show it, doesn't make them actually dangerous, does it?'

'And you're prepared to take the risk, are you?'

'Of course not. Anyway, you're the one with the sure-fire gut instinct. You know I'll go along with you what-ever.'

'And so you should.' Marie gave him her best schoolmarm glare. 'So, where are we now with Leah?'

'I've had a quiet word with a friend in uniform. He's got a couple of bodies keeping a general eye on her college. The university has been informed,' he looked at his watch, 'and right now she's being bored to death in a two-hour tutorial. She has a special cell phone that is linked directly to Control *and* her auntie. Personally I don't think we are going to get too much from what has already happened. The best we can do is to keep watching her, and hope he shows himself again.'

A young civilian stood by the desk, holding out a large printed black-and-white photograph.

'Sarge? Orac sent this for you. She said it's crap and don't blame her for the state of our street cameras.'

Marie grinned. The head of IT was always acerbic.

Carter took the photo and stared at it. 'Bloody hell! Is this the best you can do?'

The man looked downcast. 'Sorry, but the film quality is rubbish. Orac reckons the cameras on that estate were last used to keep tabs on Jack the Ripper. They belong in a museum.'

Carter nodded. 'Well, thank Orac for trying.' He stared long and hard at the grainy, indistinct picture.

'Hand it over,' Marie demanded.

'It's seriously pants. Look.'

She took it and swore softly. 'You're right. I'm not even sure if it's a male.' It was the stalker, she was sure, but to get identification from it was impossible. It could have been any of a hundred local yobs.

'Oh, I think it is,' said Carter, '*And* I think it's probably Leah's admirer, but we'll have to find a better shot. This is just about useless.'

Marie put down the picture. 'Any joy from the street cameras around Superintendent Crooke's house last night?

'Nothing. It's as if he dropped out of the sky directly into the super's herbaceous border.' Carter shrugged.

Marie pursed her lips. 'Then it looks as if our surveillance boys aren't going to faze him any. He's really determined to get to Leah, isn't he?'

'Oh yeah, he's persistent alright,' said Carter.

'So what now?'

'I guess we wait to see what he does next.' He smiled grimly. 'Ten to one he won't keep us waiting very long.'

'You reckon?'

'I reckon.' Carter sank back into a chair and stared up at her. 'I'm going back to the boat tonight. Want to come?'

'Can't this time. Sorry.' Marie bit her lip, but remembered Laura's words. She badly needed some downtime. 'Gary's cooking dinner tonight. It would have been his sister's birthday today, and he said he wanted to do what he always did and cook something special.'

'Ah, I see. That's nice.'

'So? What's the plan then? Dismantle the Eva May, plank by plank?'

'Dunno, but that doesn't seem like a bad idea.'

'Silas Breeze.' Marie surprised herself. The thought had literally just come to her.

'Silas? What about him?'

'Go talk to him before you turn your precious Eva May into matchwood. You say he got on with Ray. Well, if you spend your time waiting for some elusive bird that's only seen once every forty years, surely you chat to pass the time, don't you?'

Elation and relief spread across Carter's handsome face.

'There are times when I could kiss you, Detective Sergeant Evans!'

'Don't even think about it!' said Marie in mock horror. 'I'll accept the accolade graciously, but let's skip the slushy bit, shall we?'

'Silas! Of course! Why on earth didn't I think of him?'

'Because it's too personal. Try looking at it like a case and do it with your copper's hat on. It's easier that way, I promise.'

'You're right, as always. I'll go see Silas tonight, and now, back to work.'

Marie watched him stride away. This was more like the old Carter. When he had the bit between his teeth, there was no stopping him. If he could use that determination to pay back his friends, then maybe they could all find some peace.

Ten minutes later he re-emerged from his office. 'Guess what? Matey-boy just couldn't help himself. He's had another stab at getting Leah's attention. This time with luxury chocolates placed inside her car. Her *locked* car.'

'Shit! How the hell did he do that? And right under our noses!'

'Mmm. He's either very lucky or very clever.'

As far as she knew, there was only one place in town where you could buy really posh chocolates. Surely they'd be able to ID the purchaser? Or did he send someone else? And how the hell did he manage to bypass the university security and get into a locked vehicle? Her mind swam with suppositions.

Carter perched on the edge of her desk. 'I've decided he's clever, not lucky. Uniform have paid a visit to the shop, and guess what? It was a cash sale, and they have no security cameras. Not considered necessary.'

'What about the CCTV in the street?'

'That end of Lytton Alley doesn't have any.' He twisted a pen around and around in his fingers. 'Clever. Oh, and the car hadn't been forced. He used a key. How do you suppose he got hold of that?'

'Obviously from Leah, without her knowledge. A party maybe? Someone nicks her keyring and either gets a copy made or finds where she keeps the spare and "borrows" it.'

'This makes him a contemporary of hers. Maybe even a college mate? Maybe I was right. It's some infatuated prat who hasn't got the balls to confess he has the hots for her.'

Marie spoke quietly. 'Attraction. Obsession. Destruction.'

'The three stages of stalking,' added Carter. 'I wonder if the super is thinking about that right now. If she is, she must be hurting.'

'I'm sure she's thinking about nothing else.' Marie felt a chill creep through her. 'She must be beside herself with worry.'

She hated stalkers. There was something unhinged about them, so out of control and unwholesome. She'd told Carter it had never happened to her, but it had. It left her looking over her shoulder for months. She knew just what Leah was going through. Right now, she would give a month's wages to get her cuffs around the stalker's dirty little wrists.

CHAPTER SIX

Somewhere a skylark soared on the evening air. Carter heard its song across the marsh, all the way to Silas Breeze's cottage. He often saw Silas at a distance, a dark silhouette against the twilight sky. Silas flitted about the marshes like a shadow, impossible to touch.

Like its owner, Silas's ramshackle cottage was part of the landscape. It blended into the reeds and shrubby trees like a part of the earth. It had stood there for decades before Carter was born, even withstanding the great flood of 1953.

He called out. His voice echoed across the water and faded into silence. No answering bark from Silas's dog. The cottage door was unlocked. Carter peered around it and smiled, transported back to his childhood and his father's gamekeeper's lodge. It was the smell, a potpourri of old leather, freshly cut kindling wood, bunches of herbs and stored root vegetables. Blood, too. That particular stink of a skinned rabbit or a recently hung pheasant. The good times. Times spent away from his father.

The old man's belongings lay scattered across the old oak table. Carter made out the stained and yellowing covers of old books, an old cigar box full of handmade fishing flies, a half chewed marrow bone, three empty milk cartons and a set of scales with a pile of rusted weights.

Two overstuffed armchairs pressed close to the soot-stained fireplace. Beside one was a tiny circular wooden table holding a grubby whisky glass and a pair of binoculars. The other wore a check blanket covered in hairs. Carter pictured Silas and Klink the dog sitting opposite one another of an evening like an old couple.

Carter noticed the picture hanging above the cluttered table. It was slightly faded by the sunlight, and speckled with the bodies of tiny thunder flies. Carter remembered his younger self carefully removing it from a pile of other framed paintings in the attic of their house. It was an old watercolour, depicting a shabbily-dressed old man lifting a salmon from a river. At the man's side was a reclining dog, some fishing tackle and a large bag. It was titled "The Poacher," and the young Carter was certain it represented Silas. He had waited for his father to go off on one of his business trips, wrapped the picture in an old horse blanket and taken it to Silas's place out on Carrion Fen. Silas had looked long and hard at it, and then nodded to Carter. It had stayed with him ever since.

Carter closed the door. He'd walk back to the Eva May and watch out for the old man's return from there.

Outside, Carter found he was reluctant to leave. He sat down with his back against the lichen covered wall and turned his face to the cool evening breeze. He felt almost "normal." The accident had tainted most of his existence, but there were parts of his childhood that seemed to have remained unscathed. Days spent with Silas and his brother Eli.

He gazed along the inlet to the point where it met the river, and saw a ripple forming on the surface of the water. A boat was coming.

Carter stood up, brushed moss from his trousers and saw Silas's small weather-worn dinghy ease its way into the inlet. He waved a greeting, and Klink responded with a joyous bark.

'Nothing wrong is there, young'un?'

'Nothing wrong, Silas. Just needed to see a friendly face, and maybe talk you into having a small drink with me?' He removed a half bottle of malt whisky from his jacket pocket and waved it in the air.

Silas's face broke into a mass of wrinkles when he smiled. 'Well now. I'd say it's a fine evening for a bit of a magg, wouldn't you?' The smile widened. 'Ee-yah, tek this.'

Carter took the wet rope from the old man and tied it deftly around the mooring post. Klink leapt from the boat and hopped madly around Carter's legs. 'Hello, fellow! How's tricks?' He fondled the old dog's ears. Such a soft beast. Yet he could terrify the life out of a stranger.

They tramped up to the cottage. Silas proceeded to clear some gardening tools from an old wooden bench, while Carter went inside to hunt for usable glasses. It was too nice an evening to be stuck indoors, and Silas knew that enclosed spaces made Carter uneasy.

The old man sat down and raised his glass towards his guest. 'So. You need to ask me something, don't you, young'un?'

Carter looked at him. 'You've known all along, haven't you?'

'Maybe. Ask the question and we'll find out.'

'Ray confided in you, didn't he?'

'Ah, a good lad that one. Dreadful waste.' Silas stared out across the river. 'Not frightened of hard work either, and he loved the fen and the birds here.' He sighed and sipped his drink. 'Aye, we talked a bit.'

'About money?'

'Amongst other things.'

Carter's expression tightened. Much as he loved the old cuss, he was in no mood for games. 'I have to find it, Silas, and get it to Joanne. She's struggling. She needs it, and Ray wants her to have it.'

'Well, he told me all about them ne'er-do-wells he called his family. But listen up. He said he had "something" he was worried about. Not actual cash. A thing.'

'So he left it with you?'

'Not exactly, but I can help you find it.' Silas rubbed his chin thoughtfully. ''Ere, why did you say "Ray *wants* her to have it?"'

Carter inhaled. He had never been able to lie to Silas. 'I see them.'

'At night? In your dreams, like?'

'I just see them, Silas. We talk.'

The old man folded his arms, and nodded slowly. 'Yes, I think you would, all things considered.' He paused, still nodding. 'I think you would.'

This was deeply reassuring to Carter, although he knew very well that seeing the dead in one form or another was part of the lives of the old "web-footed" fen men.

'Recall that night, young'un? When you were coming up ten years?'

Carter stared into his glass. Yes, he remembered. Carter had never understood what he saw that night, and he still didn't.

He had been just a boy . . .

Carter was woken by the sound of gravel thrown against his window. He scrambled from his bed. He looked down and made out the figure of Silas standing in the shadows of the courtyard. He was beckoning.

He pulled on his jeans, dragged a sweater over his head and crept out of the house. Silas led the way in silence, down the lane and into the old churchyard. He put a hand on the boy's shoulder and together they crouched behind a crumbling, ivy-choked wall. Silas held a finger to his lips and pointed towards the church path.

For more than a quarter of an hour, tiny flickering lights danced along the path that led from the lychgate to the church door. The wind didn't extinguish them and they grew brighter just before they disappeared.

'Corpse candles,' whispered Silas. 'There'll be a death in the village.'

Carter almost forced the reluctant Silas up to the church door, but there was nothing there. No candles, no lanterns. Nothing. On their way back to the house, Carter plied his companion with questions, but Silas said little. They were there to lead the way for the coffin bearers. Some saw them, others didn't. Simple.

And that was that. The following Friday, Carter's mother's car skidded off the road on the Westdyke Bridge, and she drowned in the Westland River.

Carter poured them another two fingers of whisky. He had wondered about those lights for years. He'd never spoken about what he'd seen. There was a rational explanation for those lights, he knew. He'd just never discovered it. Silas would never have played a trick on him, he just wasn't like that. Eventually he concluded that it was methane gas. The wetlands emitted marsh gas when the conditions were right. It was a strange but perfectly natural phenomenon. But Carter was never entirely convinced. Maybe he had spent too much time with old Silas when he was a kid.

He spoke softly. 'I still wish it had been my father. The bastard.'

'Now, boy. Don't speak ill of the dead,' said Silas sternly.

But Carter didn't want to get onto the subject of his family now. He wanted to know about Ray's money. 'So, my friend, are you going to help me find my mate's nest egg?'

The old man set down his empty glass on the bench beside him and stood up. 'Fancy a walk?' He reached down and patted the dog's head. 'Come on, Klink, lad. Let's take this impatient young whippersnapper to find the buried treasure, shall we?'

* * *

Jackman's office was a haven, a refuge from the bedlam of the CID office.

He had made it his own, bringing in scavenged furniture. There were no official police photographs on the walls, just rows of books and a picture of his beautiful and sadly long-gone horse, Glory.

He put his finger to the decorative globe on his desk, and watched the countries of the world revolve in a many-coloured blur. 'If only real life was as beautiful,' he murmured.

'It is, if you look in the right places.'

Jackman looked up. The elfin face of Laura Archer peered around his partly open door.

'You're working late. Come in.'

Laura sat down opposite him and smiled grimly. 'I was summoned to help the FMO with a situation in custody.'

'Ah, I heard we had a difficult customer. Everything okay now?'

'He's on his way to hospital, but he's much calmer.'

'Good. And were you just passing? Because my office is in a dead end corridor, so . . .'

Laura laughed. Not for the first time, Jackman noticed how beautiful she was — in an unassuming kind of way.

'I should know better than to try and outwit a detective, shouldn't I?'

He raised an eyebrow and waited for her to continue.

'As you know, I can't discuss a patient with you, but I wanted to tell you that I am still keeping a close eye on Detective Carter McLean. Barry Richards and I were originally quite happy to allow him back to full duties, but we are aware that he still has issues. I'm just not sure whether those issues will resolve, or get worse.'

'My sergeant knows Carter very well. In fact I suspect she is closer to him than anyone, and she has expressed her concerns about him.'

Laura nodded. 'I know. I worry that she is taking on too much. The words "rock and hard place" come to mind.' She sat forward in her chair. 'That's actually why I'm here. I wanted to tell you that Marie Evans is under considerable pressure. Carter does not mean to impose on her good nature and their friendship, but he leans heavily on her, and I don't want her buckling under the strain.'

Jackman hadn't fully appreciated Marie's situation. 'Forewarned is forearmed. Thank you for telling me.'

Laura stood up, 'Excellent. I feel happier now that you are aware of the full picture. Just don't tell her I enlisted your help, will you?'

Jackman drew a finger and thumb across his lips. 'Zipped tight. And thank you, Laura.'

He watched her leave and wondered if she was married.

He sat back in his chair. He knew that Marie had sometimes accompanied Carter when he went for psychological evaluation, but he didn't realise how much time she was spending with him. She and Laura must have spoken recently. He tapped his fingers on the table. It was unlike Marie to do anything without telling him, but she was looking exhausted, so maybe she had just forgotten. He shook his head. No, it was more probable that she didn't want to lumber him with her problems.

Well, that wasn't going to continue. He'd talk to her tomorrow, and make a few gentle suggestions. Jackman gnawed on his bottom lip. Marie had always seen the very best in Carter, but Jackman himself had, once or twice, seen a different side to the enigmatic detective. There had been times when Carter McLean had been too ruthless in his determination to get his man. He just prayed that the terrible things that had happened in Carter's life did not exacerbate that particular trait. Carter had always been a bit of a loose cannon, and Jackman could handle that. As the super had admitted, he got results. But what he didn't want was Carter suddenly operating completely outside the box, and taking Marie with him. He nodded to himself. Yes, tomorrow he and Marie would definitely have to talk.

* * *

Silas and Klink led Carter towards the river and Stone Quay. So, he had been right all along. They were going back to the Eva May.

'Better get a move on,' muttered Silas. 'We need the light, so I'd like to get this done before darklings.' He glanced up. 'And it's coming in fast tonight.'

'But there's power on the boat, Si. I can fire the generator, no problem.'

Silas grunted. 'It's not on the boat.'

Carter gazed across the fields. The smell of charred stubble hung in the air. He knew what it was now, but it still made him uncomfortable. He shook himself. Think about the money. If it wasn't on the Eva May, where the hell was it?

Silas was now stepping onto the quay. 'Gonna need those muscles of yours. Last time I did this, it nearly killed me. Not quite as tough as I used to be.'

The old man walked towards the rear of the old store-room, and began to pull back a knotted clump of brambles, nettles and dead weeds.

'Your turn, young'un. We have to move that.' Silas pointed to a heap of broken chunks of concrete and builder's rubble beneath the vegetation.

'It's under there?'

'In a manner of speaking,' said Silas. 'If you get a move on, you'll see for yourself, won't you?'

'Then I'd better get some tools or I'll be here all night.' Carter went into the storeroom and returned with a large, battered shovel.

He worked until the sweat ran down his back and dripped from his forehead. This was not how he had foreseen spending his evening.

'There! Look.' Silas pointed again. Carter saw a lump of old scrap iron. 'Give it a tug. Oh, and mind. It's heavy.'

The iron bar was actually a curved handle. Carter braced himself and heaved.

Silas had been right. It was damned heavy. With a loud groan, he pulled it up out of its seating, and found that he was staring down a shallow flight of stone steps. 'Well, I'll be . . . !' He let the trapdoor fall backwards and stared into the darkness below.

'A torch would help. Unless you want to break your neck.'

With a grunt, Carter went back to the storeroom and returned with a battery-powered storm lantern.

They stood at the entrance to the old cellar. Carter switched on the lantern. Silas had been right. Darkness was falling fast.

'How come you never showed me this place before? I've lived here all my life and I never knew that there was anything beneath the storehouse.'

'For your own good, lad,' said Silas. 'When you were a boy, smuggling was rife out here. Boats went out on the high tides to meet the Dutchmen. Came back loaded with gin and cigarettes, they did. This spot was safe from the coastguards.' Silas gave a throaty laugh. 'Then the boy became a policeman, so I decided best to let sleeping dogs lie.'

'But I'd never have blamed *you* for anything, Si! You were like family to me.'

Silas shrugged. 'What you didn't know wouldn't hurt you, *or* put you in any difficult situations. It was no big deal. It hasn't been used for a decade and anyway, only a handful of people ever knew about this place.'

'And you were one of them?' Carter smiled. So the Breeze family were not just poachers, but smugglers as well.

'Eli and I built it,' said Silas flatly. He looked troubled. The lantern light deepened the furrows etched into his face. 'On your father's orders.'

Carter froze. His father? When he said his father was a bastard, he meant the drink, the lies and the deceptions, not actual criminal activities.

'I'm sorry. I shouldn't have said that.' The old man looked angry with himself. 'I should have kept my own counsel.'

Carter gave a harsh laugh. 'Don't worry, Si. Nothing my wonderful father did would really surprise me.'

'All the same, it wasn't my place to open my mouth.' He looked up at the rapidly darkening sky. 'But time for that later. We should find your friend's bag before nightfall.'

Carter nodded. He stared down at the small dark space beneath the ground. Claustrophobic, and with no other way out.

He saw in his mind that other door. In his dreams, the plane door crashed shut with a terrible reverberating sound, like a steel vault being sealed. In reality he had heard nothing, the raging storm had carried away all sound. But the memory was always accompanied by that awful, final slam.

Carter tried to swallow. His throat was parched dry and icy shivers trickled down his backbone. He concentrated on the old trapdoor. Come on, Carter. There was no possible way it could accidentally slam shut. Could it? He knew it was illogical but he still had visions of a freak gust of wind lifting it, and closing it on top of him. 'Silas, I don't think I can go down there.' His voice cracked. 'I'm sorry but I can't . . .'

'Don't have to. Klink! Go find!' Silas smiled and watched the dog leap into the cellar. 'He'll get it. It's the only thing down there with any scent left on it.'

'But it's been there for over a year,' whispered Carter shakily.

'I checked a month or two ago to see that it was safe. There'll be something left for that dog of mine to pick up, never you fear.' He peered into the darkness. 'See! What I tell 'ee? Here, boy.' Silas bent down and helped the dog drag an old leather sports bag up the last few steps. 'Good lad! Leave.'

Carter reached forward, his hands trembling slightly. 'That's Ray's bag?'

'Aye. I let him hide it there. I knew it were safe from his thieving family.' He handed it to Carter. 'Many's the time I thought about handing it over to you, but I'd promised him I'd say nothing to a living soul. Finally I decided to wait until the time was right. I knew it would come, and now it's up to you to do what the boy wanted.'

The bag was in remarkably good condition, just musty-smelling and covered with patches of whitish mould. Silas leaned over his shoulder while Carter carefully undid it. Inside were dozens of small rolls of notes, wrapped in Clingfilm and held together with elastic bands. Carter unwrapped one. The perished rubber disintegrated and a wad of ten pound notes opened like a paper flower.

Carter was elated. Another of his friends was about to have their wish granted. All he had to do now was take it to Joanne and give her Ray's message.

Silas glanced at him. 'Must be near on five thousand pounds there, wouldn't you think?'

Carter nodded. 'Probably more. Whatever, Jo will be grateful for it.'

'I wish her well,' said Silas. 'Now, let's get this place closed up again, perhaps for the last time, hey?'

Nothing pleased Carter better. He lowered the trapdoor, grabbed the shovel and soon Silas was settling the thick mat of scrubby weeds back over the rubble.

'All done. Home, Klink.'

Carter locked up the storeroom and loped after the old man. 'You're a bit eager to get away, Si?'

'Can't deny it.' Silas strode in the direction of his cottage. 'To be honest, there's been a bad feeling about this place of late. It's even affected Klink. Right unsettled, he's been. I'll be happy to be behind my own door for the next couple of nights, until the moon goes on the wane.' He glanced back at Carter. 'But don't you worry about your boat. Old Klink'll listen out for intruders.'

Carter wondered what could have spooked the old poacher so badly. He was normally at his happiest traipsing around the marsh in the dead of night. 'What's happened, then?' he asked as casually as he could.

'Oh, nothing. Just a bad feeling, that's all.'

'I've never known you to be spooked before,' said Carter.

'Me neither. Maybe I'm getting old.'

'Well, I think if you're worried, it's some*one* and not some*thing* that's behind it,' murmured Carter suspiciously.

'Well, you hold on to that thought. I'll just hedge my bets, if it's all the same to you.'

Carter knew better than to argue. Silas's world was still filled with folklore, legends, mysteries and superstitions. Carter watched Silas and his dog go into his cottage. He waited until he saw an oil lamp lit, and then walked slowly back towards Stone Quay.

Maybe he should keep watch himself? The Eva May was very special to him. After all the work his friends had done on the old lifeboat, he would willingly do time for the man who deliberately vandalised her.

He unlocked his vehicle and sat inside, unsure of what to do next. He had never known Silas to be jumpy and it unnerved him. Silas was a loner. He loved the solitude of the marsh, and had always relished the coming of eventide. This was so out of character.

He switched the engine on and wound down the window. No one in their right mind would stop here if they saw a damn great 4 x 4 parked on the quay, so there was no chance of catching them red-handed. Carter guessed he might as well go home and leave the guard duties to Klink.

He sniffed the evening air, on which the whiff of burnt grain still floated. Then he coughed and held his hand to his mouth. The stink of smoke filled his nostrils and his lungs. It was them.

He turned off the engine and jumped out of the Land Rover, clutching Ray's bag to his chest. He spun round and stared into the shadows, but all he saw was the wind-stunted trees and the straggly bushes surrounding the quay. He took a few steps towards the Eva May, but apart from the whisper of the night breeze and the water lapping the shore, there was nothing.

'Guys? Ray? Tom? Jack? Where are you?'

The breeze suddenly cooled. Tendrils of cold air stroked his face. Carter shivered and pulled up his shirt collar. 'Guys?' He swung round in a full circle. 'Ray? Where are you? I've found it! I've got your money. It's safe. Look.' He held the old leather bag up over his head.

An unnatural silence descended over the quay. Carter moved carefully back to his motor. Suddenly he was horribly aware of what Silas had called the "bad feeling." He opened the door, threw the bag inside and climbed hurriedly in after it.

What did it mean — the burning smell, and no friends? He shook his head, turned on the ignition and roared off the quay. Home was not his favourite place these days, but right now it was looking pretty good.

* * *

Carter woke at three in the morning and pushed aside the covers. His sleep had been fitful at best, and now he was too alert. He had the usual three choices open to him. Go for a run, watch all-night TV or go into work. With a deep sigh, he stood up and padded towards the shower. He couldn't face the run and he had no interest in reality TV. That left work.

74

Carter took a shower and smiled as the hot water coursed down his body. It had been worth the blisters from that old shovel. He would ring Joanne from work, and maybe go see her in her lunch break. She worked at a newly opened DIY store just outside the town, and he could be there in ten minutes, traffic permitting. The money wasn't a fortune, but he was sure it would make a welcome difference to her. Maybe he should add a bit more? Maybe another grand, to top it up a bit?

'Sod that for a game of soldiers, mate.' Ray's voice penetrated through the hissing water and Carter gasped. He stepped out onto the cool marble floor of the shower room.

'It was just a thought,' he muttered apologetically, trying to ignore the pungent smell.

Ray and the other two were across the room, perched on the edge of his bath. 'It would spoil it, mate. No offence, but just give her the bag as it is, with my message, okay?'

Carter nodded. 'Sorry. Sometimes I think throwing money at things makes them better, but I guess that's not always the case.'

'Sometimes, but not always. Nice thought though. Just not appropriate this time,' said Ray kindly.

Carter stared at them. They were different now. When he'd first seen them in the hospital, it had been indescribably horrible. They'd appeared to him like something out of a horror film — deformed, disfigured and terribly maimed. Now they were . . . he peered through the steam. Well, they were kind of normal, not so much disfigured as out of focus. He could still make out the burns, but it was like looking at a reflection in a shop window. They had a vagueness, a shifting quality as if they were made of liquid light.

He suddenly noticed that Ray seemed more indistinct than the others. He was still speaking, talking about Joanne. Carter frowned. Ray should not be here at all.

After all, he'd had his wish granted. The money had been discovered, it was right here in the apartment with them.

'Finish the job, Carter,' said Ray. 'The money is important, but the fact that she hears from you that I truly loved her is even more so. Understand?'

He understood. 'I'll talk to her later today, I promise.'

'Thanks, mate. I appreciate it.' Ray had practically disappeared. His smile, like that of the Cheshire cat, was the last to fade. The vile smell went with them.

So, Ray's task was almost complete. He shuddered with apprehension. What would Jack ask him?

CHAPTER SEVEN

'What the hell time did you get in this morning?' Marie was staring open mouthed at Carter's almost empty desk.

He looked up at her wearily. 'You really don't want to know.'

'Another bad night?' Marie felt a rush of concern for him. No matter what Laura advised, her anxiety about Carter would always be there.

And he looked awful. He was hollow-eyed, and his skin had a sickly pallor. Even his hair lacked its usual healthy sheen. He needed sleep. Everyone needed sleep to function properly.

He grinned at her. 'So, clever clogs, how did I manage to get all this work put to bed? I've collated six files of evidence reports and witness statements for the Cannon case, *and* I'll challenge you to find any cock-ups in it.' He jerked his thumb towards a neatly stacked mountain of files.

'You can do that office stuff with your eyes closed, and you know it. It's one of the things I've always hated about you.' She looked at him. 'It's not the reports, it's all the rest that bothers me.'

He pushed back his chair and summoned up the energy to smile at her. 'Sorry, Mother. I do have some good news though. Drag up a pew and I'll fill you in on exactly why I'm so knackered.'

Marie pulled a chair towards his desk. 'Do we need a couple of strong coffees for this?'

'Oh, we do, but I'll send one of the rookies out for the real thing, not that dishwater our machine produces. Fancy a Danish?'

'Why not?' Marie stared down at her slightly rounded stomach. 'What's a few thousand calories between friends? I'll have a pecan and maple syrup, if they've got one.'

Carter went to his open door and shouted, 'Whoever wants a trip to Pierre's can treat themselves to a fresh coffee and the bun of their choice!' Then he stood back and waited for the thunder of policemen's boots.

A young DC with jet black spiky hair and a fierce grin beat two others to his door. He held out his hand. Carter passed him a twenty, rattled off their order and returned to his desk. 'While we wait, you can tell me all about your special dinner for two with Gary Pritchard.'

Marie rubbed her hands together. 'Oh my! Can that man cook! Homely stuff, but he's definitely in the wrong job. People would pay good money to taste food that good.'

'So your bijou residence is about to become a select village restaurant?'

'No way. He's mine! All mine!' She looked towards the door. 'Hell, Carter, I can't wait for Kieran to get back. What's this good news?'

He leant towards her and whispered, 'I found Ray's money.'

She let out a whistle. 'Great! And was it with Crazy Silas?'

'As good as.'

Marie sat back and listened to Carter's story.

'I've already spoken to Joanne. I caught her before she left for work. I'm going to see her in her lunch hour. Would you come with me?'

Marie's heart sank. He looked so hopeful. 'But I don't even know the girl, Carter. I'm sure she won't want some stranger sitting in on your conversation.'

'Please?' Carter bit his lip. 'It's going to be very emotional for both of us. I'd be much happier if you were there with me.'

Marie stared at him. His exhausted pallor accentuated that "little boy lost" expression of his, and haggard or not, he was still scarily handsome. Carter McLean was exactly the kind of man that would have attracted her — if she had been on the lookout for someone, but after Bill . . . once again, she felt her resolve fading away. 'Oh, okay. But lunch is on you, right?'

'Absolutely. Scarlett's Deli. Anything you want.'

'This could cost you, my friend.'

'It'll be worth it.' Carter looked up as the spiky-haired constable entered the office. 'Thanks, Kieran. Did you get something for yourself?'

The lad nodded and waved another small bag. 'Thank you, sir. Iced Belgian bun.' He left, pulling the door closed after him.

'Door! Leave the bloody door! How many times do I sodding well have to tell you?'

Marie took a deep breath. She'd heard it a hundred times since the accident, and every time she cursed the youngsters for their thoughtlessness. It was a small thing, after all.

'Sorry! Sorry, sir.' Kieran pushed the door right back against the wall and beat a hasty retreat, clutching his bag to his chest.

'Okay, so where are we meeting Joanne?'

'Uh? Oh yes, she works for the big DIY store on the Fenton Estate.' Marie could see him pulling himself together. 'There's a garden and a seating area on the river bank, right next door to the store. I said we'd meet her there.'

'Do you have any idea what you are going to say? Or are you winging it?'

'I've got a vague idea, but I guess it'll depend on how she reacts. She's a down-to-earth sort of girl. I think she'll be pretty overwhelmed by it all.'

Marie puffed out her cheeks. 'Yeah, a year and a half down the road, and she suddenly gets given a bag of money that she never knew existed. *I'd* certainly be overwhelmed.' She shook her head. 'Just keep it simple, okay. It'll be a shock, so don't overdo the explanations.'

'Fair enough. That'll make it easier for me too.'

Marie sighed. It was going to be awful. She wished he had decided to mail the bag to the girl anonymously. She took a bite from her Danish and chewed thoughtfully. 'So who is next?'

'Jack. Jack's next.'

'And?'

Carter shrugged. 'I haven't a clue, but—'

'No, Carter! Don't say it. I'm really struggling with your bloody conversations with the dead.'

He bit his lip. Immediately Marie felt bad. 'I'm sorry, that came out all wrong.'

'Nothing to apologise for.' He sighed. 'I expect far too much from you, Marie. It's me who should be saying sorry. I just assume you're going to understand, even when I do and say things that are completely off the wall.'

Marie gave him a weak smile. 'Forget it. It's okay. We'll go see Joanne, and then we'll deal with Jack's unfinished business, whatever that is. Okay?'

Carter nodded. 'By the way, the super has kept Leah at home today. By all accounts she's practically walled her up. Luckily, she's working on her dissertation, so she can do it from the safety of Crooke's house.'

Marie snorted. 'I bet she loves that! She struck me as being a pretty independent kid, even though this has shaken her up.' She thought for a moment. 'Has anyone interviewed the boyfriend yet?'

Carter sipped his coffee. 'Uniform had a word, but they have no concerns about him. He's a bright student, well adjusted, with no weird hang-ups. Plus he has water-tight alibis for most of the occasions when the stalker was at work. He seemed genuinely concerned for Leah's welfare.' He set down his coffee. 'Another dead end.'

'I have a feeling our creepy crawly will relish all the attention and take it as a challenge, don't you?'

'Almost certainly,' agreed Carter. 'He'll bide his time but he will act again.'

'And we just wait?'

Carter shrugged. 'I can't see what else we can do. I tried to check on the money he used in the chocolate shop, but it had already been banked.'

'That was convenient!'

'A bit too convenient, if you ask me,' muttered Carter. 'He timed it perfectly.'

'Just like he timed gaining access to her car in the university car park. He's damned clever.' Marie stirred her coffee slowly, then looked up. 'But maybe a bit too clever? Carter, don't you think this is all a bit calculating for a stalker?'

'How so?'

'Well, if he's just some student, isn't all this perfect timing and detailed planning a bit extreme? Doesn't sound like some nerdy creep in an anorak to me. You don't think we may be dealing with something a bit more sinister, do you? Someone with a bigger agenda than just trying to get into a pretty girl's knickers?'

Carter frowned. 'Like someone intent on actually doing her harm?'

She shrugged. 'Or maybe abducting her?'

'Whoa! Let's not get too far ahead of ourselves.' Carter held up a hand. 'There's been no indication of anything *that* serious.'

'Yet.'

'You really do have a bad feeling about this, don't you?' Carter stared into his coffee. 'I still believe it's some horny kid who is infatuated with Leah and is prepared to confront the wrath of Lincolnshire's finest to get his girl. Just relax, I'm certain this will all blow over really soon.'

Marie didn't answer. Usually they worked together well on a case, and occasionally they were so in tune that there was no need for discussion. She wondered why this case was so different. 'Well, I sincerely hope you are right, Detective Sergeant, I really do.' She stood up. 'And now I need to tie up with Jackman before he takes the morning meeting.'

'How goes it with Suzanne's case? Has he said?'

His voice was even and his tone casual, but she saw the keen glint in his eyes.

'Badly, by all accounts. His exact words were that they were up the proverbial creek, and not a paddle in sight.'

'If there is anything I can do, he should ask me. I didn't know Suzanne well, hardly at all in fact, but I might know some of the people who were around her and Tom at the time. It could help provide more background.'

'Thanks. I'm sure Jackman will talk to you if things don't get any better.'

Marie left Carter's office. At the door, she glanced back briefly. There was a very strange expression on her friend's face.

* * *

The small park was almost empty, and Carter recognised Joanne Simms immediately. She was sitting alone on a bench close to the river's edge. She wore a shapeless, beige jacket over a minty green blouse and a calf-length floral print skirt. She was considerably thinner than the last time he had seen her. When was that? Six months ago? Could be longer. Initially the victims' nearest and dearest had clung to each other like debris caught up in a tornado, bound to each other by the memory of their dead loved ones and the awful thing that had happened to them. Then, as each one began to rebuild their lives, they drifted apart. They grew awkward with one another. After three months, Carter avoided all of them.

He strode towards her, hoping his fear and panic didn't show. Beside him, Marie squeezed his arm. 'It'll be alright,' she whispered.

He swallowed. 'Hey! Joanne! You look great.' He hugged her briefly. 'I don't think you ever met Marie? She's my old partner Bill's wife. She's a detective too.'

Joanne shook Marie's outstretched hand, and they sat down. 'You said you had something to tell me?' Carter sensed that Joanne didn't want this meeting any more than he did. The discomfort came off her in waves.

'Yes.' He took a long breath. 'Actually I have something for you.' He placed the bag, now clean of mildew, on the seat between them.

Joanne stared at it. 'It was Ray's, wasn't it?'

'I found it.' He paused. 'Close to the Eva May.'

'Can I . . . can I look in it?' Her voice shook slightly.

'It's yours, Jo. Ray meant it for you.' He pushed the old sports bag closer to her.

Her hands were unsteady, and she took a long time to undo the fastenings.

Carter couldn't wait. 'It's money, Joanne. Money Ray was saving for your wedding. He was scared that his brothers would steal the lot, so he hid it. I only found it last night and I brought it straight to you.' Joanne stared into the bag, saying nothing. 'I don't know exactly how much is there. Quite a bit, I guess,' he said lamely. 'Whatever, it's yours.'

Now came the hard part. 'You do know he really loved you, don't you, Joanne?'

She raised her eyes to him. 'Of course I know.'

'He just wants you to be sure of that.'

Her eyes grew wider. 'What do you mean, he *wants* me to be sure? Did you speak to him before he died? My God, Carter! Did he talk to you? You never told me that!' She was half out of her seat.

He grasped her hand. 'No, no! You misunderstand! It's just that we used to talk when we were working on the boat. He told me he was never very good at expressing his feelings. That's all, honestly. He often said he ought to tell you more often how he felt. To your face, that is.' Oh God, what a mess he was making of this.

Marie came to his assistance. 'All he's saying is never, even in your darkest moments, doubt that your Ray was deeply in love with you.'

'I'm sorry, Joanne, really.' Carter let go of her hand. 'At least this is safe with you now.' He touched the bag lightly. 'And we better go.'

To his relief, Marie put her arm around her. 'Will you be alright, Joanne? We can walk you back to work if you like? You've had a bit of a shock, haven't you?'

'You could say that.' Her voice shook but she managed a small smile. 'I'm fine. Luckily I'm owed a few hours off, so I think I'll go straight home, have a cup of tea and try to get my head around this.' She looked across at Carter. 'And I'm sorry too. You've been kind enough to bring me this, and then I go and shout at you. It's silly I know, but I'm still having a hard time accepting he's gone. From the, way you spoke, just for a moment . . . I thought . . .' Her voice faded. There was nothing more to say.

When they got to his vehicle, Carter glanced back. Joanne walked slowly, holding the bag wrapped in her arms, as if it were a baby.

Carter started the Land Rover and pulled out of the car park. The task was complete. Would Ray be with the others when they next appeared?

* * *

Danny Hurley lay on his bed and thought about his girl.

There was very little he didn't already know about her, but he loved to lie quietly and try to think of small things that might have escaped his attention. Today he could think of nothing at all, and that made him feel good. He thought of the police running around chasing their tails and smiled contentedly. Knowledge really was power.

He turned his head to look at the wall, and the dozen photographs he had taken of her. He was proud of them. His camera was his most treasured possession — after his girl of course. He had acquired the Nikon D3 digital SLR for his previous job. It was top of the range, shot up to eleven frames per second and would probably have set him back a few grand if he'd had to pay for it. He reached up and stroked a stunning close-up of her face, imagining the touch of her skin.

What a girl!

Danny stretched and stood up. No time for thoughts like that right now. There were plans to be made. Poor little Leah had been grounded by her granite-faced aunt. He knew her quarantine wouldn't last long. She was a teenager, and teenagers got bored quickly. He gave her two days, max. Then the game would start in earnest.

Carefully locking the door behind him, he strolled out of his room and along the narrow corridor to the kitchen. He ran his hands along the walls either side of him, as if trying to push them out, widen the cramped space. He wouldn't mind leaving here soon. He had never thought of it as a home, just somewhere to hide. There was more to life than this so-called "bijou flat." If his plans worked out, there would be.

In the cramped galley kitchen he took a bottle of Newcastle Brown from the fridge and flipped off the top. He drank very little, but he did enjoy a cold bottled beer in the late afternoon.

What had he done today? He had ditched his runner and taken on two new ones. It wasn't difficult, they were two a penny, and he wasn't known for being mean. He swigged back the beer. He had a day or so to rest and get his next strategy organised, and then he would be able to spend some quality time with his girl. He closed his eyes and sighed.

CHAPTER EIGHT

Carter was depressed, angry with himself for handling the meeting with Joanne so badly. Marie had told him so, but he knew it anyway. Why had he spoken about Ray in the present tense, and upset Joanne that way?

'I'm off now, Carter.' Marie leaned against his office door frame and smiled. 'I need to get to the supermarket and stock up. Do you need anything?'

He shook his head. He hadn't cooked a proper meal in a long while. Mrs Mitchell, his daily, always bought the cleaning materials and gave him the bill, and when he was hungry, he ate out. He even ate breakfast at his desk. 'Can't think of anything, but thanks all the same.'

Marie stepped inside. 'Cheer up, Carter, and don't beat yourself up over Joanne. She's okay with everything now.'

'Yeah, I guess so.' Carter yawned. 'God, I just wish I could get a night's sleep.'

'Have you tried a little helper? Nothing strong, maybe something herbal.'

'In the first few months I took enough drugs to keep a pharmaceutical company solvent for a decade! I cannot face another pill, herbal or otherwise.'

'Mmm. I'd probably feel the same, but you *have* to sleep.'

'Hopefully I will, as soon as I know about Ray. If he's moved on, then I'll know I can do the same with the other two. Then we can all rest.'

Marie opened her mouth to speak, and then closed it again. Finally she nodded and said, 'Yes, let's hope so.'

Carter sat on, completing a few outstanding reports and answering emails. When he could no longer focus, he pulled his jacket from the back of his chair and stood up to go. Would he have visitors tonight, or would they keep him in suspense? Half of him was desperate to know if his good deed had paid off, and the other half dreaded finding out that it hadn't.

He flopped back down in his chair, floored by deep sadness. He thought of Marie, so eager to get home, even though her husband was no longer there to share it. It was a home she loved, full of things she and Bill had saved for and chosen together. She had happy memories, a classy powerful motorcycle, a cat, and now a friendly companion to chat to about the ups and downs of the day, someone to share a meal with, and a glass of wine. She was a very attractive woman. When the time was right, he was sure that Marie Evans would fall in love again.

All that was closed to him. He would never have a relationship now. Who would put up with all his freaky symptoms, all his fears and phobias, not to mention his obsessive tidiness? No one. And what if he never managed to get rid of his old mates? How would he explain that?

He remembered Laura Archer's words: "You have to be prepared to face the fact that relationships will be difficult. You may find, in the early stages, that they are impossible. Just remember, all things change. Let nature take its course, let the healing begin, and who knows what the future may bring."

At the time he hadn't given much thought to relationships, he just wanted to hold onto his sanity. Now he wasn't so sure. All at once, and for the first time in his adult life, Carter felt terribly lonely.

* * *

Robbie Melton leaned forward and peered at the pile of printouts on his desk. He was the duty CID officer on night shift, and he revelled in it. During the day, the main office was clamorous with noise, resounding with ringing phones, clattering printers, mobile phone ringtones, and officers laughing, cursing and shouting across the room. At night the room belonged to him. The only sounds were the low hum of the air conditioning unit, and muffled voices drifting in from other parts of the building.

Unlike some of his colleagues, Robbie didn't use the quiet time to doss down in a corner, or watch a film on his phone. Robbie worked. Tonight, the streets and back alleys of Saltern were peaceful, and there were no calls to go out. He was able to give his full attention to Suzanne Holland.

Trouble was, he wasn't getting very far. All he knew for certain was that this woman had secrets.

He had discovered quite a lot about her sexual preferences, but nothing about the woman herself.

He looked again at her photo and whispered, 'There's got to be more to you than this.'

He skimmed his notes. It appeared that the only people willing to talk about her were some of her many casual lovers from before her marriage to Tom. Everyone else — relatives, neighbours, workmates — either refused to talk about her or simply declared ignorance.

Robbie sighed. The sarge had wanted to know about Suzanne's relationship with Tom Holland, but once again, he had hit a brick wall. There was only one person left that might know something about their life together, and be prepared to discuss it — Carter McLean. The one person he could not ask.

He considered the facts. Suzanne's first marriage to the Spanish holiday rep, Harvey Cash, had failed. Their

88

marriage seemed to have been short and not very sweet, ending in a divorce and a court case over some missing money. And that was all.

Why would no one talk to him?

Robbie pulled out a few sheets of paper dealing with Harvey Cash. If he couldn't talk to Tom Holland, he'd have to make do with the first husband. If he was awake, or more to the point, sober.

He picked up the phone, having decided that maybe Cash would be more inclined to talk if he was drunk. Last time he had caught him in a stupor. If he could catch him in the early stage, when he was on a high, he might be chatty.

Harvey Cash told Robbie in no uncertain terms what he thought of being disturbed at four in the morning. Robbie apologised profusely and launched into his semi-prepared speech. He really didn't know who to turn to, he said. Only Cash could help them. Slowly, Cash began to respond.

'Yeah, well, you're right, of course, I did know her better than anyone, but I don't want to talk about the bitch.' He paused. Robbie heard a glass clink. 'I'll just say that when you find her, dead or alive, I won't be sending any flowers.'

'Most people seem to think that she was just a fun-loving, sexy, good time girl,' said Robbie.

'Hah! She was certainly that to some people all right! But you want to speak to the ones who got close. They'll tell you a different story.'

'Why don't you tell me?'

'Because . . .'

Robbie was certain he heard a strangled sob.

'Just go to hell!'

The line went dead.

Robbie stared at the picture of Harvey Cash. 'It's about time I took a short holiday,' he mused. 'Spain might be pleasant at this time of year. And you, pal, can be my guide.'

* * *

Carter had brought home a Chinese takeaway and a bottle of the best Merlot that his local convenience store stocked. It was pretty bad, but the bottle was now almost empty. The sweet and sour pork, the spring rolls and the egg fried rice were unopened in the waste bin.

He sat on the terrace and stared out across the gardens. The view never bored him, but now he wished there was someone to share it with. He wondered where all this had come from. Maybe it was thinking about Joanne and Ray, or remembering Marie and Bill. The world seemed to be all couples suddenly, except for him. He sat watching the sky put on its nightly display, until only the darkest indigo and deepest grey were left. Time to turn in.

His bedroom contained a king-size bed, built-in wardrobes and matching furniture, all of it polished, all the surfaces clear.

He showered, and switched on the wall-mounted flatscreen television. He'd be decadent, lounge in bed with the last of the wine and watch TV until he fell asleep.

The wine finished, Carter turned onto his stomach and closed his eyes. Maybe tonight he would get a few hours of peaceful sleep. He drifted off.

An ice-cold, bony hand fastened itself around his ankle like a vice.

'Hey! Got you, Carter, old boy!'

The room filled with the familiar stench of burning.

'Jesus Christ!'

'Couldn't resist it! Sorry.' Jack's laugh echoed hollowly around the room. 'Remember the game, Carter? "Do You Dare?" The kids loved it, didn't they?'

Jack was reminiscing about the old days when they had supervised a group of deprived kids at an adventure

90

camp. 'Yeah, and then you'd organise a campfire, sit down with them and tell them scary ghost stories until their eyes were wide. Then you'd send them to bed, daring them to leave one exposed foot hanging out of the bed for the bogey man to grab! It's a wonder they didn't wet themselves!' He laughed again.

Carter's ankle still felt as if it was packed around with dry ice. He stared at it. 'That wasn't funny,' he muttered.

'Yes it was,' said Jack. 'Like it was with the kids. You scared the shit out of them and they loved you for it. Every night they came back for more stories and more dares.'

It was true. They had, and Jack was also right about those times being good. Carter sat back on the bed and looked around him.

Jack was perched at the bottom of the bed. Where was Tom? Finally he made out his friend's outline slouched against the wall close to the door. So far he had said nothing. He certainly had not joined in with Jack's jolly jape.

'You okay, mate?' Carter asked, not really wanting to hear the answer.

Tom seemed to nod, but remained silent. Then Carter realised that Ray had gone. He gasped, and peered into every shadowy corner.

'You can put the light on if you want,' said Tom sullenly, 'But you won't find him. He's gone.'

Tom moved forward out of the shadows. 'The question is, which one of the two of us is next?'

Carter flicked the switch on his bedside lamp, and then recoiled in horror and dismay. His friend looked like something that belonged on a butcher's block. Carter gagged and fought back the rising bile. He couldn't be sick! He just couldn't. He swallowed hard, jumped up, and ran to the kitchen, where he splashed water over his face and neck.

It was another legacy from the accident. Weird, but there it was. Carter had a morbid fear of vomiting. Laura said it even had a name. Emetophobia or something like that.

He leant back against the kitchen sink and breathed deeply. It was passing, thank God. He just needed to try not to think about Tom. What the hell had happened? They had been so much better. If he half closed his eyes, they looked as they always had. But now! He shuddered and concentrated on his breathing.

He had to get himself back into the bedroom. Tom had asked him a question, and he needed to answer it. When he reached the door, he hesitated.

'Come on in, mate.' It was Tom. 'Sit down, and look at me.'

Carter reluctantly did as he was told. There was Tom, smiling apologetically at him.

His face was not perfect, but it was recognisable now.

Let's get this over with, thought Carter. 'You asked who should be next. I thought perhaps it should be Jack. Whatever I can do, I'll try to do it.'

'I thought you'd say that, and that's cool by me.' Tom nodded slowly. 'In fact it's probably better that way, because my own dilemma is not exactly straightforward. Is it?'

Carter's heart sank. This didn't sound good. But first, Jack. He turned to his other friend, preparing himself for what he was about to ask.

The room was empty. Carter sat on the bed and put his head in his hands.

CHAPTER NINE

Carter was about to start his car and go to work. He reached out to switch on the ignition and saw a figure sitting next to him in the passenger seat. Jack. Tom was sitting in the back, humming a sad tune. In the confined space inside the car the smell of burning was almost unbearable.

'I've been thinking, mate.' Jack sounded almost apologetic. 'I know Ray said throwing money at things wasn't always the answer . . .' He stopped, as if he were too embarrassed to go on.

'Just ask. If I can do something to make you feel better, anything at all, I'll do it, I promise.' That was no longer quite true. Now he would do whatever it took to make them go away.

'There's something that's worrying me, mate. I know I've never told you this, but I've got a kid.'

Tom broke off his humming for a moment, as if in mild surprise. Then he continued.

'A little girl. Her name is Phoebe. Her mum, well, it was complicated. I guess I wasn't quite what her parents wanted for their daughter. We came from very different backgrounds, so . . .'

Carter shook his head. 'No, Jack, you didn't tell me. Does the mother know you're . . .' He stopped.

'Dead? Yeah, she knows.' Jack sounded utterly miserable. 'But Kim, that's her name, has fallen out with her parents, and I don't know how she's going to look after Phoebe. She loves her to bits, but she's struggling. I was going to help her, but . . .'

'*I'll* help her. Just tell me where I can find her.'

Jack gave him a surname and an address. 'Don't just hand over money, Carter. I think there's some bad people around her right now. Find another way, will you?'

Carter nodded. He knew a lot about financial arrangements. This was one task he could achieve without help and he could sort it quickly and efficiently. 'Don't worry, Jack. Leave it to me. Your little girl will have everything she needs, and a good education, rest assured.'

Carter turned to smile at his friend, but the passenger seat was empty, and apart from the faint echo of a melancholy song, he was alone again.

The stench of burning flesh abated, and Carter leant back against the headrest. He could do this with his eyes closed! Which just left his fourth friend, Tom. Carter's relief gave way to concern. Tom had said that his request was complicated.

* * *

In the CID room, Jackman stared from one to the other of his detectives. 'Anyone got *anything* more on Suzanne Holland?'

The only response he got was a low murmur of dissent.

'Max? Any luck with tracing her movements in the week before she disappeared?'

Max shook his head. 'Apart from a couple of nocturnal assignations after her husband walked out, absolutely nothing. It's like she was some kind of vampire that slept all day and went on the hunt at night.'

94

'Surely she had to show up at work?'

Charlie raised a hand. 'I spoke to her boss at the tanning salon where she worked. He confirmed that Suzanne called in sick a couple of weeks before she vanished, and never went back.'

'Not too sick to go on the pull though,' Max grumbled.

Robbie Melton stood up. 'I've had a thought, sir. Well, it's just a hunch really.'

'Out with it. Whatever it is, it's more than the rest of us have come up with.'

Robbie explained his theory that Harvey Cash, her first husband, knew a lot more than he was admitting. There was possibly a very dark side to Suzanne Holland, one that maybe got her killed or abducted. 'We can't force him to talk, especially over the phone. He'd just do what he did last night and hang up. So I thought I might go and see him.'

A chorus of catcalls and jeers echoed around the room.

Jackman smiled, and held up his hand to silence them. 'They have a point, Robbie. I have to account for every single forensic test carried out and decide whether we can even afford to do a bloody £1.10 credit search or not. I don't think you spending a few days under the Spanish sun will fit in too well with the super's budget.'

Robbie laughed too. 'I wasn't expecting it to come out of the force budget, sir. I'm due a few days' leave, so I thought I might go and top up my tan in Sanxenxo.'

'Right!' Max grinned at Robbie's night-shift pallor. 'I think it would take more than a couple of days to turn you into a bronzed Apollo.'

'Then maybe I'll just check out the sangria, with a man who knows the area.'

'Or we could get the Spanish police to talk to him,' Max threw in.

Robbie shook his head. 'I reckon he'd clam up, and I'm not sure who we would contact anyway. I don't know much about the Spanish police system.'

'The Guardia Civil would be my first port of call,' Jackman said thoughtfully. 'The Policia Municipal, the local guys, usually just deal with petty stuff. This is part of a murder enquiry, so I think they'd pass it up the ladder, and that would take time.' He looked at Robbie. 'Do you really think you could get something out of him?'

'Yes, sir. When I talked to him last night I picked up some very odd vibes. He seemed scared for some reason, and he was *very* relieved that she was out of the picture.' He drew in a breath. 'I'm sure a late-night heart-to-heart over a bottle of something strong would produce results.'

Jackman raised his hands. 'Well, it's up to you what you do and where you go in your time off. Is your passport up to date?'

'Oh yes.'

'How long does it take to get there?'

'London to la Coruna? Just over two hours, I think.'

'Then you'd better go pack your sunglasses.'

'Jammy git,' Max growled. 'Why didn't I think of that?'

'Because your only brain cell is too busy concentrating on a certain WDC.' Charlie grinned broadly at his friend.

Max and Rosie had been going out for several months now, and Max was clearly very smitten.

Jackman called his detectives to order. 'Back to work, guys! We need to keep at this. There is only so much that her ex can tell us — *and* it's past history. I want to know what Suzanne did just before she disappeared.'

The team returned to their desks, and Jackman called Marie to his office. 'How are things going with the super's niece?'

Marie told him what she knew. 'I really don't like it, sir. The stalker is too damned clever. It's far too organised.

Carter still thinks it's a kid who is totally infatuated with Leah, but . . .' She shook her head.

'You think otherwise.'

'I do. But we've hit a brick wall. Although I don't like it, we've no alternative but to watch the girl and wait until he tries something else.'

'Well, I'm about to take a look at the Holland home. It's remained empty since the night she went missing. Want a short break from obsessive admirers?'

'Sure, I'll come with you. I'll grab a pool car.' Marie turned to go.

'Hold on.' Jackman beckoned her back. 'How is Carter today?'

'Last time I saw him he was heads down with Rosie. They seem to be really coming to grips with getting the Cannon family drugs case ready for presentation.'

'That's a relief. If anyone can make it watertight, McLean can, but we all know what the Crown Prosecution Service is like.'

Marie nodded grimly. She had seen numerous cases thrown out or stopped by the prosecutor in what was called "discontinuance." Some of these had taken months, even years of painstaking work. It was galling and disheartening, and she hoped it wouldn't happen to the Cannon family case.

'He seems happy enough working with Rosie, don't you think?' Jackman asked.

Marie thought for a while. 'Yes, but as I said before, it's a double-edged sword. He needs to prove to himself, and us, that he's fully capable of doing whatever is asked of him, yet he's scared to move forward. Hence he's accepted the soft option to help out Rosie. But I'm certain part of him wants to be back in the thick of it.'

'I get that, don't you?'

Marie nodded. 'I also get the feeling he's a time bomb waiting to go off. Whenever I walk past him I swear I hear ticking.'

'In that case, I'm going to leave him where he is for the time being. I don't want to be the cause of a good detective imploding.'

'He has to get back in the saddle at some point, or he'll never know if he can ride again. But I'm mighty glad you are taking it slowly.'

'Damage limitation, that's all it is. Now, go get a car.'

* * *

Half an hour later, Marie and Jackman were making their way along the Black Sluice towpath. Few people used this lonely stretch of path, which wasn't exactly pretty.

Jackman looked at the greenish-brown water of the river. 'Oh dear, what a miserable place to live.'

'Or die?'

'Most likely.'

'Even if it was an area of outstanding natural beauty, violent death is violent death,' said Marie. 'It's horrible no matter where it takes place.'

'Agreed, but look at this spot.' He pointed to a dirty piece of police tape still strung across the gateway to an old fen cottage. 'It's beyond dismal.'

'We could have driven down the slip road to the back of the cottage. It's the only way to get to it in a vehicle.'

Jackman smiled at Marie. 'I wanted to get an idea of the setting. And I thought a walk might help blow away some of the cobwebs from that overworked brain of yours. I've never seen you look so preoccupied. And so bloody tired.' Marie said nothing. 'Oh, I know what is worrying you. I just don't know how to help.'

'It'll all come out in the wash, as my mum always says.' Marie shook her head. 'I appreciate your concern, Jackman, but I think this is one of those awful times when you just have to wait and see what happens.'

'How do you see the future for Carter?'

Marie sighed. 'I dread to think.'

Jackman stared at the sad old property, weathered, tired and unloved. 'If things are really so dire, Marie, I might have to recommend that he be retired out.'

'No! You can't do that, sir! He's working through it, I know he is. He just needs a bit more time.' She took hold of his arm. 'Please, he's really trying hard. I know I shouldn't bring all my worries about him to work with me, but with our support, he'll get stronger. Then he'll be able to decide which is the right way for him to go.'

Jackman squeezed her hand. 'Okay, that's fine by me. But talk to me, Marie, because a problem shared and all that? Don't shoulder all this alone. I'm here, aren't I?

'It's difficult when someone shares their innermost feelings. You kind of feel you're betraying them if you talk about it.'

'I know. But try dumping some of the more mundane stuff on me. I have broad shoulders, you know.' Jackman flexed an invisible muscle.

Marie smiled. 'I might just do that.' She looked over to the old cottage. 'I like rural, and I like traditional, and sometimes I even like isolated, but I do not like this place.'

Jackman nodded. He turned in a circle and gazed out at the surroundings.

There was the river, with a footpath on both sides. Then an expanse of reeds and water grass that was sometimes covered at very high tide, and then a grassy overgrown bank. Finally, mile upon mile of arable fields, broken only by the odd tree or clump of scrubby bushes. In the distance lay the marshland and the grey waters of the Wash. 'I can only count three other dwellings in the whole area,' said Jackman. 'And the reports state that uniform covered those on a house to house that started right at the beginning of the towpath.' Jackman took a small pair of birding binoculars from his pocket and focused on the largest of the three homes. 'That's Bittern Lodge. I went there once for a charity ball. Very posh indeed.'

Marie stifled a laugh. It sounded odd coming from Jackman, who looked every inch the wealthy landowner.

'The Lodge is empty this month. Douglas Fitzpatrick, the owner, is out of the country. He left his contact numbers before he left, so that uniform could do a drive by every so often.'

'What? No servants?' Marie pretended to be shocked.

'None that live in. Times is 'ard, milady, didn't you know?'

Marie borrowed Jackman's glasses and surveyed the country house. 'Doesn't look that way. Does he use nail scissors to manicure that lawn? There's not a blade of grass out of place.'

'He does keep it nice. It wasn't his family home or anything. He purchased it when the original owner went bankrupt and had to sell up.'

Marie turned the glasses on the other two properties, 'And those two? Isn't that Mallard's Farm, the old Curtis place?'

'It is, and it's been a building site for months. They've just finished revamping it. Bit too modern for me now, but each to their own, I guess.'

'And the other?' Marie squinted through the lens at a cluster of dilapidated barns.

Jackman shook his head. 'Not sure. We'll check it when we get back.'

'It looks deserted, but it's a bit far away to be sure.'

Jackman pursed his lips. 'Then maybe we should drive round and take a look.'

Marie handed back his binoculars. 'Definitely. Five minutes across the field pads and you could reach that place from here.'

'Shall we go inside?'

'Can't wait.' She gave an exaggerated shiver.

Jackman took a key from his pocket and walked up the overgrown path. 'With the husband tragically killed, and the wife mysteriously missing. No wonder no one comes here.'

'Jackman? I've not read the old reports fully, but why did Tom Holland fly off on a jolly "boys' outing" with his mates, three days after his wife's blood was splattered across the lounge carpet?'

'It's not very clear, but it seems they'd had a falling out. Tom had walked out and was staying at his mate's place — Ray Barratt? The groom?'

'Ah, another of Carter's dead friends.'

'That's the one. As far as we can tell, Tom never knew that anything had happened to his wife.'

'He can't have done, can he? He'd hardly have been jetting off on a stag weekend if he knew she had been hurt or abducted.'

'We have a character profile on Tom Holland, and it would be more than out of character. He was a decent, hardworking lad. I think he would have been devastated, even if they'd had a tiff.'

'So who found the crime scene?'

'We did. Well, the local bobby came to break the news of the air crash, but got no answer. When he came back for the second time, he looked through the windows and saw the blood.'

'And no one had reported her missing?'

'Apparently not, but then she wasn't universally liked, or so it seems.'

'And what was the assumed timescale?' asked Marie.

'Forensics thought the incident must have happened about three days prior to the crash.'

Marie gave a little shiver. 'This is not a lucky house, is it?'

They spent around fifteen minutes in the musty, deserted cottage. Jackman stood for a while longer in the lounge, staring around him and trying to imagine what might have happened. Apart from the discoloured patches on the floor and walls, there was nothing to indicate an altercation or a fight. Whether she was killed or abducted, Suzanne Holland hadn't struggled. He turned to go. 'Seen enough?'

Marie nodded. 'Nothing to see.'

Even so, Jackman hung back. He looked again, trying to absorb every last ounce of atmosphere. Outside, he stared at the ground, at the river, at the sky, and then hurried to join Marie. 'As I said, a miserable place to live . . . or die?'

CHAPTER TEN

In his lunch break, Carter rang his family solicitor, his financial advisor, his bank manager, and an acquaintance in the property business. If his dead friend could not help the mother of his only child, then Carter McLean most certainly could.

Because of Jack's warning about the people around Kim, Carter made a few discreet inquiries before he set the wheels in motion. Jack had been right, so cash was out. He would need to set up a series of trusts.

'They need a safe place to live, too,' whispered Carter to himself. 'For a fresh start.'

His property-dealing friend made a few suggestions, and one sounded perfect. There was a small affordable housing complex recently built in one of the fen villages. The village itself had a nursery, a school, a couple of churches, a post office, a bus service and best of all, a bloody good fish and chip shop. What more would she need?

It wouldn't be done overnight, but in an hour, he had laid the foundations.

This time he would be honest about things. He would go and see Kim as soon as he finished work, and tell her that Jack had been very concerned about her and his daughter and had asked his rich friend Carter for help. End of.

Carter sat back, satisfied. By the end of the day he would know whether his plans for Kim and Phoebe Walker were viable. And if they were, Jack's child would have a good future to look forward to, and Kim could ditch the vermin that were creeping around her and enjoy being a mother.

He sipped his cooling coffee. Matt's marathon had been great. Finding Ray's money had been exhilarating, but helping a mother and child to live a better life had been the most rewarding of all.

Then his shoulders slumped. Because as soon as Jack faded away, it would be time for his fourth friend's task. He was dreading it.

* * *

Laura Archer was having trouble concentrating on her last consultation of the morning.

The officer concerned ostensibly had multiple problems, but Laura was almost certain that he was trying to work his ticket and get out early with his pension intact.

All the indicators pointed one way. This was not a serious mental health issue at all, just a man desperate to find a way out of a job he could no longer handle. It was sad, but it also made her angry when she thought of Carter McLean.

At last her client left. Laura walked to her desk, flopped down and let out a sigh.

She was still thinking about Carter.

She was happy that his boss, DI Jackman, was aware of her concerns, but even so, she felt uneasy. Laura was certain there was something seriously amiss that she had failed to see. She sighed again. Perhaps she should seek a second opinion.

Laura rubbed her eyes. The first person that came to mind was her old professor, Sam Page. Sam was retired now. He lived close to a bird reserve on the marsh, and spent his time watching his beloved waterfowl. He was always ready for a chat with his star pupil.

Sam was the most astute man Laura had ever met. He was kind, too. He reminded her of her elderly uncle Frank, who had often taken her fishing, and who'd taught her the patience she still used in her work.

She knew Sam's number by heart.

'Today I found a nesting Pochard, my dear! You often find them in winter, but a few do stay to nest. I am so lucky! They are an Amber list species, you know, quite beautiful! Will you be coming over to see them?'

Laura gave a little laugh. 'I'd love to. How about tomorrow afternoon? I have some time free then.'

'Wonderful! You can grill me about your worrisome patient while we drink tea and watch for Pochards.'

'What makes you think I have a problem patient? I might be desperately missing your company.'

'And pigs might fly.' The old man laughed heartily. 'But I'm happy to help anyway. I'll see you tomorrow.'

Laura shook her head. Sam could read her like a book.

She stood up and stretched, hoping he would read Carter McLean as easily.

* * *

Rosie pushed a thick file of statements across the desk to Carter. 'This is pretty awesome, Sarge.'

'It's Carter, according to the new protocol.'

'No thanks, but whatever, it's still awesome. I've read these half a dozen times and I can't see a single loophole. You are very good at this, aren't you?'

'You're no slouch either, kiddo. You've done a lot of work to bring this together. I'm just mopping up, using a fresh pair of eyes on it.'

'If the CPS throw this out, I'm going to quit and get a job as a dog food taster.'

'Nice! Then we'd better hope they accept it.'

Rosie yawned. 'I'm done in.'

'Me too,' said Carter. 'All this paperwork is as tiring as doing a cross-country run.'

'Fancy a drink after work, Sarge? Max and I were going to call in at the Sea Witch on the way home.'

'Love to, but I've got an appointment. Rain check?'

'Sure.' Rosie looked at him. 'But don't leave it too long, okay? I know you.'

Carter saluted. 'Understood.'

He pulled out another file and opened it. One more hour and he would be off to look for Kim Walker, and give her what he hoped was the best news she'd had in years.

* * *

Kim Walker was as cagey as a street kid. It took Carter several minutes to persuade her to let him through the door.

'It's a con, isn't it?' Kim was slender, in skinny leggings and a graphic T-shirt. Her black hair fell halfway down her back, and her eyes were narrowed to slits.

'It's no con, Kim. I really need to speak to you privately.' Carter heard a thump followed by a string of swear words coming from the room above. 'Preferably somewhere else.'

'Tell me exactly who you are again?'

Carter explained that he was Jack's friend, and the only man to survive the crash. He took out his warrant card and held it out to her. 'I'm DS Carter McLean from Saltern Division, Fenland Constabulary. I think Jack might have told you about me?'

Light suddenly dawned. 'The rich git?'

'That's me.' He gave a wry smile.

'But why now? He's been dead for eighteen months.'

Good point, thought Carter. Maybe because he only told me yesterday? 'There has been a lot to sort out, Kim, and I was injured myself. It's taken me till now to find the courage to deal with everything.'

Her expression relaxed a little, and she nodded. 'The only one to survive? Yes, I suppose that would take some getting over.' She looked around. 'I'll get Phoebe. Where do you suggest we go?'

'If it's all right with you, we'll take a ride in my car, because there is something I want to show you.'

The distrust returned. 'A ride? I don't think so.'

'Five miles from the town centre, no more. I promise.'

She sighed, went inside and returned with a small dark-haired girl of about three. She was dressed in dunga-rees with rabbits embroidered on them, and a cowgirl's check shirt.

'Howdy, pardner!' Carter knelt down and stuck out a hand. So this was Jack's little girl. She needed to get out of this hole, and she was going to need his support to do it. He felt an unexpected surge of emotion. 'Hello, Phoebe. I'm Carter.'

The child stared at him.

'She's not good with people she doesn't know.'

'Nothing wrong with that.' Carter smiled. 'Do you have a car seat for her?'

Kim nodded and went back inside. The seat she produced was top of the range. 'My parents still haven't got the message that you can't always buy yourself out of a bad situation.'

Hearing her say that, Carter took a deep breath and wondered how she would feel when she heard his proposal.

She handed the seat to Carter. 'Okay, we'll come. I carry pepper spray, so no funny stuff, alright?'

'You do know they are illegal?'

'It's defence spray, smart-arse.'

Carter grinned. He was beginning to see why Jack had liked her.

'So where are we going?' she asked.

Carter led the way out and opened his car door. 'Sutterthorpe Village.'

'Why?'

'Have you eaten?'

'Not yet, why?'

'I'm going to get you both fish and chips. And like I said, I have something to show you.'

It took only a few minutes to reach the village and collect their supper. The three of them walked across the green and sat on a bench overlooking a children's play area. To an outsider, thought Carter, we must look like a nice little family enjoying the evening together.

Kim looked around. 'It's nice here, isn't it?'

'I hoped you would think so.' Carter's tone had grown serious. 'Kim, before he died, Jack wanted to make some sort of provision for you and your daughter. It was always a joke between us. I was the rich git, and he was just a poor sod.' He drew in a deep breath. 'The thing is, I *am* well off, and now Jack *can't* help, I want to.'

Kim ate slowly, listening to his words.

'My mother died when I was a kid and my father was an evil bastard. I have no family and no close relatives. The only thing I do have is money.' He exhaled. 'See that new development over there?' He pointed to a cul-de-sac of small new-build starter homes on the far side of the green. 'Quite small, only two-up two-down, with fitted kitchen, bathroom and shower, oh, and a nice little garden and a garage in a block around the back. If you want one, it's yours. For Phoebe, from her father.'

He ate a chip and waited for her reply.

Kim said nothing. Then he saw that tears were running down her face. 'I wondered, that is, I thought that maybe . . .' She sniffed. 'Please tell me my parents aren't behind this. They're not, are they?'

Carter shook his head. 'I have no idea who your parents are, Kim. This is just me. I'm trying to find a way to say sorry to Jack.'

'Sorry that you are alive and he isn't?'

'Something like that.'

'You should give thanks that you *are* alive. You can't live feeling guilty all the time. That's how things are, Carter McLean. You win some, you lose some.'

'Will you let me help you?'

'I'd be a real idiot if I said no, wouldn't I?'

Carter breathed out. 'Phew! Well, here's the plan.'

It took a while to explain how the trusts and allowances would work, but by the time their supper was finished, Kim Walker looked like a different woman.

'I did love Jack, very much.' She looked at him from dark brown eyes. 'But my parents put enormous pressure on us. I left home after they split us up. I went a bit wild for a while.' She pulled a face. 'Hence my present lodgings, and the people there.'

'It shouldn't take too long to sort out. And in the meantime, I suggest you pack your things, and I'll check you into a local hotel.' He gave her his most winning smile. 'And no funny stuff, I swear!'

She smiled back. 'Jack trusted you, so I guess that's good enough for me. And he told me all about you and your friends rebuilding the Eva May. He promised me a trip to see it, but we never got there.'

'It's nearly finished. If you like, I'll take you one day, just so you can see what he was talking about.'

'I'd like that.' She looked at her daughter who was unsuccessfully chasing a duck around the green. 'I was terrified of what would happen to her. Now . . .'

'Now you can forget about worrying. She'll be well provided for. You both will.' He paused. 'I wonder why Jack never talked to me about you and his daughter. We talked about so much. It seems odd that he never brought you to see me.'

'Well, he must have talked about his plans for us, or you wouldn't be here, would you?'

Carter experienced a moment of panic. He had done it again, let his mouth take over. 'I . . . I mean he never explained how serious the situation was with your parents, and he did keep you secret. He only came clean when we were on our way to Holland.'

Kim seemed satisfied with that. 'My mother and father came down really heavy on Jack, almost to the point of serious threats. We decided to keep our meetings hidden from absolutely everyone, so I guess that meant you guys too.' She looked sad. 'After that, I went off the rails a bit. I never thought things would get better again.' She rubbed her eyes. 'But this is like some kind of modern day fairy story. I still can't believe it.'

'Believe it. I'm just sorry that I'm no Prince Charming.'

She leant across and pecked his cheek. 'Well, you're not a frog, and you *are* my knight in shining armour.'

'No, Kim, that's Jack. It's all down to him.'

He handed her a tissue.

* * *

Robbie hadn't really looked forward to his "holiday." He wasn't a big drinker and he never went clubbing, so the understated nightlife in the Spanish town of Sanxenxo came as a pleasant surprise.

And the Galician coast was unbelievably beautiful. He had arrived at night, but everywhere he saw flyers and leaflets describing the numerous hiking trails, impressive scenery and wild landscapes. Robbie loved walking, and he decided he would come back here one day.

The nightlife turned out to be rather cosy and casual. It seemed to revolve around bars, cafes and lounges. He found Harvey Cash in a quiet backstreet bar. He was pretty drunk, but Robbie already knew that this was more or less normal.

He noted what Harvey was drinking, went to the bar and ordered two large gin and tonics.

'I hate it when someone hangs up on you, don't you?' Robbie pushed one of the tall, frosty glasses towards Harvey. 'So I thought I'd come and take a closer look at the man who put the phone down on me last night.'

Harvey's eyes widened. He made an attempt to stand, but Robbie pushed him back into his chair. 'I paid for my flight myself. So I'm sodding well going to make it worth my while. I'm not leaving your side until you tell me why Suzanne was such a bitch . . . as you put it last night.'

Harvey seemed to deflate. 'You aren't going to go away, are you?'

'Nope.'

'Well, I'm not talking here. We'll finish these, then you are going to buy a bottle, correction, you are going to buy two bottles, and we go back to my place. And that's the only way it happens.'

'I can live with that.' The only thing that Robbie was unsure of was how he was going to keep a clear head. After watching his parents get paralytic on far too many 'social' occasions, he had steered clear of alcohol. In fact the last time he'd had an alcoholic drink had been at Christmas. This was not going to be easy.

'When I heard you were a holiday rep, I kind of expected an 18-30 resort full of raucous drunken Brits throwing up all over the place.' He glanced around. 'But this place is really nice.'

'Some of the quieter coves are the best on the coast. I lived here for a while, way back. Now I've come full circle. I don't think I'll be moving on now.' Harvey ran a hand through his thinning hair, picked up his drink and downed it. He belched loudly. 'Ready?'

Robbie watched in horror. 'Sorry, mate. No way can I do that!'

'Then I'll help you. It'll be just like magic! You get two bottles of Ribeiro from my friend Mateo at the bar, and by the time you've paid and given Mateo a generous tip, this will have disappeared, abracadabra!'

Twenty difficult minutes later — Harvey kept insisting that they should go to another bar — Robbie and Harvey arrived at the apartment.

Robbie was surprised. The place was quite respectable. Apart from a few odd empties in various slightly obscure places, it was pretty tidy.

Harvey flopped down onto a brightly coloured sofa. 'Glasses in the kitchen cupboard over the fridge. The wine is very good. Local stuff, but *excelente*, so maybe you'll do better with that than the gin.'

Robbie poured the wine and took a sip. Not bad at all. He handed Harvey his glass, and then sat down on an oversized bean bag.

'You must be pretty desperate to come here, what did you say your name was?'

'Robbie. And, yeah, pretty desperate.'

'Why me and not her next model? Er, Tom what's-his-name.'

'He's dead, Harvey. Tom Holland was killed in a plane crash.'

'Trying to get away from her, was he?'

'No. Although I understand from our files that he was not living at home when she went missing.'

'No surprise.' He took a long slug of his wine. 'So, what about her creepy brother? He was always hanging around her. He could probably tell you more than anyone.'

Robbie looked at him. What brother? How come he wasn't mentioned anywhere? How many more surprises was he going to uncover about Suzanne Holland?

'He's a new one on me, Harv. Who is he?'

Harvey puffed out his cheeks. 'Ah, well, can't say I remember. They had different surnames, but she called him . . . Oh, yes, Ralphie. That's right, Ralph Dolan!'

Robbie scribbled the name into his notebook. 'Why did you say he was creepy?'

'Had that pervy look to him. Not the kind of guy you'd leave alone with anyone, not even your dog.'

'Do you know where he is now?'

'Rotting in hell with his half-sister, hopefully.'

'He's dead?'

Harvey grinned wickedly. 'Sorry, just wishful thinking. I have no idea where he is.'

'But you do think she is dead?'

'I really do hope so.'

Robbie sipped his wine. He was beginning to feel almost mellow, and at least he had a new name to chase up when he got back. 'I hate to do this to you, mate, but could we talk about why I've come here?'

The smile vanished.

'Okay.' Harvey sighed. 'Have another drink, Robbie. Then sit back and I'll tell you all about the lovely Suzanne . . .'

* * *

That night Carter slept until four in the morning. He woke to see the lone figure of Tom, sitting at the foot of his bed. The stench was appalling.

'Tom?' He eased himself up and rested on his elbow, trying to focus on his friend. 'Well, I guess it's finally your turn, mate.'

The figure slowly faded. Carter stared into the darkness, a single word ringing in his ears.

Suzanne.

CHAPTER ELEVEN

'Sir!' Charlie called across the CID room. 'I've got a man on the line here, who might have some new information about Suzanne Holland!'

Jackman hurried over to Charlie's desk, and took the receiver. 'Detective Inspector Jackman here. I believe you have some information regarding the Holland disappearance?'

'My name is Alan Pitt. I've been working away from home for a while, but I've had to come back to receive a course of hospital treatment. That's where I saw the TV appeal for witnesses. I'm due to be discharged tomorrow morning.' There was a throaty cough, then Pitt said, 'I think I saw something that night.'

'We'll come and talk to you, sir. What hospital are you in?'

'Lincoln, but I'd appreciate it if I could be allowed to finish my treatment first. It's pretty exhausting. Isn't this what you call a "cold case?" Surely it can keep for one more day.'

It sounded like the man was in the oncology unit, so Jackman did not insist. 'Of course, sir. Shall we see you at your home, or would you prefer to come here?'

'I'll come to the station. I'll make it as early as I can, unless there is any holdup here.'

'Thank you, sir.' Jackman paused. 'Can I just ask, did you actually see something happen?'

'I saw two men acting strangely on the towpath, at the spot described in the appeal.'

'I know this is a long shot. It was a long time ago. But do you think you would recognise either of them if you saw them again?'

'Funnily enough, yes. Well, one of them. He reminded me of my cousin.' There was another bout of coughing. 'I need to go, but I'll come in tomorrow.'

Jackman took his details and thanked him. 'Charlie, go inform the desk sergeant about this man, and tell him to call CID the moment he arrives.'

Charlie hurried off.

A lead! It sounded like a valid one too. Jackman turned and saw Marie looking at him expectantly. 'Well, let's just hope he's got an eidetic memory, *and* is a descriptive genius!'

Marie raised her eyebrows. 'Let's not get too excited. Most people can't recall someone they saw two hours ago, let alone eighteen months. I reckon it's a very long shot indeed. Still, Orac tells me there's much better software available these days.'

Jackman nodded, and shivered slightly at the mention of Orac.

Orla Cracken, known to everyone simply as Orac, was a computer wizard who ruled her underground domain with a rod of iron.

Jackman was terrified of her.

'Yes,' he said. 'Maybe we should pin our hopes on Robbie, and hope he has some luck with Suzanne's ex in Spain.'

'He's a really good copper, isn't he?' said Marie. 'I mean totally dedicated.'

Jackman nodded. 'Yes, he is. I'm glad we took him on board.'

'I like him,' Marie added. 'I like the whole team, but Robbie's a one-off, isn't he?'

'Sometimes I think he's trying to prove something. I'm just not sure whether it's to us or himself.'

Marie nodded. 'I think he's trying to be the best he can for his old crewmate. Stella North had to give up the job she lived and breathed for after she was injured, and Robbie, well, I think he's taken up her baton. He's doing it for her.'

'I'd rather he did it for himself. But I'm not complaining! He's a credit to us, no matter who he's doing it for.' He glanced at his watch. 'He managed to get a ticket for yesterday evening and flew out at eight thirty. He reckoned the bars would just be hotting up when he arrived.'

'Ah, sun, sea, and sangria! I think Max was right, he *is* a jammy little git!'

'If the ex gives him what he's looking for, he'll be catching a flight straight back this evening. Not a lot of time for clubbing.'

'Ah, shame.'

'Said with feeling, I *don't* think.' Jackman smiled. 'Why don't *you* try to get a holiday sometime, Marie? You look so tired.'

'Maybe. When the investigation is over, and when . . .'

She left the sentence unfinished, but Jackman knew what she was about to say. *When Carter is back on an even keel.* 'Somewhere hot, I suggest.'

'I was thinking more of spending some time with my mum in Wales.'

Jackman winced. 'You like rainy holidays?'

'Not much, but I do like my mum,' said Marie with feeling. 'She refuses to take off for sunnier shores, so I guess it's Cymru or nothing.'

Marie returned to her desk. Jackman wished he could buy her two tickets to the warmest, most beautiful place he could think of. He had seen officers burn out in the past, and he didn't want it happening to one he cared for, not to

116

mention one that was so damned good at her job. He took a deep breath. They needed to get this case out of the way, then he'd try to ensure that Marie took some badly needed R&R.

* * *

It was Carter's day off. It didn't feel right, but he knew that if he didn't back off occasionally, he'd pay for it. He got up late, and after breakfast decided to go down to the Eva May.

Before he went, he rang Marie. 'Even the slightest hint of anything occurring with Leah, you ring me, okay? I'll be on the boat, so I can get to you in fifteen minutes.'

Marie told him to forget about everything. Between her and uniform, *and* the super, Leah was well looked after. She promised faithfully to ring him if anything did happen.

Down at Stone Quay, the sunshine glistened off the Eva May and Carter felt a jolt of pride. He and the lads had done a bloody good job.

When they first got her to the quay, they had almost despaired. But as the months went by, the lovely old lifeboat had begun to show signs of coming to life again. Carter had enlisted the help of a group of owners and enthusiasts of wooden boats. He'd even asked some of his father's old business colleagues to help with equipment for lifting and turning her. Matt was a master carpenter and he had been invaluable. He had soon stripped away the rotten planks on her hull and replaced them with new mahogany ones that he had needed to steam into place. He remade oak fenders and strengthened the gunwale. He had set Carter and Jack to work cutting and planing wood for the deck panels.

The engine had been Ray's baby, and he was a genius. They had managed to acquire an old second-hand engine, which Ray had stripped down, repaired and installed.

Tom had tackled the bronze and metal work. He taught the rest of them all about galvanised centreboards, mast tabernacles, prop shafts and propellers.

The work had never seemed to end. They needed sails, spars and a new engine canopy and then, all at once, they were painting the hull.

Now there was little to do, and Carter was alone. But he needed to finish what they had all started.

He climbed up the ladder and saw Silas standing on the quay.

'I've got some time to spare, young'un. Want a hand? I'm still good with a paintbrush.'

Silas had been working on boats all his life. Carter swelled with pride when he saw the admiration in the old man's eyes. At first Silas had laughed at their efforts, but he kept an eye on their progress and offered some invaluable advice.

'Come aboard, Si.' He helped the old man climb aboard.

'When's the big day?' Silas asked.

'Next week. John Baxter from the Greenborough Marina is bringing down some lifting equipment and hoists on Tuesday.'

'And then?'

Carter breathed in deeply. 'And then, I take her out.'

'Alone?'

Carter wasn't sure how to answer that. He was rarely alone these days. Tom Holland seemed to dog his every footstep. 'Not sure, Si. Maybe.'

Silas made no comment.

They spent the next couple of hours tidying up and putting small finishing touches to the paintwork. Carter heard Klink barking from the quay.

A Sportage was pulling in next to his Land Rover. He squinted into the sunlight. What on earth was Laura Archer doing here?

Klink eyed her suspiciously, but made no move.

'Well, I should be getting along now.' Silas wiped his hands on his trousers and stood up.

'Thanks for your help, Si. I appreciate it.'

'I'm always here if you need me.' He looked intently at Carter. 'Always.'

Carter touched his shoulder and nodded.

Klink and his master disappeared from sight.

Carter waved across to Laura. 'Come up and take a look!'

Laura climbed the ladder into the boat and ran a hand over the smooth paintwork. 'I thought she was going to be a wreck, but she's beautiful!'

'She *was* a wreck when we started.'

'What an achievement!'

'It's just a shame the lads can't see her.'

Laura nodded.

Carter suddenly frowned. 'There's nothing wrong, is there? Only you've never been here before.'

'I had an hour spare, and I thought it was time I checked out what you've been up to for so long.' She looked at the planed and polished wood and gleaming brass fittings. 'I didn't expect anything like this.'

'We did have help, but basically the Eva May was ours. Blood, sweat and tears.'

'I think you should contact some marine heritage group. This should be seen, and maybe even used by people who love our island history. I bet she has one hell of a story to tell.'

'She does. Tom did some research on her life. She was involved in lots of heroic rescues, and many of her crew drowned at one time or another. You wouldn't believe the kind of seas this little vessel braved in order to rescue others.'

'I would. I used to live in Northumberland, close to a lifeboat station. I used to pray whenever I saw it go out.' She looked at him. 'Why not use it? Maybe for river trips or seal watching, or something like that. It could be a memorial to your friends. What better way to pay tribute to all their hard work?'

He tried to look as if he were considering her suggestion, but he had something else entirely in mind for the Eva May. 'Want a beer? We have a small fridge on board. All mod cons, you know.'

'No thanks. I've not had lunch yet, and some enthusiastic copper might stop me on the way home.'

Carter pulled a face. 'I used to think like that too.' He sat down and patted the seat facing him. 'Can I ask you something?'

'Of course.'

'At the moment I am involved in a case where a young woman is being followed by an amorous admirer. I honestly believe that she is in no real danger, but nevertheless we need to sort it out — especially as it's the super's niece.'

Laura listened in silence.

'The thing is, the others are working the Suzanne Holland disappearance. They are getting nowhere fast, although if anyone can help them, it's me. But they refuse to let me work with them.' He leaned towards her. 'I *need* to get on that case, Laura.'

'Need is a very strong word, Carter. Why do you *need* to be on the case?'

'For Tom.' Carter tapped his fingers rapidly on the side of the boat. 'They have all gone but him. Matt, Ray and Jack, all gone.'

Laura didn't ask him to explain. After a while, she said, 'You've done something for each of them, and you believe you've allowed them to rest. Is that it?'

Carter nodded. 'Except for Tom, and . . .' He wanted to cry. He swallowed. 'The thing is, I know what he wants me to do, and he'll keep haunting me until I do it.'

'What does he want?'

'He hasn't said it in so many words, but he keeps whispering "Suzanne," over and over. He wants me to find out what happened to her, I know he does, but I'm not on the case! How can I help him if I'm shut out of the investigation?'

'Have you spoken to DI Jackman?'

'And tell him what? That my dead friend won't get off my back until I've tracked down his wife's abductor, or maybe murderer? How would that sound?'

Laura spoke calmly. 'Perhaps you could just offer to assist, since you knew Tom Holland so well?'

'I've done that. They don't say it, but they want me well away from the case. Even Marie was as wary as hell when I broached the subject.'

'They are trying to protect you, Carter. They don't want you being overwhelmed with memories from the past. Jackman will want to ease you back into the job, not chuck you straight in at the deep end.'

Carter shook his head. He still felt like crying. 'I know, but you have no idea how horrible it is, not being able to help.'

Laura smiled gently. 'You do know that your "seeing" Tom is part of what we call survivor guilt? It's a common reaction, Carter. When others have tragically died and you have survived, it has a massive impact on you. Many people in similar circumstances try to keep the memory of the deceased alive.' She leaned a little closer to him. 'Actually you have devised a brilliant way to move forward, and you did it without anyone's advice. Lots of therapists recommend finding a way to memorialise the deceased. The way you've done it is by helping their loved ones, and that is wonderful. It's a very positive action, Carter.'

Carter rubbed his eyes. 'Maybe. But why does he seem so real? And why do I always smell burning?'

'It's all part of the terrible thing you witnessed. As I recall, Tom was the last face you saw before you lost consciousness?'

Carter's expression hardened. 'I don't want to go there.'

'And I don't want to take you back, but you asked for a reason, and that is the answer. Carter, you're making incredible headway considering what happened, you *are* getting there. You are functioning well at work and generally holding things together. Please, please, do not be so hard on yourself. The past is immutable, but you can learn to find a new future.'

'That won't happen if I can't give Tom what he needs in order to rest. We have to find Suzanne. I can't handle this much longer. I need to fulfil the last challenge, Laura, I really do.'

Laura sat back. 'Then we'll have to see if we can get you involved in the investigation.'

'Will you talk to Jackman?' Carter asked urgently.

'I'll need to think about it. Leave it with me, and I'll do what I can.'

Carter drew in a shaky breath. 'Thank you! Thank you.'

Laura left. He had seen her expression. He had put her in a very difficult position, but what choice did he have?

There was no way Laura could actually interfere with police procedure. It was not her responsibility or her business. But Carter knew that for his sake, she would talk to Jackman. He just prayed that she could convince him.

Carter leaned back against the side of his beloved Eva May and heard it again, whispered above the lapping of the water. 'Suzanne . . . Suzanne . . .'

He choked back a sob. 'Leave me alone! I'm doing my best! What more can I do?'

CHAPTER TWELVE

Robbie touched down at Heathrow in a daze. Had his trip been a waste of money? Maybe not. At least he'd found somewhere new and beautiful to go hiking. Robbie didn't travel abroad much. In his childhood he had been dragged from one resort to the next by his gold-digging, social climbing parents, and had vowed never to get on a plane again. But he had fallen in love with the coast of Galicia.

He thought about his new drinking partner, Harvey Cash. After three hours drinking together, Robbie had begun to like this bitter, disillusioned man. By the time he left the apartment, he felt truly sad that he could do nothing to help him.

The beautiful young Suzanne had been the end of the road for Harvey. She'd tricked him into marriage, bled him dry and tortured him with stories of her unfaithfulness. When she divorced him, he thought it was finally all over. But then she took him to court, accusing him of stealing thousands of pounds from her savings. 'Should have known, should have realised.' Harvey had paid a high price for simply loving her.

Harvey hadn't provided much real evidence, but at least Robbie knew more about Suzanne Holland's character. It wasn't pleasant. He walked out to the car park wondering about her marriage to Tom Holland. It didn't fit with what Harvey had told him. He wondered if Harvey had been honest with him, but he had seemed genuine enough. Robbie desperately wanted to talk to Carter McLean. The two had been best mates, and Robbie was sure Tom would have confided in him. Maybe that final argument had been more than a simple tiff. Perhaps Tom and Suzanne were not as blissfully happy as they'd seemed to have been.

Robbie recalled what Harvey had said, shortly before he put his head back and began to snore. 'She hurts the ones she claims to love. And I mean *hurts*, Robbie-boy. Hurts.'

Robbie wasn't quite sure what he meant. An old song had briefly flitted across his mind, *You always hurt the one you love* . . . But Harvey seemed to mean more than this. He had kept repeating the word "hurts." By then it was too late to ask. Harvey Cash was out cold.

Robbie was convinced that Suzanne's past had caught up with her.

He drove away from the airport, full of a fresh enthusiasm for the case. He had copies of all the original investigation reports on his desk at work, and suddenly he felt the need to read them again, especially the ones about Tom and Suzanne's marriage. He glanced at his watch. Just after ten. By the time he got back it would be around midnight. Yeah! He'd call in and frighten whoever was on CID night cover, and spend a quiet hour reading up on Saltern's own Black Widow.

He entered the CID room to the sound of gentle snoring coming from behind a desk.

Charlie Button was fast asleep. For a moment he was tempted to drop a filing tray onto the desk, or yell "fire!" in Charlie's ear. Robbie smiled and went across to his own desk. The kid had been working long hours. Let him grab a bit of shuteye while he could.

Robbie sifted through the papers, took out those that referred to her marriage and settled down to read.

It took around thirty minutes to get the picture, and it did not coincide with Harvey's story in any way. There had indeed been that acrimonious divorce from Harvey, followed by a string of casual affairs. But from the moment she met Tom, Suzanne seemed to have become a model wife. Until the week before Tom's death, they seemed to be the perfect couple. Apart from the time Tom spent working on the old lifeboat, they spent every other moment together. So what had happened to shatter love's young dream?

Robbie turned pages and checked statements but found nothing. Then he remembered that Ray had been about to get married. They had died on their way to his stag do. Robbie logged into his computer and accessed a site that gave a report of the aftermath of the light aircraft crash. It listed the mourners at the remembrance service.

Joanne Simms, Ray's heartbroken fiancée. He nodded to himself and scrolled through again, watching for the name Joanne.

And there it was.

'Can you tell us the reason why Tom Holland was staying over at Ray Barratt's flat?'

'He and his wife had had a bit of a falling out, that's all.'

'Do you know what about?'

'A something and a nothing was all Ray told me. He was sure it would all blow over quickly, but then . . .'

Then they all died, thought Robbie.

'How long did he stay?'

'Four or five nights, yes, five I think, and then it was the stag . . .'

In the quiet of the big room, Robbie almost heard the girl sobbing through Charlie's soft snores.

A something and a nothing. It clearly wasn't serious as far as Joanne was concerned. But maybe Tom thought it was. Or Suzanne. Maybe he hadn't walked out. Maybe she had thrown him out.

Robbie yawned. If he couldn't ask Carter, Joanne seemed the best place to begin. He scribbled her name on a memo and left it on his desk.

He closed the door quietly behind him. Charlie Button slept on.

CHAPTER THIRTEEN

Jackman was pacing the office. 'No news about our witness?'

'Not yet.' Marie looked at her watch. 'The duty sergeant said he would notify us as soon as he arrives. Maybe the traffic's bad.'

Jackman didn't answer. He had spent half the night worrying about Alan Pitt. He wished now that he had disregarded the man's wishes and just gone to the hospital. This Pitt was the only person who might have seen something that could move the case forward, and now he was thirty minutes late.

Marie nibbled on her lower lip. 'There's a lot of reasons why he could be held up, sir. He didn't even give us an exact time, so let's not give up hope. He'll be here.'

Jackman knew Marie, and he knew she was trying to buoy him up, while feeling just as concerned as he was. 'We should have got to him yesterday, the minute he rang.'

'We should have, but we didn't. Spilt milk and all that.' She heaved a sigh. 'Want a coffee?'

'*Another* coffee?'

She shrugged. 'It's something to do.'

Then the phone rang. They looked at each other. 'Jackman.'

'Your man is here. I've put him in Interview Room 2, okay?'

'Thank you, Sergeant. We'll be down immediately.'

'Saved from the coffee!' Marie smiled.

Jackman nodded. 'I really thought . . .'

'Me too, if you must know.'

'I did. Right, let's go. We have a possible witness.'

* * *

As soon as Marie saw Alan Pitt, she knew Jackman had been right. He had been undergoing chemotherapy.

Pitt wore a woolly beanie hat with the Lincoln Imps logo embroidered across the front. He was painfully thin under his several layers of clothing. His face was sallow and his cheekbones protruded. She was very pleased that they had not bothered him yesterday.

Jackman introduced them, and she offered Pitt a cup of tea or coffee.

'Just water, please. The drugs make anything else taste really odd.'

'It's very good of you to come in, sir. We'd have been happy to visit you at home.'

The man looked around the cold, grey room and grinned. 'Funnily enough, this makes a refreshing change from looking at those sterile hospital walls. I've never been in a police station before. It's quite exciting.'

Marie wished she could feel the same about the place.

Jackman switched on the tape machine, raced through the introductions and explained that it was just an informal interview. Afterwards, Mr Pitt would be asked to sign a statement affirming that what he had said was correct to the best of his knowledge.

'You believe that you saw two males on the evening of Tuesday, February 9, in the vicinity of the missing woman's home, is that correct?'

Pitt nodded. 'Oh, I need to speak, don't I? I did. Yes.'

'Can you tell us why you were on the towpath at that time of night? And what time you were there.'

'Ten fifteen. I know because I usually walk my dog then. We go out at ten o'clock, walk along the towpath for a quarter of an hour, then walk home.' He sipped his water. 'I was just about to turn around when I heard voices, and I saw these two men on the lane leading to the Holland Cottage garden. They were just off the main path, by the gateway that leads across the fields to Mallard Lodge.'

'Did you speak to them?'

'I was going to, but they seemed to be talking in a rather heated manner, so I left them to it. I don't think they even knew I was there.'

'And you never saw them again?'

He shook his head. 'I went straight home and no one passed me.'

'Now we come to the million dollar question, Mr Pitt. Could you describe them for us?'

'Oh yes. Well, as I said, one of them.'

Marie wasn't holding her breath. She'd heard that so many times before.

'It was a clear night, and almost a full moon. He was tall, around six foot I think, good physique. By that I mean he looked a pretty powerful guy.'

'Hair colour?' asked Marie.

'Moonlight distorts colour, doesn't it? But he had pale hair. I think it was blond, but it could have been silver grey.'

'Style? Long, short, straight, curly?'

'Ah, that one's easy. He had a long ponytail, you know? Like some of the foreign footballers have? That's why I remember him so well. My cousin Henry went through a period of wearing his hair long and tied back like that. This man looked just like Henry, and he wore similar glasses too.'

Jackman let out a whistle. 'That's a couple of very specific points of identification. Can you recall what he was wearing?'

'Dark clothing, but I couldn't say what.'

'And the other man?'

Pitt shook his head. 'He stayed very much in the shadows. He was tall too, but I never actually saw his face.' He drank some more water and gave a rasping cough.

Marie looked anxiously at Jackman. 'I think that's all for now, don't you, sir?'

Jackman agreed. 'Mr Pitt, would you recognise him again?'

'Absolutely. I saw his face quite clearly.'

Jackman gave him a satisfied smile. 'Then if you are up to it, we'll get you to come back in and work with our IT experts to make up a composite likeness.'

'I'll go home and have a rest and take my midday medication, so maybe later this afternoon?'

Marie looked at him. 'Only if you are well enough, sir.'

'The word "well" doesn't feature too often in my vocabulary right now. I have good days, like today, and not so good. I never know what it's going to be, so the sooner I do this the better, if you see what I mean?'

Marie nodded. She understood exactly what he meant.

* * *

Marie returned to the CID office and rang around to see if there were any further developments regarding Leah's persistent admirer.

One of the officers on observation rang her back. 'He's gone to ground, I reckon, Sarge. No more silly games or sightings.'

'I'm beginning to think the police presence has scared him off.'

'Let's hope so, cause I'm bored rigid. There are only so many Mars bars you can eat in one shift.'

Marie thanked him and leafed through her list of people that had been interviewed. None of them seemed suspicious or obsessive. Maybe Carter was right after all. Marie closed the folder and nibbled on her bottom lip. Carter was being unusually blasé. Normally he was very cautious in his approach to a case.

Marie's phone rang.

'I'm not sure how much longer I can keep my niece under lock and key, Sergeant.' The super sounded fraught. 'She has decided that the whole thing has been blown up out of all proportion. She thinks she probably just overreacted to someone's ham-fisted attempt to get her attention.'

'And what do you think, ma'am?'

'She's the closest thing I have to a daughter, so give it a guess.' Ruth Crooke gave an irritable sigh. 'But even I'm wondering if we see so much bad stuff in our job that we always think the worst, especially when something threatens our nearest and dearest.'

'And I think that because of all the bad stuff, we can't afford to take risks.'

'True. Any suggestions, Sergeant? If I have to play one more game of Monopoly, I think I'll lose the will to live.'

'What does Leah want to do?'

'Go back to Uni. Or at least go back to her flat and sort some things out there.'

'Why don't I come over and pick her up? I'll accompany her wherever she wants to go and then bring her home later. I'll let uniform know exactly where we're going to be. At least it would give her a break, and you too, ma'am.'

'Where's Carter?'

'He's in his office, ma'am. He can watch out for anything that comes in here and keep me updated.'

'I suppose you're right.' Ruth drew in a breath. 'I hope I don't regret this.'

'Her admirer is hardly likely to try anything with me on her heels, is he?'

'Look after her, Marie.'

'Of course I will, ma'am.'

She hung up and went to find Carter.

'Best thing. The kid will go stir crazy shut in with her aunt all day.' He gave her an evil grin. 'I know I would.'

'Why are you so laid back about this, Carter?'

He shrugged. 'Just don't have your gut feeling that something is seriously wrong, I guess.'

'Well, for once I hope you are right.' She turned to leave. 'I'll keep in touch.'

She went back out to the main office and found Jackman talking to Gary Pritchard. 'I'm off to do a spot of babysitting, or should I say, police protection duty.' She told him about the super's dilemma.

'Okay. Just keep your eyes peeled, and don't let her out of your sight.'

She threw Jackman a withering look. 'I have done this before, you know.'

He laughed. 'I know. It's just that she's a relative of a high-ranking officer, and a rather prickly one at that, so it would be prudent to be doubly cautious.'

'Wilco.'

* * *

Robbie Melton was deep in conversation with Max.

'So, considering all the people you've spoken to about Suzanne Holland, what would you say was their overall attitude to her?'

Max didn't even stop to think. 'Wary, mate. Dead wary.'

'Me too. I know my "interview" with her first husband was somewhat unorthodox and totally off the record, but he seemed to be consumed with hatred for her. He said she hurt people, and he meant it.' He chewed on the end of his pen. 'I think what he actually meant was that she *destroyed* people.'

'I saw a film about a woman like that once. All sweetness and light on the surface but really a cunning, evil bitch. Do you mean that kind of woman?'

'Well, it was her who seduced him to begin with. Then she married him, took him to the cleaners, and then accused him of robbing her. So I guess the answer is yes.'

'Was she going to do the same to the next husband, Tom Holland?'

Robbie scratched his neck with the pen. 'If that was her plan, she hadn't got the ball rolling yet. The pictures of them together show a happy couple.'

'Perhaps Tom Holland was her one true love, and she turned over a new leaf when she met him?'

'You know what they say about leopards and spots.' He frowned. 'And if they were so blissfully happy, why is no one telling us that?'

'Search me. And where the hell is this half-brother that your pissed-up travel rep told you about? I've been trying to track a Ralph Dolan all morning, but I'm damned if I can find him.'

'How are you spelling it?'

'D-O-L-A-N. As you've written it.' Max pointed to the memo Robbie had given him. 'And I tried it with a E, and with two L's as well.'

'It's an Irish name, I'm sure.' Robbie remembered an old school friend. No one could spell his name correctly because it was pronounced so differently. 'Let's Google it.' He clicked the mouse and pulled up variations of Dolan. 'Here we are. I've got a few more suggestions for you to try. There's Doland, Dooley, Dowling, Doolin, Doolan, O'Dooley and a whole load more.'

Max pulled a face. 'Thanks a bunch.'

'Sorry, but it might help to check the sex offenders register too. Harvey swore he was weird and he didn't trust him any further than he could throw him.' He stood up. 'I'm going to get my head stuck into Suzanne and Tom's financial history. If she was squirrelling away money from their accounts, maybe she did have a master plan for her beloved husband.'

'But a bloody great storm got him first.'

Robbie couldn't think of an answer.

* * *

Alan Pitt returned looking much more rested. Jackman hoped the treatment was working.

The worst thing about what they were about to do was that it involved Orac, and Jackman had foolishly let Marie go out with Leah. Marie was always there to act as a buffer between himself and the scary IT manager. Today he had to face her alone.

The truth was, he found her fascinating, but had no idea what to say to her.

Orla Cracken, Marie had assured him, was not the intimidating cyborg that he believed her to be. Her appearance told him otherwise.

Orac had white-blonde hair, cut in a GI Mohican style, and she wore mirror contact lenses. They glinted at him like polished steel. That alone was enough to make Jackman delegate anything IT to one of the others. The other thing was that Orac took great delight in paying him an inordinate amount of attention, which made him ten times more uncomfortable.

For Alan Pitt's sake, Jackman took the lift down to the basement, where the IT unit was housed. He paused in the doorway, took a deep breath and entered.

'DI Jackman! You came in person. I'm honoured.' Orac sat in front of a bank of computer screens and flashed those disconcerting eyes at him. 'Please, do come in.'

Jackman swallowed and tried not to stare. How did she do it? Already he seemed to have lost the ability to speak coherently. And where did that stammer come from?

'And you must be our witness.' She held out a hand to Alan Pitt. 'Mr Pitt, I'm Orla, but my friends here all call me Orac.'

Alan Pitt smiled. '*Blake's Seven*, wasn't it?'

'I'm just as valuable as that supercomputer. I'm probably also just as terse, short tempered and unhelpful.'

She gave Jackman a disparaging look. He swallowed.

'Please take a seat, Mr Pitt, and we'll begin. It's a simple process, and the computer does most of the work.'

'I wondered if this might help.' Alan passed her a head shot photo of a fair-haired man of around forty. 'It's my cousin. The man I saw has so many of the same features that I thought we could work from that.'

'Clever idea, Mr Pitt.' Orac took the picture, scanned it, and brought up the image in the identification program. 'Now, talk to me about your man.'

It took only ten minutes to arrive at an image that Alan Pitt declared to be "as near as damn it." Jackman stared at a serious-looking man wearing glasses with fashionable dark hipster frames. His long, ash-blond hair was tied back in a full ponytail. He looked vaguely like a footballer.

'And that is all I can tell you, I'm afraid.' Alan seemed quite sad that his session with the enigmatic Orac was coming to an end.

'You've helped us a lot, Mr Pitt. It's the first time we have had something to go on.' Jackman was already inching towards the door. 'Uh, and thank you, Orac. Much appreciated.'

'Anytime, Detective Inspector. *Anytime*. It's my pleasure.'

Jackman almost ran to the door.

'Wow! She's quite something, isn't she?' Alan Pitt shook his head in wonder. 'Are those eyes for real?'

'I'm told she is blind in one eye. She hides it with those weird lenses.'

'She likes you, doesn't she?'

Jackman coughed loudly and muttered something like "utter nonsense."

Alan Pitt grinned, but wisely dropped the subject. 'Do you think those men were involved in that woman's disappearance, DI Jackman?'

'Possibly. The timing fits perfectly.'

'How will you use the EFIT picture?'

'We'll circulate it to all forces, get it into the local and national newspapers, and on the TV too.'

Alan Pitt exhaled. 'I hope I've got it right then. I'd hate for someone to be wrongly accused because I didn't give a good description. It was a long time ago.'

'I think your description was excellent, sir, and we are very grateful to you.' He stopped. 'By the way, if you ever see that man again, maybe close to your home, please contact us immediately.'

'Of course, but I hope that doesn't mean you think he's dangerous?'

'No, I was thinking more that he might be local. If you saw him once, there's a possibility you could see him again. He could be completely innocent, in which case we need to talk to him and eliminate him from our enquiries.'

Alan Pitt nodded. He seemed to be fighting for breath.

'Are you alright?'

'Get a bit breathless. I'll be fine in a minute.'

Jackman thought Pitt looked far from fine. He waited with him, and walked him slowly out of the station. 'Take care, sir, and thanks again.'

'Will you let me know if you find him?'

'We might need you to identify him, if that's okay with you?'

Pitt nodded. Then he said, 'Just don't leave it too long, if you catch my drift?'

CHAPTER FOURTEEN

Carter looked up from his desk. Through his half open door, he watched Marie stride into the CID room. He had known her for many years, but she still made him look twice. She was one of the most striking people he had ever seen. Tall and strong, with beautiful chestnut hair and an air of absolute confidence. She lived as she rode that damn great motorbike — assured and controlled, but with a dash of daring.

But not now. He watched her talk to Robbie. Her usual energy just wasn't there. She wasn't lethargic, she just lacked her spark.

She looked up and gave him a brief wave.

He lifted a hand in acknowledgement. After a while she came into his office.

'Safely home, and in a much better frame of mind.' She flopped into the only other chair. 'She's a nice kid. I like her.'

'Nothing like Ruth Crooke, thank heavens. So, no more funny goings-on in the flower beds?'

'Nothing so far.'

'Good.'

'What are you working on?'

Carter pushed a pile of paperwork across the desk. 'Oh, it's still the Cannon case. But we are getting there. I'll

137

soon be looking for something else to occupy my time. I can't see this taking more than a day to wrap up.' And knowing that he would be moved to another case set him wondering whether Laura would visit Jackman in person, or ring him. Whatever, he hoped it would be soon.

Before he could continue, his desk phone rang.

'She's gone! McLean! Leah has been snatched!'

'Ma'am?' Carter pressed the loudspeaker button so Marie could hear the conversation.

'Slow down! Marie delivered her back safely just now, and uniform are still on obo outside. Are you sure she's actually been taken?'

'I'm not bloody stupid, Detective! I've just got in. The French window has been forced, and there's a broken mug on the floor of the conservatory. There are signs of a struggle, and Leah is gone. Get yourself over here, now!'

Carter stared at Marie. This could not be happening!

Together they ran from his office. Marie hurried off to find Jackman, and Carter raced to the staff car park.

By the time he had brought the car round, Marie was waiting for him.

'This is all wrong!' he stammered. 'I don't understand.'

Marie stared at him. 'Hell, Carter, she's had a stalker breathing down her neck for days! We *knew* this might happen. Why so shocked?'

He drew in air between his teeth. He couldn't answer her.

'Because you got it wrong? So what? We all get it wrong sometimes. Just calm down.'

Carter's mind was racing. He needed to get to the super's place and see for himself.

* * *

Ruth Crooke's house was a modest four-bedroom property. No two houses in her road were the same, but they all had long back gardens and a rear entrance out onto a narrow leafy pathway that led to a children's recreation park.

Uniform were already there. Ruth Crooke had radioed in as soon as she realised what had happened.

'We spoke to Leah about five minutes prior to the super turning up,' said a breathless PC Connor Waite. 'And we'd done a walk round of the gardens a few minutes before that. He must have been watching from somewhere, but heaven knows where.' He looked around and shook his head. 'We haven't relaxed for a minute. I just don't get it.'

'And you never heard anything?' Marie asked.

'Nothing, skip.'

Marie grimaced, and turned to Carter. 'Time to go face the music.'

* * *

The superintendent was incandescent. She began by declaring that she had made a serious error of judgement in asking Carter McLean to find the pervert who was threatening her niece.

Marie watched Carter, ready to jump in if the old animosity boiled over again. But Carter just seemed bemused.

After a while, he simply said, 'I'll get her back, Ruth. I swear to God, I'll get her back.'

The super stared at him. She didn't seem to know how to react to this. She left them and went back out to the uniformed officers in the garden.

Marie took Carter's arm and gave it a shake. 'Talk to me, Carter.'

He looked at her long and hard, apparently incapable of uttering a word.

Marie followed him out of the hall, through the lounge and towards the conservatory.

A young WPC stood at the door, blocking their entrance.

'We've left the scene uncontaminated, Sarge. No one in, no one out. SOCOs are on their way.'

139

Marie gazed around the bright, airy room where she and Leah had so recently been chatting. She glanced at her watch. Was it only an hour ago? 'He's never stopped watching this house. He was just waiting for us to let our guard down. He knows an awful lot about our routines, doesn't he?'

'How did he force the doors without alerting Leah to the threat?' Carter seemed to be slowly returning to earth from wherever he'd been for the last half hour.

They walked around the house, looking for something to help them. Then Marie saw Leah's mobile phone plugged into a charger on one of the kitchen units. 'Just as I left her she said she needed to charge her phone.' She peered at the battery icon. 'Not fully charged. And there's music playing in here. If he was quick and quiet, there's a good chance she came to plug this in, and never heard him at all.' She exhaled loudly then clenched her fists. 'That poor kid! I really let her down.'

'No! You haven't! I let her down, not you,' Carter shouted. 'But I'll get her, by God. I'll get her back by nightfall.'

Marie stepped back, shocked.

'I'm taking the car. Get uniform to run you back, or ring Max or Charlie.'

'Where are you going?' Marie was beginning to be afraid.

'I'm not sure, but I think I know someone who might just point me in the right direction.' He swallowed, then gripped her arm. 'Trust me, Marie. I'm going to sort this.'

Marie made to follow him, then stopped. Whatever he was going to do, he clearly didn't want her along. For a moment she had no idea what to do. Then she pulled out her phone and called Jackman.

* * *

'I've never seen him like this,' Marie told Jackman.

Jackman knew Marie very well. He'd seen her in a dozen different frames of mind, but he'd never seen her as confused as she was now.

They were sitting in his car, waiting for the forensic team to arrive, and Marie told him of Carter's strange reaction to Leah's abduction.

'Do you know, just before this happened I was about to give him the go-ahead to talk to us about Suzanne and Tom Holland. I've had Laura Archer bending my ear about his final task.' He ran a hand through his hair. 'Now I'm really not sure what to do.'

'I was going to ask you the same thing. He's been going on and on about helping with the Holland inquiry. He knew the Hollands. Tom was his best friend. We need his help, and he wants to give it. If he has a major setback, it could happen over anything. Maybe this is it.'

Jackman sat back, stared out of the window and watched the uniformed police officers securing the scene and knocking on neighbouring doors. 'Maybe this outburst actually stems from his frustration about the Holland investigation.'

'That, and the fact that Ruth Crooke asked him for help, and he believes he failed her.' She grunted. 'The super really tore into him, sir. And he just stood there and took it.'

'I'm very twitchy about him going off like the Lone-bloody-Ranger. I've never liked having a loose cannon on the team, but I thought I could handle him.' He looked at Marie. 'Any idea where he might have gone?'

Marie shook her head. 'Not a clue. All he said was someone he knew might have information that would help him find Leah. A snout, I guess.'

'Do we have a list of names?'

'I do, although he's been office bound for quite a while now, so it might have changed. Street people do move on.'

'Anyone you can recall who was well in Carter's pocket?'

'Not especially.' She looked up. 'SOCOs are here.'

A big white van with "Crime Scene Investigation" emblazoned on the side was pulling up outside the property.

'Okay, let's go sort this, then we'll see if we can get a fix on our masked avenger, shall we?'

CHAPTER FIFTEEN

Danny Hurley paced the big empty storeroom.

His heart raced. For the tenth time in as many minutes he checked his watch. They had said two hours. And those agonising hours were now up.

He listened for the sound of an engine, but all he heard was a tractor churning up and down some distant field.

Had something gone wrong? Had the police changed their observation routine? He doubted it. They had been doing their checks on the dot. He checked his phone, then shoved it angrily back into his pocket.

They should be here.

His own car sat waiting, ready to carry his girl away from this horrible town. They were going to a place where they could be alone and get to know each other properly. He laughed, and it echoed around the high, timbered ceiling. There was very little he didn't know about Leah Kingfield, but she had a lot to find out about him.

He laughed again, then resumed his pacing. He checked his watch one more time.

* * *

Carter drove across town and drew up outside a seedy-looking house on the edge of Saltern's only council estate. The place was pretty rough, but not too bad, considering. The residents tended to be older, and they did their best to keep it looking reasonable.

Carter slammed his car door shut and locked it. He loped up the garden path, skirting a rusty wheelbarrow and a rustier bike, and hammered on the door.

The moment it opened, he pushed his way in and grasped the man inside by the shirt front, propelling him back into the hallway.

'A word, my friend, and I'll be gone.' The man was short and overweight, and he put up no resistance. Carter bundled him inside and threw him down onto a tattered sofa.

'I'm in a hurry. I haven't got time to mess around.'

The man stared up at him open-mouthed. Carter never behaved like this.

'I need to find someone, and fast. I'll give you a name, and you tell me exactly where I can find him *and* do not say you don't know, because I know you do.' He leant closer and smelled sweat. 'This is no joke, so don't piss me about.' He whispered a name.

The man licked his lips nervously. 'He'll be at Ramsey's Bar. The snug.'

Carter believed him. 'And the other one, if you please?'

This time the man looked worried. 'He doesn't have a regular routine. I'll tell you where he lives, but that's all I know.'

'That will do.'

The man reeled off the address of a small house on the edge of the estate.

Carter nodded and backed off. He reached into his pocket and pulled out a note. 'For your troubles.' He flung the ten-pound note onto the sofa and strode out of the house.

He started up the car and thought for a minute. He had to get this right. His fingers beat out a tattoo on the steering wheel. Why had this happened? He had been so sure. His face was set hard as granite. No point in recriminations now. He needed to sort this bloody cock-up before Leah got hurt.

* * *

Marie stared at a long list of names. 'When he and Bill were working together he always had a lot of people on the ground. He used to say that if you managed them right, they'd save you a lot of legwork.' She gave a half smile. 'Carter's motto was "speculate to accumulate." My Bill wasn't all that happy about the way he manipulated some of them, but he did get results.'

Jackman stared at the list and shook his head. 'There's too many. We can't go tearing round Saltern hunting them down on the off-chance. We'll be better off getting some vehicles and bodies out there watching for a sighting of him or his car.'

'I've already told uniform. They are all aware he's done a caped crusader, but I have told them to back off if they see him, and ring us. If he really is onto something, we don't want to gatecrash his party.'

Jackman massaged his temples. 'What the hell is he doing?'

'My best guess is that he's mobilising his informants. I reckon he's calling in old favours, big time.'

'Has he got that much clout with the villains?'

'He certainly had back then. Carter was never snow-white. But now?' Marie shrugged. 'Who knows?'

'Maybe we'll find out. By nightfall, is that what he said?'

She nodded. 'By nightfall.'

'Not too long to wait, but *we* have to go by the book. Grab the team and we'll try to find her the regular way, shall we?'

Danny was beside himself. He'd finally received a text saying there had been unforeseen holdups, but all was well. They just needed to lie low for an hour or so, then they would meet him as arranged. The merchandise was safe and secure.

Dark thoughts crept into his head. If they had harmed one hair on his girl's head, he swore he would kill them.

Danny sat down on a pile of plastic storage boxes and put his head in his hands. Never in all his life had he been so utterly consumed by desire. This waiting was purgatory. He wanted to touch the face he had photographed so many times, the skin that looked so much like porcelain. He pulled a crumpled photo from his jacket pocket and stared at it. She was the most beautiful thing he'd ever seen. Soon . . . oh, soon . . .

He straightened up. An engine!

He ran to the big double doors and peered out. The security lights came on, illuminating the grey VW hire van that was pulling in. Danny pulled back the heavy doors and waved the vehicle inside.

As soon as the truck came to a halt, the driver and passenger doors opened and two men almost fell out. 'Money!' hissed one.

'When I see that she's unharmed.' He took two fat envelopes from his pocket, but held them close to his chest.

'Money. Now. The girl's in the back. We need to get out of here.'

Danny gritted his teeth. 'If she's hurt, you can forget the money.'

'She's not hurt. See for yourself.' The driver nodded towards the back of the vehicle.

Danny glared at them, took hold of the back door handle and pulled it open.

Carter's body struck him with the force of a steam train.

146

Together they hit the floor with a thump that took the breath from his lungs. Before he knew what was happening, his wrists were in cuffs and he was face down in the dirt.

'I'm DS Carter McLean, and you are nicked.' He picked up the two envelopes from where they had fallen, and tossed them to the driver and his mate. 'Here. Now beat it!'

They were gone in seconds. Danny lay on his back and watched as all his dreams came crashing down around him. The man read him his rights. Then he was on the phone telling the police that two IC1 males were on their toes from a yard in Cray Lane and making off towards the east end of the town on Fendyke Road.

Danny tried to stand, but a boot smashed into the lower part of his back, and he crumpled, gasping in pain.

Helpless, he looked on while the man jumped into the back of the van and gently carried out his girl.

'Leah!' Danny cried. 'I love you!'

'*Love?*' Carter McLean glared at him, and his face contorted. 'You don't know the first thing about it, you twisted little creep!'

He drew back his clenched fist, and Danny tensed, waiting for the impact, but Carter turned aside and spat.

The two-tones screamed to a halt outside the building. To a chorus of sirens, Danny Hurley's dreams of running away with the most beautiful girl in the world faded away forever.

CHAPTER SIXTEEN

'I'm sorry. I know I shouldn't have gone off alone, sir,' Carter said to Jackman.

Carter looked apologetic, but Jackman didn't believe for a second that he really meant it. 'Well, you've certainly put the super in a difficult position. Half of her wants to tear you limb from limb, and the other half will forever be in your debt.'

'The girl is safe. I'd like to leave it there as far as Ruth Crooke goes. The fact is, I should have listened to her, and to Marie, but I didn't.'

'Sit down, Carter. We have to talk about what happened.'

Carter sat, still looking contrite.

'How in heavens name did you find the abductor so quickly? We had half the station watching that girl twenty-four/seven, and found nothing. *You* found nothing either, before the balloon went up. So what changed?'

'*I* changed, sir.' He puffed out his cheeks. 'I was so involved with my own problems, and with worrying about the Holland case,' he shrugged, 'I just never took the threat seriously. I was never really committed to it.'

'Well, I can't argue with that. But how did you manage to nail Danny Hurley?'

Carter looked down. 'I'm not proud of this, sir, but before the accident I wasn't averse to bending the rules to get a good result. Back then we had a pretty free rein with our informants. We can't work that way now, there's a form to fill out for every single bloody thing. But I've kept in touch. I've got a long memory, sir, and I know a lot about the bunch of thieves I used to work with. And I know who will grass up who, and who has old scores to settle.'

'Marie thought as much. Although she put it rather differently.'

Carter nodded. He looked up at Jackman. 'I found someone who knew that Danny was throwing money around, using gofers and runners for something devious. Danny's not the sharpest knife in the drawer, and he didn't cover his tracks or pay well enough for his hired help to pledge him eternal loyalty. After two house calls I had the full story. I caught up with his drivers en route to their rendezvous at the storage yard.'

'Danny is saying some very odd things about how he got his info on Leah.'

'I heard, although he's not exactly reliable, is he? I don't think he's the full shilling. It hadn't even crossed his mind that Leah might not actually *want* to run away to fairyland with him.'

'I agree, but some of the things he's implying are cause for concern,' said Jackman.

'I haven't heard his exact words, but he's saying that it wasn't him who started the whole thing. Is that right?'

'He swears he was paid to do it.'

Carter looked puzzled. 'But he admits he was going to run away with her. From the way he was yelling his undying love as they took him away, I don't think there is any doubt that Danny was the one obsessing over her.'

'No doubt at all. It's just unsettling.'

'So where has a little rat like Danny got the money to pay for this kind of thing?' Carter frowned. 'I checked on the database. He's been done for a fair bit of small-time stuff, mainly theft, but nothing big enough to fund this sort of caper.'

'Maybe there's a grain of truth in what he's saying. Especially when you consider how well planned it all was. The timing was perfect, and he had a disturbing amount of knowledge about both Leah and how the police operate.'

'Could be right, sir. Danny isn't bright enough to have worked all that out on his own. He's had help from someone alright.' His face darkened. 'But are we thinking his benefactor was a villain who knows our ways better than we do, or someone on this side of the fence?'

Jackman tensed. 'Let's not get ahead of ourselves, Carter. A villain with a grudge against Ruth Crooke would be my first guess.'

Carter nodded. 'I don't like the woman and I've never pretended otherwise, but this was nasty.'

'Very, and I think it's really shaken her. She's a tough woman, but one's brain goes into overdrive when a youngster gets taken.' Jackman put his elbows on the desk. 'Now, if I can just get one thing straight about what happened. You took off alone in order to keep Marie out of your shady dealings with your informants?'

Carter nodded. 'Yes, sir. Marie is straight as a die, as was Bill, her husband, but . . .'

'As you said, *you* used to bend the rules. And now?'

'We work for a different kind of force now, sir. I'm aware that things have changed, and the old ways don't work anymore. I know I pulled a fast one today, but it won't happen again, I promise you.'

Jackman sighed. 'It had better not, Carter, because your behaviour was unacceptable. We are team players in this office, every one of us. But . . .' he looked hard at Carter, 'you did get Leah home safely and unharmed.'

'And before nightfall.' There was the hint of a smile on Carter's face. 'I can't believe I actually said that. How melodramatic!'

'Where are you with the Cannon drugs case?'

'End stage. Rosie and I are pretty well through.'

'And your opinion?'

'If the CPS throw this out, there truly is no justice in this world. We've sewn it up tighter than a duck's proverbial.'

Jackman made his decision. 'Okay. Then when you are ready, perhaps you would talk to the team about Suzanne Holland? I believe our good intentions to wrap you in cotton wool were somewhat misguided. And we've been missing a trick by not using your knowledge of the Hollands.'

'I'm on the case?'

'*If* there is anything left of you after you've seen the super, yes.'

Carter sat up straighter, looking determined. 'Talking about the super, is she back from the hospital yet, sir? I think it's down to me to apologise this time,' Carter inhaled, 'even if it does go against the grain.'

'I think that would be a very sensible career move, Sergeant. And, no, she's still with Leah.'

Carter smiled. 'She wasn't harmed, sir, and she was very switched on. As soon as she knew she was no longer in danger, she was well up for staying in the back of that van and taking a look at the creep who had had her abducted. She's one feisty young woman.'

'What about the two men that Danny hired to bring her to him?'

'Got away.' Carter scowled. 'I was on the radio almost immediately, but they must have had a car close by.'

'You know who they are, don't you?'

Carter didn't answer immediately. 'I, er, made a few promises, sir. I had to, in order to catch Danny red-handed. I could have just taken Leah home, but then Danny would have scarpered, and she would still be looking over her shoulder. So I convinced his two foot soldiers to complete their job.'

'In return, you develop amnesia, and maybe give them a head start?'

'Me, sir?' Carter assumed a shocked expression.

'*You*, Carter. It stops right here, okay? I don't want to know how you manipulated this little scenario. All I want is this CID office running as it should do — within the boundaries of the law.'

'Understood. You'll get no more trouble from me, sir. I promise.'

'You will still have a lot of explaining to do to the superintendent, so I suggest that you make sure your story holds up.' Jackman knew that Carter's debriefing would be as tightly sewn up as the Cannon case. He was very good at tidying up loose ends, and if Ruth Crooke's niece backed him up, he would be off the hook. 'Right, final warning, Detective, just behave! No solo missions, okay? Or it's back to that desk for you, and you'll never leave it again.' Jackman was beginning to feel like a headmaster forced to admonish one of his star pupils. 'And one last thing, if the Holland case proves to be too much, you *must* talk to me. That's an order. Plus, I want you to have regular chats with Laura Archer while you are working it.'

Carter nodded eagerly. 'Received and understood. And thank you, sir.'

CHAPTER SEVENTEEN

'Isn't that Suzanne's brother — or half-brother rather? Is he in the frame for this?' Carter stared at the image displayed on the whiteboard.

Marie and Jackman looked at each other.

'Suzanne's brother?' Marie asked.

Carter looked puzzled. 'Well, yes. Why?'

'Do you know him?' asked Marie.

'No, but I've seen him two or three times.' The corners of his mouth turned down. 'Not the kind of guy I'd fancy socialising with.'

'How so?'

'Deep. As in he doesn't talk much but he watches people. Looks like he's analysing everything they say and do. Creepy.'

Jackman stared at the picture. 'Did you ever talk to him?'

'Not directly. He was waiting for Suzanne one day when Tom and I got back from a day on the boat. Tom had a few words with him, but I stayed back. He put my hackles up the moment I saw him.' He frowned. 'And then he was at a barbeque at Tom's place. I don't think he was actually invited, but he came anyway. That's when I clocked him observing people.'

'We believe his name is Ralph Dolan. Is that correct?' asked Jackman.

Carter tilted his head. 'I heard him called Ralphie, but I never got his surname. Tom didn't like him at all, reckoned he had a thing for Suzanne.'

'His sister?' Marie looked at the picture with distaste. 'Oh, yuk!'

'Sums him up really.' Carter shrugged, 'As I said, creepy.'

'Do you know where he lives?' asked Jackman.

'Sorry. I was never interested enough to ask.' He turned to Jackman. 'Why is he on the board?'

'We have a witness who places a man of this description close to the Holland house around the time that Suzanne disappeared. Until now we had no idea who he was.'

Marie glanced at the clock. The others would be here in a moment for the morning meeting. It felt good to have Carter here with them, instead of being shut away in his office. 'Cannon case concluded?'

'Almost. We've passed it upstairs for a second look before we kiss it goodbye.'

Marie touched his arm. 'Good to have you back.'

'Good to be back.'

Marie thought he seemed rather apprehensive. Understandable, she guessed, although he seemed to function very well on the streets, going by yesterday's unauthorised escapade. She told herself to stop trying to understand Carter McLean.

The next fifteen minutes were taken up with a report on the previous night's activities in the town. Marie really wasn't too interested. She half listened in case a name came up that might be useful.

Then it was Jackman's turn, and the Suzanne Holland investigation.

'As some of you know, DS McLean and the late Tom Holland were friends, so we are grateful to him for joining

154

us, and perhaps filling in some of the gaps in our knowledge about Suzanne Holland.' He looked towards Carter. 'He has already given us a possible identity for the mystery man who was seen in the area on the night Suzanne disappeared. So I suggest we make our priority the search for this Ralph Dolan. Max? Anything on him since yesterday?'

Max stood up. 'I've confirmed his name, sir. It's Ralph Edward *Doolan*. The spelling confused me at first, but so far I've had no luck in tracking him down. He was last living at an address in Nottingham, but he's since moved with no forwarding address.'

'Do we know *anything* about him? What he does for a living? Has he ever been in trouble?'

Robbie raised a hand. 'We checked the PNC and found nothing, sir.'

Jackman looked at Carter. 'Anything at all that you can tell us about him?'

Carter told them about Tom Holland's suspicions that the man was too interested in his half-sister, and what he himself had observed. 'I have no idea where he worked or what he did.'

Robbie raised a hand. 'So it would be reasonable to believe, if this man *is* Doolan, that he could have had a legitimate reason for visiting his sister that evening?'

Jackman shrugged. 'He could, but we don't know that. Did he go there purely to see her? Or to abduct her? Kill her? Did they argue and things got out of hand?'

'Or did he discover her body?' said Marie. 'But if that were the case, why not just dial 999?'

'And who was with him?' added Carter. 'You say he was talking to another man?'

'Alan Pitt saw Doolan clearly, but not the man he was with. He stayed in the shadows.'

'Sir?' Marie said.

Jackman looked to Marie and raised an eyebrow.

'It's Alan Pitt, our witness. How can he be so certain, not only of the description, but of the date too? After all, it was eighteen months ago.'

'Ah. Well, knowing how unreliable witness statements can be, I did ask him that question.' Jackman exhaled. 'He told me that the date is etched in his brain because it was the day the hospital gave him his diagnosis and he knew for certain he had cancer. He said he was in a state of shock, but still tried to carry on as normal — walking his dog and so on. He said he was totally absorbed in his own problems, and hearing the men's voices made him jump. He wanted to speak to them, but they sounded pretty angry, maybe arguing, so he backed off. He said he felt quite disturbed, and for a moment he thought Ponytail was his cousin.' Jackman paused. 'I think that's sufficient reason to remember that night and what he saw.'

'But it was at night.'

'If there's no cloud cover, go out late tonight, Marie. It's a full moon. I'm betting you'd spot a ponytail and designer glasses without artificial light.'

Marie smiled. 'Fair enough. You've answered my query. Poor guy.'

Jackman beckoned to Carter. 'Come up here and tell us anything you think might be helpful about your friend Tom, and Suzanne.'

Marie watched Carter amble towards the front of the room. This was the deep end they'd been trying to avoid all these months. Would he sink, or swim?

'Tom was my best mate. We went to school together and we remained friends afterwards. The only thing I ever recall disagreeing with him about was when he told me he was going to marry Suzanne Cash.' He swallowed, but carried on. 'I'd heard rumours that she was, well, an easy lay. And I thought Tom deserved better. But,' he shrugged, 'Tom was adamant that he knew all about her past and it didn't matter. He said she had changed. She loved him, and that was that. And for the first year they were together

I had to agree. Everyone said she was the perfect partner, with eyes only for Tom. And then they got married.'

Marie recalled Carter saying that he hardly knew the woman. She asked, 'Were you his best man?'

Carter flashed her an odd look. 'They married in a registry office, with no guests. They used council workers as witnesses and there were no photographs. Tom said that was how they wanted it — no fuss.' He sighed. 'I stopped spending so much time at his place after that. We still met, went out, did stuff and worked on our boat, but I rarely went to their home.'

'You still had reservations about her?' asked Jackman.

'I just couldn't take to her, end of. So I stayed away. And, well, being a copper I made a few discreet enquiries about her first marriage. I found out roughly the same as Robbie did, although I had no proof. It isn't a pleasant story.'

Robbie gave a grunt of assent.

'Then after another year went by, Tom got kind of quiet, but he wouldn't say what was wrong. He swore everything in the garden was rosy, but I didn't believe him. You know when someone says, "I'm fine!" too often? You know damn well they are lying.'

Like you, thought Marie, and nodded.

'And that's all I can tell you. Nothing concrete, but an undercurrent strong enough to sweep away a herd of cows.'

'Do you know what they rowed about, Carter?' asked Jackman. 'It must have been serious, since he packed a bag and went to Ray's house.'

'And why Ray?' Marie added. 'You were his best buddy. Why not stay with you?'

'I was off on a stakeout the night he had the row. And I think he knew I disliked her, though he never bad-mouthed her, not once. Maybe he didn't want to tell me what had happened.'

'And he *never* told you?' Max sounded surprised. 'We blokes usually like to chew over things like that with our mates.'

'Not if we are embarrassed, or know we are in the wrong,' said Carter.

'Mmm, good point.'

'I'd have thought Ray would have said something to you,' Jackman mused.

'He told me it would blow over. Storm in a teacup.' Carter pulled a face. 'Ray was pretty blunt, bless him. He said I'd probably open my big gob and make things worse.' He gave a little laugh. 'So even on our way to the stag do, it wasn't spoken about.'

Marie glanced at Jackman and ran a finger across her throat. *Cut it now, sir. He's had enough.*

Jackman coughed. 'Well, we appreciate all that, Carter. Now, I suggest that Robbie, Max and Charlie keep up the search for Doolan, and Marie and Carter tackle Suzanne herself. I've got a broad outline of what she did during the week prior to her disappearance. Work from that, and find out all you can about her and the people she fraternised with. Don't hold back either. No one has been willing to talk about her, and I want them to stop pussyfooting around. We need someone to be straight about that woman.'

'Anything I can do to help, sir?' asked Gary Pritchard.

'You are with me, if uniform can spare you, Gary. I'd like you to keep up with what is going on with Danny Hurley. I know the girl is home and dry, but his story still bothers me. We need to know about this mysterious third party who apparently orchestrated and possibly financed the whole weird scheme.'

'Fine, sir. I'm cleared for a few days.' Gary winked at Marie.

She responded with a smile. She knew how pleased he was when he managed to get himself seconded to Jackman's office.

'Excellent. Right, let's see what we can achieve by the afternoon meeting, shall we?'

* * *

Marie and Carter decided to start with Suzanne's last place of work. Soon they were sitting outside the Tan-Amazing salon in East Market Street.

'Lovely,' said Marie sarcastically. 'Really nice.'

'I suppose it's work, isn't it? And all the free rays you can soak up.'

'Glad to see you are looking on the bright side.' Marie released her seatbelt. Before she could get out of the car, Carter took hold of her arm.

'I just wanted to say thanks for not objecting to my getting back into the CID office, especially after the way I acted yesterday.'

'Ah, is this where I get the apology?'

'I know I was an arse.'

'Yes.'

'It was just that the only way I could sort the situation fast was to go the back route, and I didn't want to land you in the shit too.'

'Very thoughtful of you, but I'd have turned a blind eye to a lot of things just then.'

'Maybe, maybe not. It wasn't worth the risk. But I am sorry.'

'Okay, accepted. But I think the straight and narrow would be the sensible way to go, at least for a while, don't you?'

'It has been pointed out to me, thank you.' He sat back and exhaled. 'You have no idea how relieved I am to be helping at last.'

Marie knew only too well. 'Your last task.'

He nodded. 'My last task.' He ran a hand over his face. 'He's with me all the time now, Marie.'

Her heart sank. *Oh no, please. Not more tales from the bloody crypt!* She turned and looked at him.

'Tom was at the morning meeting, leaning against the back wall, all the time I was speaking. I'm surprised the stink of burning didn't set the alarm off.'

'There was no smell in that room, Carter, other than the usual coppers' sweaty armpits and a few farts.' Her attempt to make light of it failed, and she added, 'Tom Holland wasn't there either.'

'I do know that. But I still see him.' His grip on her arm tightened. 'He'll go, Marie, he will move on, I know it! Just like the others have. Let's get this case sorted, then maybe I can get my life back. Or some of it.'

She looked into his eyes. Carter was pleading with her.

At least he had admitted that the manifestations were all in his head. All he wanted was to rid himself of the last ghost from the past. Marie knew that somehow she had to find the strength to see him through it.

She made her decision. She would be his rock. Together they would find out what the hell happened to Tom's wife, and then he could move on without her. 'What does he say to you now?'

'"Suzanne." Just that one word — Suzanne.'

'Then we need to stop wasting time sitting in this sodding car, and find out what happened, don't we?'

Carter lit up as if he'd been plugged into a socket. 'Yes, Sergeant Evans, we bloody well do!' His smile widened. 'Let's go!'

CHAPTER EIGHTEEN

Danny Hurley had complained of feeling unwell. He wasn't supposed to be interviewed until the FMO had okayed it, but Jackman wasn't wasting time. While his officers were out on the Suzanne Holland case, he was going through every word of the original reports.

When he was on his third coffee, he picked up the phone. 'Professor Wilkinson?'

'The same. I think I hear the dulcet tone of a detective inspector in trouble. How can I help, DI Jackman?' Rory Wilkinson replied.

'I'd really value your opinion on a case I have inherited.'

'Then I'm all yours. Is it a macabre and gruesome murder? Lots of blood?'

Jackman smiled. He could just imagine the tall, hook-nosed man rubbing his hands in glee. 'I have no idea. I don't even know if it is a murder.'

'No body? No blood? Oh dear.'

'Body, no. Blood? Gallons of the stuff.'

'How old?'

'Eighteen months plus.'

'Intriguing.'

'If I sent you the CSI photographs, would you take a look for me? Oh, and the scene is still pretty well intact.'

'After all that time? Did the attack occur in some kind of time warp?'

'It's a strange case, Rory. The cottage was owned by a husband and wife. The wife, whose blood is spread all over the lounge, is missing. The husband was killed in a light aircraft crash three days later, so no one can do anything with the property. It's in limbo.'

'As are you, by the sound of it.'

'Totally.'

'Then I'd be happy to take a look. Who did the original forensic examination?'

Jackman squinted at the scrawled signature. 'Looks like . . . Squires?'

'Ah, the Squirrel! Good man, if a trifle odd.'

Jackman stifled a chuckle. They didn't come much odder than Rory himself.

'Did I ever tell you why we call him the Squirrel? Other than the obvious play on his surname.'

'If it has anything to do with nuts, I don't want to know.'

'Spoilsport! You are getting as bad as DI Nikki Galena. She's always ruining my fun.'

'Sorry. So can I send you the reports?'

'I can do better. Have them ready and I'll call in. About an hour?'

'If you're sure? I could take you to the crime scene, if it helps?'

'A trip out with the delectable DI Jackman? Is the Pope a Catholic?'

Jackman hung up, still grinning. Despite his camp patter, the Home Office pathologist was one of the sharpest professionals that Jackman had ever met. The thought of getting his opinion on what might have happened to Suzanne Holland cheered him up enormously.

* * *

The beautiful town of Sanxenxo was awash in glorious sunshine, but Harvey Cash was struggling just to wake up.

The hangovers were part of life now, like breathing. Except even that hurt. Drawing in a breath made his head thunder like a steam hammer.

He felt his way slowly and carefully to the fridge, and downed half a bottle of cold water. The shock made him gasp.

He stood for a moment, holding onto the heavy door, trying to regain his balance and control his heaving stomach.

After a few moments he was able to sit on a kitchen chair and think about eating. He couldn't face it. He shouldn't consider another drink either, but he couldn't face being sober.

Since that Brit cop had visited him, he had been possessed by thoughts of Suzanne.

He'd told the guy a lot, more than he'd ever told anyone. But he hadn't told him all of it. Now Harvey was wondering if maybe he should have done.

A yellow-and-green magnet with a shield and a canary on it pinned the young detective's card to the fridge door. Right now Harvey was a very long way from Norwich City and his beloved Canaries.

He stared at the card and pondered. Should he call? Should he tell that persuasive copper the awful truth about Suzanne? Or should he have another drink?

Harvey opted for the second option.

* * *

The overwhelming response to the EFIT picture in the papers and on television had come as a shock.

Superintendent Ruth Crooke tapped her finger on the massive pile of typed sheets. 'I'm sure it has something to do with social media. The whole world and his bloody brother think they know this man.' She scowled at

163

Jackman. 'Are there really that many men who wear their hair like that?'

'A reliable source called Max tells me that long hair is very popular nowadays. A lot of women think it's pretty hot.'

Ruth snorted. 'Sorry, but I think it's ridiculous. They just look . . . oh, never mind. The thing is, I've had to allocate about a thousand civilians to this. We can barely cope.'

'It's frustrating I know,' Jackman said reasonably, 'but maybe one of them really does know him. Let's just hope the sorting process filters something of use.' He noted the dark circles beneath Ruth's eyes. 'How are you?'

'Me?' There was a long pause. 'I'm shaken, Rowan. Shaken to the core.'

'I'm sure you are. And Leah?'

'That girl is amazing. She's gone from being all nervous and unsettled to some kind of super hero since she was actually abducted. It's bizarre.'

'It's a good way to be. Where is she now?'

'Business as usual. Back to uni, although I've insisted she stays with me until we know whether or not someone else was involved.'

'I'm taking Professor Wilkinson to see the Holland house, and after that Danny Hurley should be fit to interview. He is my number one priority.'

'Good. Thank you, Rowan. I appreciate it. Just the thought of some shadowy figure waiting in the wings to make another attempt on her turns my blood to ice.'

'Uniform still have her under surveillance, don't they, ma'am?'

'Oh yes. I would never have let her go back otherwise.' She gave him a weak smile. 'Just keep me updated regarding Hurley, would you?'

'Absolutely, ma'am.'

* * *

Rory Wilkinson took his time. He walked slowly around the cottage, looking constantly from the forensic photographs to the stains themselves. Uncharacteristically, he made no comment.

Finally he turned to Jackman and said, 'Bloodstain evidence has always fascinated me. It's far more complex than the layman would believe.'

Jackman looked at him with interest. Rory hadn't made a single sarcastic or humorous comment.

'I'm only guessing, but I think our Squirrel was covering his back somewhat when he submitted his report. This woman died right here. There's no doubt at all.'

Jackman digested the news. 'Can you give me any idea what happened?'

'Luckily, the record of the bloodstain and spatter patterns was beautifully done. If you give me a little longer I can probably reconstruct the scene, using some spanking new technology, and tell you exactly what happened.' He grinned. 'I am a genius, after all.'

'You won't find me disagreeing.'

Rory put the photographs and reports in his brief case. 'I'm going to enjoy this. I have already ascertained that we have spatter, transfer, cast-off *and* drag marks, plus an arterial bleed with its distinctive rhythmic spurts. It's a positive haemo-cornucopia of delights!'

'Glad you think so,' said Jackman drily.

'Give me until tonight, and I will present the next episode in this nail-biting drama.'

'You're a diamond, Prof.'

'I am rather, aren't I?'

* * *

Marie and Carter were back in the car, considerably more relaxed than before.

Carter passed her a bag containing a jam donut, and balanced a cardboard beaker of coffee on the dash. 'They didn't like her, did they? Not one of them.'

'They did not. And we've spoken to a lot of people this morning. Work colleagues, people she met in different places, like her gym and her hairdressers, and not a single one of them liked her.'

'Yet poor Tom idolised her.' Carter sounded very sad. 'Or he seemed to.'

'What was Tom like?' Marie just managed to stop herself from looking over her shoulder.

'Gentle. That's the first word that comes to mind. Kind, thoughtful, and a great laugh, but never in an unkind way. The kids in our outward bound group all loved him.'

Marie bit into her donut. 'Was he maybe *too* soft? As in almost naïve? You said he thought love was all that mattered, not his wife's dubious past.'

'No, not naïve. He was quite simply a good person. He preferred to think the best of people. Not like us cynical coppers, who always expect to find the worst.'

Marie brushed sugar off her trousers. 'I'm so sorry you lost your friend, Carter. He sounds like a really great guy.'

'He is — uh, he was. One of the best. I miss him. I miss them all.'

Marie felt tears forming and changed the subject. 'So what do we make of Suzanne?'

Carter slurped his coffee. 'That my initial impression was bloody right. Tom Holland was a fucking goofball to marry the tart. He must have had shit for brains.'

Marie burst out laughing, and after a moment, Carter joined in.

CHAPTER NINETEEN

'I don't know who he was! How many times do I have to tell you?' Danny Hurley raged.

Jackman looked on impassively.

Jackman had studied sociology at university, and he hadn't forgotten what he'd learned. He listened, of course, but he also watched. Body language and mannerisms spoke as loudly as words. Sometimes they positively shouted.

'So, you were *paid* to follow and abduct the very girl you were obsessed with. Can you see how that looks to us, Danny?' He turned to Gary Pritchard. 'Wouldn't you say it's just a little bit far-fetched, Constable?'

Gary nodded sagely. 'Oh dear yes, sir. Quite a stretch of the imagination.'

Danny punched a fist into his cupped hand. 'No! You've got it all wrong! Why won't you listen?'

'We are listening, Danny, but what we are hearing doesn't make too much sense.'

'I was paid to do a few things. Send her flowers, chocolates and stuff like that.'

'But you don't know who the person was?'

'I never met him.'

'Him? You know it was a man? How?'

Danny stammered. 'Well, I don't, but a woman wouldn't be doing that, would she?'

'How did you get paid?'

'Cash and instructions arrived with a parcel delivery service.'

'You've got to be kidding! No one sends money with a man with a van!' Gary exclaimed. 'What company was it?'

Danny stared at the scratches on the table and mumbled, 'I dunno. It was an unmarked car.'

Jackman shook his head. 'Better and better. So, where are these "instructions?"'

'I burnt them. It was part of the deal.'

Jackman leaned forward. 'Why not start telling us the truth, Danny? You really liked the girl, didn't you? And you wanted her. We've seen the pictures on your wall, Danny. You didn't take them for someone else, did you? They were just for you.'

Danny's eyes narrowed, but he said nothing.

In the ensuing silence, Jackman decided to try a different tack. 'Okay, Danny. Let's say I believe you. I don't, but let's assume I do. Did you know Leah before Mr Anonymous contacted you?'

'I'd never seen her before.'

'Right, so he sent you money and you started . . . what? Putting cards through her door? Something like that?'

Danny nodded. 'Cards, yes. And notes, then roses.'

'So they weren't really from you, but from another guy who fancied her?'

Danny didn't seem happy with this idea. 'It wasn't like that.'

'How do you know? It sounds like it to me. Someone giving you money to spend on an attractive young woman? I'd say they definitely wanted something from her.' He shot a knowing glance to Gary. 'What I don't get is why, if you had the hots for someone, you would take them flowers and love tokens from another man?'

Gary rubbed his chin thoughtfully. 'Well, *I* certainly wouldn't.'

Jackman could almost hear Danny grinding his teeth.

'Help us out here, Danny. We are struggling.'

'It's about revenge! Alright! It was payback time! Then I saw Leah and, well . . .'

He threw up his hands, and then his voice fell to a whisper. 'I'd only ever heard of love at first sight. They didn't care about her, they never did. It wasn't about her at all, just revenge. But for me, it was a dream.' He slumped forward and put his head in his hands. 'A dream.'

Jackman nodded towards the door and he and Gary stood up. 'Interview suspended at fourteen hundred hours. DI Jackman and PC Gary Pritchard are leaving the room.'

Outside, Jackman beckoned Gary into an empty room and closed the door.

'We need to get Leah out of uni and back under close observation. Do you agree?'

Gary nodded. 'Someone is after the super, aren't they?'

'I'm sure of it. Danny Hurley is infatuated with Leah, that's a fact. But I reckon he was telling the truth about a retribution thing.'

'Me too.'

'I'm going to see if there is anything in his statement that could point us to the villain who is behind this. You speak to your sergeant and get Leah taken to a place of safety. Danny might have cocked up, but she's still in danger.'

Gary turned to leave. 'Let's hope that Danny's bungled mission and his arrest have scared the bastard off.'

'Let's hope so, but in the meantime, belt and braces.'

'I'm on it, sir!'

'And for heaven's sake, hurry! Whoever paid him is still out there.'

* * *

169

Three-quarters of an hour later, Jackman sat opposite Ruth Crooke, wondering how much more the woman could take. The invincible superintendent he was used to seeing had gone. He understood why, but found the transformation dispiriting.

'I never told you, Rowan, but my sister did not have a good death, if there is such a thing. That is probably why I try to compensate when it comes to Leah. I only want the best for her, and whereas we can't ensure the easiest passage through life, I did want her journey to be a safe one.' Ruth pushed a stray lock of hair behind her ear. 'She found her mother's body.'

Jackman already knew that Ruth's sister had taken her own life, but not that her daughter had found her. 'I am so sorry, Ruth. That's a terrible thing to happen to someone, especially a young person.'

'I think that's why she's studying psychology. She wants to help save others from the same fate.'

'A very good reason.' He smiled. 'I thought she was a very strong young woman. Now I'm certain of it.'

'So, what have you gleaned from the Hurley creature?'

Jackman explained about the interview. 'The second time I went in, I took Rosie with me, and we found out a bit more.' He leaned forward. 'We believe that this mystery man only intended to put the frighteners on you via your niece. It was Danny Hurley who upped the game. We've pieced together what he was actually instructed to do, and the rest he did off his own bat. Both Rosie and I believe that the intention was never to kidnap or abduct her, but Danny changed the plan.'

Ruth frowned. 'So he was out to scare me, not take Leah.'

'That's what I think. The instructions this man, if indeed it is a man, left were quite convoluted. Danny had to use gofers and keep himself in the background, out of sight. He was to conduct the orchestra, not play the instruments himself.'

'Well, that didn't work, did it? They really should have done their homework before hiring him.'

'Yes. He, or she, certainly picked a wrong one there.'

'Hearing this makes me feel a little easier, although we can never assume anything, can we?'

'Of course not, ma'am. But I feel the same. Danny's unpredictability could have caused some really serious damage.'

'So how can we trace his unknown "employer?"'

'Well . . .' Jackman hesitated. 'I was thinking I'd deploy Carter out on the streets. He knows more about the local thieves and villains than all the rest of us plods put together.'

'And has more connections in higher circles than the chief constable.' There was a hint of bitterness in Ruth's words. 'He's an enigma. But like it or not, he's a valuable asset. Just never, *never* let him know I said that.'

'As if!'

'Okay, let him go digging, but for God's sake, keep him on a short rein.'

'I'll do better, ma'am. I'll hand over the reins to Marie Evans.'

CHAPTER TWENTY

Carter looked worried. 'I'll do my best, but I've probably used up most of my loyalty points tracking the bastard down in the first place.'

'Try money.' Jackman looked around. There was no one within earshot. 'I've made a few minor adjustments to my budget sheet.' He held out an envelope.

'I don't need that, sir. I think Ruth should have this one on me, after all she's gone through.'

'Take it. She was the one who authorised it.'

Marie took the envelope and pushed it deep into her jacket pocket. 'Well, while you two are forming the Saltern debating society, I'm making the decisions. Come on, Carter, let's get back out there.'

Carter threw up his hands in surrender. 'Gotta go. Orders.'

Jackman watched them walk away. They were clearly comfortable working together. He just prayed that Carter's issues didn't affect Marie any more than they had already. Perhaps, just perhaps, finding out what happened to Suzanne Holland would draw a line under this whole episode.

Jackman went back into his office and closed the door. When something terrible happened, there was always more than one victim. Disaster had a ripple effect, like a pebble thrown into a lake, drawing in many more people than those directly involved. Jackman sighed. He had a feeling that things were going to get a whole lot worse before they got better.

* * *

'At sodding last! Got something, lads!' Max snatched an email from the printer. Robbie and Charlie hurried over.

'Doolan is in Scunthorpe General Hospital. He was in an RTC yesterday.'

'How bad is he?' asked Charlie.

'Not good, but not critical either. We need to go see him.' Max grinned at Robbie. 'And even though there's no sun, sea, sand *or* sangria, like some people's recent trips, this one is mine.'

Robbie held up his hands. 'Scunthorpe is all yours.' He grinned back. 'Although I am *bitterly* disappointed.'

'Yeah, I'm sure. Bitterly.'

Max hurried off to tell the boss, and Robbie and Charlie returned to their desks. It wasn't over yet. They still had to place him at the scene of the crime. But at least they now knew where he was, and by the sound of it, he wouldn't be going anywhere any time soon. Another link in the chain.

Robbie stood up. 'Want a coffee, Charlie-boy?'

'White with two, please.' He put a hand in his pocket.

'Forget it, it's my turn.'

Robbie strolled along to the coffee machine, wondering how his expat friend was doing. If Harvey had been local, Robbie would have visited him again. He had a distinct feeling that all was not well with HC. Not only that, he knew he had been holding something back. What was it? Could it be important?

Robbie carried the two coffees back to the CID room and set one down in front of Charlie.

'Thanks.' Charlie looked up from his monitor screen. 'I've been thinking. What if Ponytail isn't Ralph Doolan?'

Robbie blinked. Charlie had a knack of saying the blindingly obvious, in a way that made you think again. 'I've been rather running with the hypothesis that there wouldn't be two Ponytails and Glasses in Suzanne's life.'

'Why not?' Charlie shrugged, 'He was a dead ringer for Alan Pitt's cousin, and the boss said he looked like an Arsenal footballer, so? She could have known two Ponytails. It's not impossible.'

Robbie stared at him. 'What the hell does the boss know about Arsenal?'

Charlie laughed. 'Sod all, as far as I know. But if Doolan comes up with a cast-iron alibi, we need to start looking for Ponytail II, don't we?'

'I suppose.' Robbie let out a sigh. 'I can hardly wait.'

* * *

Sam Page had just finished a long stint on the riverbank, watching great crested grebes. As soon as he entered the house, he checked his answerphone. No messages.

He went into the kitchen and put the kettle on. He was worried about Laura. She had been so interested in hearing his opinion of her complex patient, and then nothing.

He made tea and took it through to the sun lounge. He had deliberately left his garden to grow wild, and it was now a haven for wildlife. Sam loved nothing better than watching his "lodgers," as he called the field mice, hedgehogs, bats and other creatures that had made it their home.

He sipped his tea and thought about Laura Archer.

She had told him the story of this patient of hers called Carter, and Sam had realised that it was one of those rare cases where the client affects the therapist in a profound way. He hated to see Laura so anxious, but he didn't know what to do about it.

Eventually he muttered to himself, 'Come on, Sam. Just call her.'

Laura answered before the second ring. She must have been waiting for a call from someone else. 'Shall I ring back at a better time?' he asked.

'Oh, Sam, no, of course not. Now is fine.'

'I was wondering if you'd managed to tie your man down to an appointment where I can sit in. I'm quite free this week.'

Sam heard a muffled grunt.

'He's not returning my calls. I've rung and left messages, and I've texted him, but he's not getting back. I'm sorry, Sam, but I guess we'll have to forget it.'

'You are very worried about him, aren't you?'

Her silence spoke volumes.

'Laura, you can't heal them all. Just as some physical injuries are beyond the help of a surgeon, injuries to the mind can have the same outcome.'

'I had a brief word with his friend, Marie. She told me that his fourth friend is with him all the time now. It has scared the life out of me. It's not something I've ever dealt with before.'

'Yet he still functions?'

'He does outwardly, and he seems to keep this friend, Tom, well under wraps. No one other than Marie and her DI are aware that anything is wrong. To most people, he's an amazing survivor — a superhero.'

Sam thought about it. 'From what you told me, he chose an excellent coping mechanism. As he no longer "sees" the other three friends, it is clearly working for him, but the fourth task is much more difficult. How long is it since this woman disappeared?'

Laura murmured, 'Eighteen months, Sam. A long time.'

'And Carter believes that this friend wants him to find out what happened to his wife?'

'That's what he says.'

'And all the time he is being haunted by the friend's restless, unquiet soul. We have to consider that this case may linger on for a very long while.' He took a breath. 'And I'm not sure how Carter will handle that. The labours of Hercules seem a bit tame compared to the task that young man has set himself.'

'That doesn't bear thinking about, Sam.'

'There is another worrying factor.'

'And that is?'

'That he has got under your skin. You are too close to this man. You *must* detach yourself. You cannot afford to let him breach your defences.'

Laura did not answer him.

Her silence told him all he needed to know. 'Can I ask, have you finished your paper? The one on psycho-social transitions?'

'I've ditched it.'

'Why?'

'Oh, you know why! He was my main case study, wasn't he?'

'Let me take over his case. I know that you are more than capable of dealing with his problem, but you are too involved with the man himself. It's not healthy, my dear. You don't need me to tell you about distancing yourself emotionally.'

Laura let out a sigh. 'God, Sam, I've tried all the tricks, even the exercises we use in training. But this time . . . nothing works.' She paused. 'You are right, Sam, but because I work for the police force I can't just hand his case over to you. You don't have clearance.'

'Then allow me to help you. Don't tackle this alone.'

'Would you? It would be such a relief! And let's pray that our boys and girls in blue solve the mystery of Suzanne in double-quick time, before we all finish up in therapy!'

Sam hung up, feeling happier. At least if he were there to guide her, she wouldn't have to worry about errors of judgement. And if things didn't pan out for Carter McLean, Laura might really need him.

* * *

Jackman was just deciding to call it a day when his phone rang.

'As promised, the full story.' Rory Wilkinson sounded excited. 'It's a shame I'm based in Greenborough, I'd love you to call into my underground kingdom. I have this really dinky little 3D graphic showing the last moments of Suzanne Holland.'

'I can get there tomorrow. But for now, can you tell me what happened?'

'Of course, dear heart! Now would you like the full cast production, or the abridged version? I recommend the full Monty because then I can show off my *huge* repertoire of regional accents.'

'I'm sure your repertoire is most impressive, Rory, but a simple synopsis would suffice.'

'Are you related to DI Galena, by any chance?'

'Not to my knowledge. Er, the story . . . ?'

'Right. Suzanne died because she hit her head against the mantelpiece. She then fell to the floor sustaining a further head injury on the cast-iron surround of the fire-place.'

'She fell?' Jackman was sure Rory had suggested a more violent end.

'Yes, she fell.' Rory paused. 'But only because she was pushed, with considerable force.'

'You can be quite irritating sometimes, Rory, did anyone ever tell you that?'

'I'm told — frequently.' He chuckled. 'I really do think I can explain much more clearly when you see the whole thing in motion.'

'Early tomorrow, if that's okay?'

'Since I practically live here, that will be fine. Oh, and I am going to do another forensic sweep of your crime

177

scene. I have equipment available to me now that wasn't around eighteen months ago. Blood spatter analysis is my passion, and I have a theory about the hearth rug that I would like to check out. Would you arrange that for me?'

'Just say when. I have access to the keys.'

'We'll sort that out when you do me the honour of visiting tomorrow. So for now I'll just say, Ciao, and hasta mañana.'

Jackman replaced the phone and saw Marie standing in the doorway.

'Any joy?'

'Maybe, maybe not.' She sat down. 'Carter has got a name for one of Danny's gofers, but the little scrote has gone to ground.'

'Maybe uniform can find him.'

'I'd leave it to Carter, sir. He's got a knack with the underbelly of Saltern-le-Fen. If anyone can root him out, Carter can.'

'Anything else?'

'There's an undercurrent out there. We both noticed it.' Marie massaged her temples, as if her head ached. 'It's hard to explain, but there seems to be a lot of bad feeling towards the police — more than normal — and Ruth Crooke in particular. First thing tomorrow I'll pull up a list of local villains that might have a grudge against her, then Carter and I are going knocking on a few doors.'

'Where is Carter now?'

'He's gone to see her.'

'Voluntarily?'

Marie grinned. 'Yes, would you believe? I could be wrong, but I get the feeling that this business with Leah is mending a very old rift.'

'Not before time.'

Marie stretched. 'Any news on the Suzanne front?'

Jackman told her about the half-brother, and what Rory had found.

'Looks like we are moving forward at last.'

178

'Let's not count our chickens, but something's beginning to emerge from the mist.'

'Good.' Marie yawned.

'Get off home, Evans! And get some rest.'

'I will. I just want a quick word with Carter before I go.'

'Don't let him get you involved in one of his long heart to hearts, please. I need you on the ball, not worried sick over imaginary dead people.'

'Er, sir. They are actual dead people. Not imaginary.'

'So remember that, okay?'

'Yes, sir. Understood, sir.'

* * *

Carter was on his way to Stone Quay, and trying to concentrate on the road. His mind was on Ruth Crooke, and the sudden change in their relationship.

At close of day, he had sat and actually talked to her for almost half an hour. And not one acrimonious remark had passed between them. Nothing had been said, but he knew that they had made their peace at last. He left her office feeling as if the wind had blown a heavy storm cloud from the sky.

He came to a halt and found the key to the storeroom. He had a couple of particular jobs to attend to this evening, and then he would be almost done.

Silas was sitting on an empty oil drum, with his dog sprawled across his feet.

'Evening, Silas. Alright?'

'Good enough, young'un. You eaten?'

Carter considered the question.

'Thought not. Come to the cottage, it won't take more'n a few minutes. You can't work with no fuel in your belly.'

Carter followed him through the long grass and reeds to the tumbledown cottage. Carter had eaten with Silas before. His meals might not pass current food safety standards but they were the most delicious he had ever tasted.

Now he sniffed the air. 'Rabbit stew?'

'Hare casserole. Get yourself a bowl.'

'And you?'

'I ate earlier. But you help yourself.'

The old man offered him a ladle and pointed towards an ancient stewpot bubbling away on the stove.

'I used a bit of my homemade wine in it. Think it worked, too. Eh?'

'I'll say.' Carter ate and ate. Being with Silas Breeze felt right, it always had. This old half-ruined cottage was his refuge from an unkind world.

He finished the bowl of food and sat back. He looked around. No Tom. Come to think of it, he never saw Tom when he was in Silas's place. 'I must get some work done, Si, but thank you for that. I appreciate it.'

'I knows that.' The old man grinned showing very few teeth. 'You'll work twice as 'ard now.'

Silas had been right. Carter worked until encroaching darkness made it impossible to do any more. All evening, Tom had been a silent presence.

He drove away, and the sound of her name followed him into the dark night.

CHAPTER TWENTY-ONE

Jackman arrived back from Greenborough just in time for the morning meeting. Marie met him in the corridor by the vending machine.

'Coffee?' She smiled, and in her eyes, he saw a spark of the old Marie.

'I'd love one. Are the troops assembled?' He nodded towards the CID room.

'All present and correct, sir.' She handed him a beaker of coffee. 'Was your trip worthwhile?'

'Edifying, Marie. Very.'

'So is what our Max dug up in Scunthorpe.'

'Then we'd better go and put our heads together.'

He confirmed that another person of interest had surfaced in the Danny Hurley investigation, and then concentrated on the Holland case.

'Professor Wilkinson is conducting further forensic work at the Holland Cottage, and until he has completed his checks it will remain sealed up.'

Jackman took several large printouts and pinned them to the whiteboard. Diagrams of the crime scene.

'These are stills from motion graphic software. You will see in the first diagram the general layout of the lounge, and here,' he pointed to an enlarged photograph taken by the first team of SOCOs, 'is the forensic photographers' view of the room. It has an old-fashioned stone fireplace and an open fire. Note, the mantelpiece is very low compared to modern, or even Victorian designs.' He pointed to the next picture. 'Professor Wilkinson believes that Suzanne was standing in the centre of the hearthrug — here.' The image showed a woman of Suzanne's height and build. She was facing away from the fireplace.

'How has he done all this?' asked Carter.

'Blood spatter and stain analysis.'

'Clever stuff.'

'He's a brilliant scientist.' Jackman gave a wry smile. 'If a little off the wall.'

There was a ripple of laughter. Rory Wilkinson was universally liked in Saltern. His camp humour often defused the tension that followed after witnessing a traumatic crime scene.

'I suggest you all come and look at these pictures when we are through here. It will give you a fairly good idea of what happened. In a nutshell, it went like this . . . Suzanne Holland was pushed with considerable force. She possibly caught her foot in the rug, tried to turn to steady herself, then hit her head against the corner of the mantelpiece. She then fell to the floor and cracked her temple on the iron surround. Prof Wilkinson says that there is no chance that she survived her injuries.'

'How can he be so sure? And how did he know it was her temple?' Marie was staring at the pictures.

'I've just come from a twenty-minute tutorial on the mechanism and classification of spatter patterns. It included low, medium and high velocity of the blood depending on the force of impact. I have learnt that blood issues from the body in many different ways. It can drip, ooze, flow, gush and spurt, and they all leave different patterns. It was worth getting a migraine. I'm telling you, there is nothing that man does not know about blood at crime scenes.'

'Heck, sir! I only asked.'

Jackman grinned, and then became serious again. 'As for the temple, Prof Wilkinson said there was an arterial spurt that most likely came from one specific artery, the left external carotid. He made that deduction from a passive bloodstain that would have gathered beneath her body after her heart stopped beating.' He exhaled loudly. 'Of course, without her body we cannot be certain about everything, but the crime scene and the evidence found there will tell us more than enough.'

Charlie raised a hand. 'So would it be classed as an accidental death, sir?'

'We do not know the intentions of the person who pushed her. Whatever, it was definitely the push that caused her to shatter her skull and sever an artery. The blood loss must have been extensive. If there had been no intention to harm, then it would be manslaughter, but if it was deliberate, well, then it was murder.'

'We need to find her body,' Carter almost whispered.

'We do.' Jackman looked across to Max. 'Come up here and tell us what happened when you went to see Suzanne's brother.'

Max took centre stage. 'Ralph Doolan is at present in Scunthorpe General Hospital. He sustained injuries in an accident, a hit and run that took place in the early hours of yesterday morning. Neither the vehicle nor the driver of the car have been traced.' He looked down at his notebook. 'I was allowed to talk to him for a short while, and then again a little later. I confirmed his name, date of birth, and the fact that Suzanne Holland was his half-sister.' Max closed his notebook and looked around the room. 'His injuries are not life-threatening, but he has some serious damage to his pins, er, sorry, his legs. With several operations planned, he is likely to be there for some time, so we know where he is if we want him. Now, the thing is,' he ran a hand through his spiky hair, 'he says he was in the Fens at the time of his sister's disappearance, but he hadn't seen her for weeks. He swears that he wasn't near the cottage on the night in question.'

'Does he look like the photofit?' asked Marie.

'Bang to rights, Sarge. And he still has the ponytail. Oh yeah, and the glasses were Ray-Bans.'

'That's good?' Charlie asked.

'Pleb! Like they would have set him back a couple of hundred smackers?'

'Alibi?' Jackman questioned.

'He's given me the name of a friend. He said he might have been with him that night, but he can't be sure. And that, folks, is that.' Max returned to his seat.

'So, no firm alibi, and he is a match for the photofit. It doesn't look good for Mr Doolan, does it?' Carter commented.

'It doesn't,' agreed Jackman. 'So we better have another word. And, Max, talk to the friend, will you?'

'That's first on my list for this morning, sir.'

'Right, people. Let's do all we can to discover what happened to Suzanne's body.'

* * *

Ten minutes later, Jackman was sitting in his office with Marie and Carter.

'Before you get back out there looking for whoever was running Danny Hurley, I'd like to get your thoughts on what happened in the Holland house, now we know she was actually killed there,' Jackman said.

'What I can't understand is, why remove the body?' Carter rubbed at his chin. 'Given the amount of blood, it was patently obvious that something dreadful had happened. Why not just ring it in?'

'Would you, if you'd just killed her?' Marie asked.

'Do you think it was Ponytail and sidekick?' Carter asked.

'Who else? Two men heard talking in raised voices on the path leading to the scene of the murder, on the very night we believe she died?' Marie raised an eyebrow, 'What more do you want?'

'A motive,' interjected Jackman. 'Okay, so she wasn't popular, and she'd had a failed marriage, then she went a bit wild and slept around for a while, but that's not sufficient motive for murder by stone mantelpiece, is it?'

Carter looked at him. 'Could she have tripped?'

'Rory assured me that so much blood loss means that she was probably flung or pushed by someone in a rage.'

'What does he hope to find from this new search, sir?' asked Marie.

'He just said he has a theory, but nothing more.'

'Curiouser and curiouser,' Carter muttered.

Jackman stood up. 'Well, thanks for the input, but I think we are just going to go around in circles until we have more information, so you'd better get back out there. Good luck, guys.'

Carter went off to make some preliminary calls.

Marie waited behind. 'We are edging closer to finding out what happened, sir, aren't we?'

'We are.' Jackman saw her expression. 'Close the door, Marie. Okay, what's wrong?'

Marie hesitated for a moment. 'Carter is really into this, really focused. I believe he is totally convinced that solving the mystery will get rid of his unwanted friend. But what if he doesn't like what we discover? What if the person who killed Suzanne was someone very close to home?'

Jackman digested her words. 'As in one of his other friends?'

She shrugged. 'Possibly. I've been wondering who that second man was, the one with our friend Ponytail. I spent a lot of the night thinking about all the people who had some connection to Suzanne. Four of them are dead, so proving where they were and what they were doing won't be easy, will it?'

Jackman breathed in. She had a valid point. 'I'll personally check the old reports for discrepancies, but I'll do it quietly, if you see what I mean?'

'Thanks, sir. It's just a wild guess really, but I still feel very twitchy about Carter's reaction if things do not go as he imagines they will.'

'You and me both, *and* Laura Archer. I saw her talking to the FMO yesterday, and she looked worried sick.'

'And we can all guess who she's worried over.'

Jackman mustered a smile. 'Thanks, Marie, now you'd better go before the closed door causes comments.'

* * *

Two hours later, Carter and Marie were sitting in a seedy backstreet café talking to an even seedier man.

Carter had told her that Sidney was one of his oldest snouts, and unlike most of the street people he used, he actually trusted him. Sidney had taken a bit of finding, but the promise of food and a hot drink had tempted him out of his hole.

Now, with a full English breakfast inside him, he looked almost human.

'He's a creep, Mr McLean, no other word for him. Danny's had these "things" about women before, but he's never gone as far as snatching them. Silly bugger.'

'You're certain he was acting alone when he arranged to take the girl?'

'Well, he used a couple of the lads to do the actual snatch.' He winked at Carter. 'As I think you know. But, yes, he was going to take her away with him.'

'Where?'

Sidney shrugged. 'No idea. But of course, it wasn't him that started the whole thing.'

'So he says.' Carter's eyes narrowed.

'He isn't lying, Mr McLean. The word on the streets is that a certain well-known family — one that's headline news at present — were just saying "thank you" to the rozzer that put three of them in the cells.'

Marie's eyes widened. 'The Cannon family?'

Sidney tilted his head. 'Maybe.'

That would make all kinds of sense. In her head, Marie went over the reports on the arrests and yes, Ruth Crooke had been the OIC. 'Do you reckon that they never meant Danny to go as far as he did?'

The old man looked shrewdly at Marie. 'They are in enough trouble, miss. It was just meant as a sort of "gesture." Not intended to be linked to them, but still, an irritating thorn in said rozzer's side.'

Carter shook his head. 'Well, they certainly chose the wrong man for the job.'

'I dunno. Even in our community, not many people know about Danny Hurley's dark side.'

Carter pulled a face. 'That's true. I've never had dealings with him personally, but it never came up on the radar.'

'And I'm guessing there will be no way to connect what happened to Leah with the Cannon family?' asked Marie.

Sidney rolled his eyes. 'Not in a million years. And as soon as I leave this place, I'm forgetting every word that was said.' His face broke into a rather sad smile. 'I'd do the same if I were you, miss, for all our sakes. *No one* goes up against the Cannons. But I'm thinking that as long as Danny is in your care, your young woman will be safe to return to her life again.'

They ordered Sidney more tea, and thanked him. Marie walked ahead, turned to say something to Carter and saw him mutter a few words into Sidney's ear and pass him a small fold of notes.

Back in the car, she turned to him and raised an eyebrow. 'Money well spent?'

'Oh yes, I think so, don't you?' His face lit up. 'Now we can get back to doing some real police work.'

He started the car. Marie watched him as he drove. From the set of his jaw, she knew that one way or another, Carter McLean was going to get to the truth of what happened in Holland Cottage. Was it to see justice done, or to rid himself of a ghost?

CHAPTER TWENTY-TWO

Robbie looked down at his growing pile of reports. He had been meaning for some time to visit Joanne Simms, the late Ray Barret's fiancée, but there weren't enough hours in the day. At last he picked up the phone, wondering if it was really the lack of time that was holding him back. Or was it his reluctance to talk to a woman whose future husband had died just days before their wedding.

Robbie arranged to meet her outside the DIY store where she worked. He drove across town, marvelling at how resilient people were. A terrible tragedy occurs and, somehow, those left behind pick up the threads and move on. He thought of his old crewmate, Stella, gunned down as she tried to protect innocent bystanders. He thought of Marie, continuing to be a damned good copper after the love of her life had died in front of her, racing his favourite vintage motorbike. Then he considered Carter McLean, and his mind went into overload.

He drew in a deep breath. *Don't even go there, Melton!*

Joanne waited for him in a small park beside the store. She looked nervous. Robbie knew that he didn't look like a police officer, which helped a lot in situations like this. He adopted his "little brother" persona, and Joanne began to relax. In no time at all, they were chatting away like old friends.

'It seems unbelievable that the wife of one of five such close friends could be attacked and removed from her home, and not one of them, including her husband, had the slightest idea that she was even missing.' Robbie shook his head.

Joanne nodded. 'But poor Tom had been staying with us, hadn't he? He hadn't been back to the house for fear of meeting Suzanne.' She shuddered. 'Initially I thought, thank God he didn't. It would have been terribly shocking to find all that blood. But now,' she tugged at her earlobe, 'I wonder if he *had* gone back, then the stag trip would have been cancelled, and they'd all be alive.'

Robbie patted her arm, afraid that she was about to break down. 'You mustn't think like that, Joanne. No one can alter what happened, and "what if?" are two very painful words.'

'You're right.' She gave a shaky sigh. 'Anyway. How can I help you?'

'I believe that it's very important that we find out what led to Tom and Suzanne having such a serious row. We have no details at all. Is there anything more you can tell me, apart from what you said — you know, about it being a storm in a teacup?'

Joanne wrung her hands. 'I haven't allowed myself to think about the things Ray said for a long time. It was all so horrible. But recently I've been starting to come to terms with my loss, and I have been trying to recall what it was all about.'

'I don't mean to cause you pain, Joanne, but we now know that Suzanne was killed in that cottage, and her body was taken away.'

'Murder?'

'Maybe, or manslaughter at the very least.' He looked at her earnestly. 'We have to find who did this, and where they took her body. Anything at all that you can tell us might help.'

Joanne's voice was stronger now. 'Some of this is just my thoughts on what happened. But, whatever. I believe the upset between Tom and his wife was serious, possibly irreconcilable.'

Robbie tensed. This was the first time he'd heard it described as anything more than "a bit of a tiff."

'Tom was with us for four or five days before they went on that trip.' She paused. 'Well, Tom was a sweetie, a real softie, and he really loved Suzanne. He couldn't understand why his friends, and Carter McLean in particular, couldn't love her too. He hated the fact that no one liked his wife. He was aware she had had a lot of men before she met him, but he swore that from the moment they got together she had been faithful to him. He thought that meant she deserved a second chance.'

Joanne glanced at her watch, but went on. 'Whatever it was, he was devastated. He and my Ray would talk well into the night, and I could hear Tom crying. It was horrible, and Ray made it worse by begging me to leave Tom alone. All he would tell me was that Tom had been hurt, and couldn't bear to talk about it.'

Alarm bells began to ring in Robbie's head. Harvey Cash had said the same thing. Suzanne hurt people.

'I should get back to work. But if I think of anything at all, I'll ring you.'

Robbie gave her his card and thanked her. He hurried back to his car. He needed to talk to Harvey Cash, and he'd damn well buy another ticket to Sanxenxo if he had to.

He ran into the office, pulled out his pocketbook and looked up Harvey's number. Sod the cost of the call, this was important.

Harvey Cash was incoherent.

Robbie gritted his teeth and desperately tried to get him to concentrate. It took a while, but finally he got his answer.

He hung up and felt a surge of excitement. Now all he needed was for Carter McLean to confirm it, and they had a motive for Suzanne's death.

* * *

When Carter walked into the CID office, Robbie Melton practically vaulted over his desk and ran towards him.

'At last! Can I take five minutes of your time, Sarge? It's urgent,' Robbie said.

'Take as long as you like. Marie is just talking to Jackman, and we think that the Leah Kingfield problem is probably sorted.'

'Oh, that's a relief, especially for the super. Can we go to your office, please? What I want to ask about concerns Suzanne Holland.'

Robbie followed Carter into his office, sat down and began immediately. 'Sarge? Is there a chance that Suzanne Holland was a husband beater?'

Carter felt as if he'd been punched in the gut. 'I . . . I hadn't considered that.'

'Then do, Sarge. Because I think she was a bully, and not just verbally. I think she may have been physically abusive.'

Carter was too shocked to speak.

'Sarge, did Tom ever say anything about his relationship with Suzanne that made you think it wasn't a . . . a healthy one?'

'Like what?'

Robbie was almost bouncing in his seat. 'As in, did he ever describe his home life as being volatile? Emotional? Crazy?'

'Kind of, although he never said much. He used to say that she was unpredictable, and he was always getting things wrong. Is that what you mean?'

'Exactly.'

'But he didn't talk about her much at all, Robbie, and that was *my* fault. I didn't like her, and that hurt him, so he kept his problems to himself, and I did nothing to help.'

If he'd just been a bit more understanding, if he'd tried harder, if . . .

'And maybe your attitude made no difference at all, Sarge. Most guys who are involved with abusive women don't talk about it, they *can't*.' Robbie threw up his hands. 'Think about it! You've lost your self-respect, you feel powerless and manipulated. You might even start to believe all the crap she is feeding you about yourself. You are traumatised by her behaviour, embarrassed by it and ashamed of being unable to stop it. Tom Holland couldn't "offload," as you put it, to anyone at all.'

Carter looked at Robbie. 'Tom did change. He got quieter and, well, a bit introverted, I guess. How did you get to this, anyway?'

'By listening to a drunk.' Robbie sighed. 'And I'm surprised to say that I've become rather fond of him.'

'Suzanne's first husband?'

'Suzanne's first victim.'

CHAPTER TWENTY-THREE

Marie and Jackman went upstairs to report to Superintendent Ruth Crooke. Carter had opted out, saying, "The girl is safe now. I know it, okay? Just tell the super that, would you? I want to get to work on Suzanne."

'I feel relieved of course,' Ruth said, 'but it's been such an unsettling time that I can't bring myself to believe it's over.'

'We have no real proof, ma'am,' Marie said apologetically. 'But I'm pretty sure the old boy was telling the truth. He and Carter go back a long way, and Carter said that Sidney's info has always been reliable.'

'And you, Marie? What's your impression? You said there was a bad feeling on the streets the other day. Is it something I should be concerned about?'

'The beat bobbies think the unrest is caused by the Cannons' relatives and friends, ma'am. There are two camps. Half are convinced that they will get off, like they usually do, and the others are cautiously expecting them to go down. They are divided, and they are taking it out on us.'

'And me in particular, I guess.' Ruth sounded exhausted. 'After all, I was the officer in charge of that investigation.'

'It's par for the course, ma'am,' Jackman added. 'It happens every time we nail a local villain.'

'Marie? You didn't answer my question.' Ruth was looking at her.

'I believe that Leah is good to go. And Carter does too.'

Ruth exhaled. 'In which case we'll just keep an eye on her for a while, but I think I can relax a little, don't you?'

'You mean, give up the Monopoly?'

Ruth gave a weak smile. 'Thank heavens! That get-out-of-jail-free card was giving me the heebie-jeebies.'

Marie left Jackman talking with the super and walked slowly down to the office. Something was bothering her. Something about the morning had hoisted a red flag. The problem was that Marie had no idea who or what was waving it.

'I know that look.' Gary Pritchard came and stood beside her.

'Mmm. It's that one that renders me totally useless for hours while I try to fathom out what is bothering me.'

Gary pulled over a chair and sat down. 'Is it a recent something, or an historical one?'

'Oh recent. Today, in fact. I'm sure of it.'

'Then retrace your footsteps. Think about every place and conversa—'

'Got it! You're a star!' Her smile faded instantly. Now she had to work out why breakfast with Sidney should have registered a warning.

'Any time.' Gary stood up. 'Wish all my queries were answered so easily.'

'Hang on, Gary.' She pointed to the chair, and Gary sat back down. 'I know you haven't been stationed here for very long, but you are local. What do you know about a snout of Carter's called Sidney?'

'Ah, Sidney.' Gary absentmindedly played with his signet ring. 'What do you want to know about him?'

She shrugged. 'Anything at all really.'

Gary said nothing for a while. Marie sensed he was uncomfortable.

'Sidney Leyton-Crowe. One-time head teacher of a public school for boys. Was at the centre of a scandal, found innocent and completely exonerated, but the impact on him was profound. He had a breakdown, Marie. Very sad, very sad indeed.'

Marie knew that many street people had heartbreaking back stories. She should have realised that Sidney was one of them. She recalled his intelligent shrewdness. 'Of course,' she murmured. 'So what was with all the "rozzers" and "silly buggers" talk?'

'When in Rome. He'd not last long out there if he acted like a "snob."' Gary made air quotes.

'How did he come to be one of Carter's snouts?'

Gary took a quick look around. There was no one within earshot. 'He was Carter's headmaster. If Carter hadn't stood up and testified on his behalf, he wouldn't have had a chance. He'd been fitted up, but everyone was too scared to take his side.'

'Except Carter.'

'Exactly. He had a strong sense of right and wrong even in his schooldays. No wonder he became a copper.'

'Thanks, Gary, and don't worry, my lips are sealed.'

He nodded and stood up. This time she let him go.

She glanced around. Apart from Charlie Button and a couple of younger pool detectives, the room was empty. 'Charlie? Has something happened that I don't know about?' She indicated the empty chairs.

'Max and Rosie have gone back to have another talk with Mr Ponytail Doolan, and Robbie practically did a rugby tackle on Carter the moment he set foot in the room. I haven't seen them since.'

'Has he found something?'

'I would think so, from the look on his face. He'd been chatting to his Spanish drinking partner.'

'Really?'

'Sounded like he was talking to a little child, or a complete idiot.'

'Then I expect Harvey was drunk again.' Marie wondered what Harvey had revealed in his inebriated state.

She decided it was time for coffee. 'Want one, Charlie?'

'No thanks, Sarge. I've got some water here. I'm training again. Decided I need to have a crack at busting Carter's time on the marathon. I still can't believe he beat Max and me.'

'You should know by now that Carter is full of surprises.'

'Isn't he just?'

Marie went to make her drink, wondering why Carter hadn't told her Sidney's story. It seemed odd that he could share so much with her, yet keep other things secret. What else hadn't he told here?

When she returned to her desk, Robbie was just coming out of Carter's office.

'Sarge, I've just been talking to Carter about a theory I had. It's something that Harvey Cash confirmed — well, sort of confirmed.' He looked at her intently. 'I think we need to talk to the DI.'

'He's still with the super. Tell me.'

Marie listened with fast growing concern. Robbie might well be right. Why else would a man clam up on those closest to him? Some of the most traumatic situations Marie had come across had involved two people living together. If Harvey was confirming it too, they could well be looking at their elusive motive for murder.

'I'll go and interrupt Jackman. He'll want to hear this.' She stood up, then abruptly stopped and asked, 'How has Carter taken it?'

'As you can imagine, Sarge, he's pretty staggered. He blames himself for not realising that Tom Holland had a serious problem.'

'Carter blames himself for *everything*.'

Marie felt a hint of concern. She decided to go and talk to him.

Then she saw that his door was closed. Carter never closed his door.

With Robbie at her heels, she hurried across and knocked. Receiving no answer, she went in. The small room was empty.

'This is not good,' she murmured.

'Damn. It's my fault!' Robbie growled. 'I should have waited and told you first. I was just so amazed at what Harvey told me that I rushed in and told Carter everything. Stupid, stupid thing to do!'

'Lord! Don't *you* start taking the blame now. You did what any normal detective would do. Let's just find him, shall we?'

* * *

Laura sat opposite Sam and stared at the heavy file on the desk between them. 'You really think I should continue with my paper?'

'I've read it, Laura, and it's good. You don't need an outcome for Carter McLean's case study. The structure of your observations will suffice. You *must* finish it, and present it too. It's an excellent piece of work.'

'Praise indeed, Professor. I am honoured.'

'Credit where credit's due, student!'

The doorbell rang.

'I know I haven't got an appointment, but . . .'

'Carter?' Laura took one look at his face and said, 'Come in, come in.'

She opened the door to her office. 'Sam, this is Carter McLean. Carter, come inside and sit down.'

Carter halted in the doorway and looked at Sam Page, obviously disappointed to find him there.

'Carter, Sam is a professor of psychology. He is my teacher and my mentor. He is also my friend.' She smiled at him. 'Even we professionals sometimes need help and advice, and Sam's the one I always turn to. You can trust him.'

Carter seemed to relax a little. She had purposely left the door open. He glanced at it and walked to an empty chair.

'You've just had a bit of a shock, or am I way off target?' Sam asked softly.

Carter made a huffing noise. 'Bullseye, Prof.'

Laura watched him carefully. He was showing signs of agitation and barely controlled anger. Was it directed towards himself? 'Can you tell us what happened?'

Carter began to rock steadily back and forth. He put his hands over his mouth and looked around the room, as if checking for an escape route.

Laura remained calm. She was thankful that Sam was here to witness this. 'If you can talk to us, it might help.'

'I've failed him. Yet again, I've failed him.'

'Tom? Tom Holland?'

Carter drew in a shaky breath. 'Tom Holland. My best mate. I've failed him twice now, but I won't do it again.' He breathed in deeply, then straightened up. 'I'm sorry, Laura.' He turned to Sam, 'I apologise to you too. I'm not normally like this, but maybe I should explain . . .'

Laura sat and listened. As if a switch had been thrown, the confused and tormented soul became the rational policeman again.

At the end of the story, he sat back, as if he were in a briefing and waiting for feedback.

Sam spoke first. 'I think that I too would feel enormous guilt in those circumstances. But if a friend is holding something back, they've drawn a line. It's not easy to know whether you should cross it or not. If Tom had given just a little, I'm sure you would have been there for him. He put up the barrier, not you.'

'I should have done more. I should have at least done *something*.'

'What exactly? If Tom was experiencing abuse at the hands of his partner, it would be very hard for him to admit it, to anyone.' Sam shook his head. 'Statistics show that the number of women convicted of perpetrating domestic abuse has more than quadrupled in the past ten years, but only a very small percentage of men actually tell anyone.'

Carter hung his head. 'I'm sure you are right, but I can't bear to think of him suffering like that, and I didn't realise.'

'But you still spent time with him, didn't you?' said Laura. 'You didn't abandon him. You worked on the boat and kind of hung out together?'

'Yes, that didn't change.'

'So you *were* there for him. It's important for someone who is in a difficult relationship to have some downtime, and you supplied that. And I'm betting you didn't slag off his wife to him, did you?'

'I never even spoke about her if I could help it. And I did sometimes make the effort to join in with something she had organised, like the odd barbeque, but it wasn't often.'

'No matter. You were still a constant in his life.' Sam paused. 'This hypothesis has not actually been proven, has it, Carter?'

'No, but it makes perfect sense. And her previous husband has apparently admitted that the same thing happened to him.'

'Do you know the man? Do you trust his word? He could have an axe to grind. I suggest you wait until you know a little more before you go into meltdown over this.'

Carter gave a dry laugh. 'I think I've already done that, don't you?'

'You reacted badly to an unpleasant suggestion,' Laura said evenly. 'It's understandable, considering the circumstances. If it were anyone else, I would say back off, leave that case to your colleagues, but knowing how much you want to do one last thing for your friend, then . . .' She pulled a face. 'Are you really up to seeing this through?'

'I have to be. I can go into meltdown when it's all over.' He stood up. 'I feel such a fool for behaving like that, but I'm okay now. I'd better get back to work and try to explain why I disappeared.'

'Don't say too much, Carter. Just keep it simple and don't make a big thing out of it.' Sam stood up and shook Carter's hand. 'If Laura should be busy and you need to talk, I'm retired now. I have all the time in the world to listen.' He took a card from his wallet and handed it to Carter. 'I hope you get to the bottom of it all.'

'Me too, Sam, and thanks for listening. Poor Laura here is used to it, but I can be a bit of a challenge, I'm afraid.'

After he had gone, Laura flopped down in her chair. 'Now do you see why I worry?'

Sam tilted his head. 'I'm not sure what to think about that abrupt mood swing. It was pretty spectacular.'

'It's a new phenomenon. He's usually very contained, sometimes almost insular. Or else he appears totally laidback and rational. He is a damned good actor, but this wasn't a performance.'

'I noticed the way he moved his head, as if he were trying to find the source of something, like a sound, or a smell?'

Laura picked up a pen and toyed with it. 'When he "sees" his dead friend, he always smells burning.'

Sam's face clouded over. 'Burning? Always the smell of burning?'

She nodded, and told him what had happened during the crash.

They fell silent, each one thinking about Carter's state of mind. Finally Sam said, 'I think that young man needs watching very carefully. I'm just not sure how you should go about it. Who is going to be there to spot the warning signs if he isn't coping?'

'His DI is very understanding, and he has a close friend who works with him. I'm just worried about putting too much pressure on her. He drains her at the best of times. Lord knows what he'll do if he gets any worse.'

'He *is* worse, Laura. And we need someone to look out for him. There's an unstable element to that young man, and it concerns me greatly. She only needs to watch and report if she gets concerned. I really think you should talk to her.'

Reluctantly, Laura picked up the phone.

CHAPTER TWENTY-FOUR

When Carter walked back into the CID room, Jackman and Marie, with Robbie and Charlie, were sitting listening to the Home Office pathologist, Rory Wilkinson.

Carter felt his chest tighten. Wilkinson had indicated that he had an idea about what had actually happened to Suzanne. 'Have I missed much?' He turned on the most charming smile he could muster. 'Sorry I disappeared. Needed to get a few things straight in my head.'

'And did you?' asked Jackman calmly.

'Yes, sir. Absolutely.' He continued to smile.

Marie looked at him with apparent relief.

'Come join the cabaret, old chum.' With a sweeping gesture, Rory pointed to a vacant chair. 'I was just extolling the virtues of the new forensic technology.'

Carter noticed Jackman glance swiftly at Marie, who nodded. She seemed worried. Probably they would rather he wasn't present.

'My second forensic sweep confirms that Suzanne Holland was pushed with extreme violence. Her heel caught in the hearthrug, which halted her backward trajectory. I discovered this from matching blood stains on the carpet with what should have been matching stains on the floor. They did not match until you rucked the carpet up, as though catching your foot in it. That meant that her body probably jackknifed back with far more force than a simple topple. Her head smashed into the stone mantelpiece, she twisted as she fell, and landed with her temple down onto the cast-iron fire surround. A real double whammy, if ever there was one.'

'This confirms what you surmised from the original forensic reports,' said Jackman.

'It certainly does. My motion graphics are incontestable. They are calculated on velocity, distance, and careful scrutiny of every single drop of blood that was shed, but I can add a bit more to the scenario.'

Everyone looked at him.

'She was left there, in the position that she fell, for over three hours before she was moved. And one person would not have been able to get her out of the cottage alone. Two men, correction, two *people*, were involved in this.'

'How do you know how long she was left there?' asked Charlie.

'Again, from our wonderfully informative blood. The blood that had seeped from the body had separated into clot and serum, so I could calculate the amount of time between her dying to the time she was dragged. It came to several hours. If she had been moved immediately and dragged through fresh blood, the drag pattern would have been quite different. Plus, the drag pattern stopped, and just a few drips were then found, indicating that she was lifted from the room, hence two people required.'

'And two men were seen talking outside in the garden,' added Carter. 'Ponytail and another man.'

'Why would her half-brother be so angry with her?' Marie asked thoughtfully. 'Wasn't he generally the fawning type? Creepy and quiet?'

'You know what they say about the quiet ones,' Robbie answered. 'And if he really was lusting after her, she might have rejected his advances, making him angry.'

Carter raised a hand. 'Something bothers me about this Ponytail, or Ralph Doolan, as we believe him to be. He was always a loner. According to Tom, whenever he visited Suzanne he always came by himself. Max's checks on him said the same. He has very few, if any, real friends. So who was with him on the night Suzanne died?'

'This is probably completely irrelevant,' Charlie smiled rather anxiously, 'but Ralph Doolan is in hospital because of a hit and run. Do you think someone was trying to get rid of him?'

Everyone turned to Charlie.

'Someone like the man who helped him dispose of Suzanne's body?' he added hopefully.

'I suggest you give Max and Rosie a ring and ask them to speak to the Humberside boys about that hit and run. You might just have a point there, Charlie-boy!' Jackman looked pleased, and so did Charlie.

Then Robbie dampened the mood. 'What if Ralph had nothing to do with Suzanne's actual death? The killer could have been the man in the shadows, and he called Ralph to come and help him with the body?'

There was a collective sigh.

Marie shook her head. 'We need more evidence. Anything come up regarding DNA at the scene, Professor?'

'Apart from some skull splinters that had been missed, the original SOCOs did a good job. There was no new DNA.'

Jackman stood up and walked over to the whiteboard. 'What facts do we actually have? Rory has now confirmed that Suzanne was killed in situ, left for several hours, then moved.' He pointed to the name Alan Pitt. 'This man saw two men. This one,' he tapped the ponytailed EFIT picture, 'and an unidentified male, in heated discussion, on the garden path of Holland Cottage, at around the time she was killed.' He pointed to Suzanne's picture. 'Harvey Cash, her first husband, has stated that she was a violent and abusive partner. Carter has confirmed that his friend

Tom Holland changed after he married Suzanne. The changes he describes are consistent with someone living under threat from an emotionally abusive bully. She was not well-liked generally, and was known to be promiscuous prior to marrying Tom Holland. We have no indications that she was still behaving in that manner after her marriage, although we think from enquiries at the time, and from people that Max has interviewed, that she did see several men after Tom left. Which means that we cannot say whether she was faithful or unfaithful.' He then pointed to the picture of Ralph Doolan. 'There are allegations that this man, her half-brother, was sexually interested in Suzanne. But apart from hearsay and several descriptions of him as creepy, that is not a proven fact.'

He stood back. 'Have I missed anything?'

No one spoke.

'Not a lot, is it?'

'Look, I hate to leave things like this, but I have to get back to my lab. I hear a cold cadaver calling me.' Rory stood up. 'If any other little morsel of information comes to me, I shall be in touch.'

'Thank you, Rory.' Jackman looked around. 'I think we are finished here anyway. Back to the drawing board, folks.'

With a scraping of chairs they all returned to their desks.

Carter hung back, wanting to reassure Marie that he was okay, but he saw Jackman beckon to him. *What? Now?* thought Carter miserably, but smiled and followed his boss from the room.

* * *

Marie watched them go and bit her lip. Laura Archer had phoned a few minutes before Carter reappeared, and told her of his unsettling "episode" with her and Professor Page. Marie had naturally agreed to be vigilant. The call was hardly necessary, she had been on red alert for weeks!

'Sarge, can I have a word?' Robbie looked worried.

'Carter looks fine, so I hope you are not still worried, are you?' She hoped she sounded reassuring. She wanted everything back on an even keel where Carter was concerned.

'Yes, Sarge, it's not that.' He pulled a chair close to her desk. 'No one seems to have mentioned that if Suzanne did abuse Tom Holland, he might just have been the one who killed her. Women like that are addicted to conflict. She could have instigated an argument that ended in her death.'

Marie leaned closer to Robbie, elbows on her desk. 'Jackman and I had come to the same conclusion. When you mentioned someone asking Ponytail — Ralph Doolan — to help him, then the only person I could possibly think of would be Tom Holland. Who else knew him?'

'My thoughts too. But I didn't want to talk in front of Carter. Not after the last time.' He looked apprehensive. 'Actually I've changed my mind. I don't think Carter should be here at all.'

'Well, we have our reasons for keeping him close.'

Robbie nodded. 'Can I get permission to go back to Holland Cottage?'

'Why?'

'I want to go through all their personal stuff. Letters, diaries, calendars, computers, the lot.'

Robbie was obviously on exactly the same track as she was. The discovery that Suzanne might have been abusive meant husband Tom was suspect number one. 'A lot of it is in the evidence storage facility. It was taken and bagged and tagged after her disappearance, but go ahead. See what you can find, and I'll call evidence storage and tell them to allow you access, okay?'

'Thanks, Sarge.' He started to get up, then sat back down again. 'One thing that doesn't conform to the usual abusive pattern is that Suzanne seemed to be okay about Tom spending time with his mates. Carter says they spent a lot of hours working on that old boat, but she didn't object.'

Marie frowned. 'I couldn't really say. I don't know too much about that kind of behaviour.'

'Sadly, I do. I had an old friend who got involved with a controlling woman, and it was one of the scariest things I've ever seen. Hence I read up on it. The thing is, they usually isolate their partner, keeping them apart from friends and family, and then poisoning their minds so that they actually become hostile towards them.' He scratched his chin. 'Suzanne didn't do that.'

'Don't these things escalate? Maybe she hadn't reached that stage yet? Or, maybe she liked to let him out somewhere safe, like with buddy Carter on the Eva May, because she was busy with other things.'

'Like going back to her old ways?'

'Bet ya!'

'Good point.' Robbie stood up. 'Don't tell Carter where I'm going, will you?'

'No intention.'

'I'll report back to you.'

'Do that.'

* * *

Carter left Jackman's office. He had done everything he could to soothe his boss's troubled mind, though it had been difficult to concentrate when he was almost choking on the acrid stench. Tom had stood like a statue, staring out of the window.

He went into his own office and pulled the door to as far as he dare without actually closing it.

He didn't like the way this investigation was going. More than anyone else, he wanted a result, but he could see which way the wind was blowing, and he was sure they had got it all wrong.

He sat down and tried to think how he could pull the investigation back onto the right track.

First, he had to speak to Max. He needed to know the outcome of the visit to Ralphie. The corners of his mouth turned down in distaste. Ralph was one of the most unpleasant men he had ever met. He was most certainly a voyeur, and possibly a predator too, although he'd never dug up any proof, and he sure had tried. He was telling the truth when he said he barely knew the man, but the first time he saw him, nosing around his half-sister, he knew that Ralph was a pervert. Even his lovely mate, Tom, suspected him of having unwholesome needs. He pitied the nurses in that hospital, and hoped that Ralph's personal nurse was either male, or tough as boot leather.

Somewhere along the way he had forgotten to ask Max if he had checked out Ralph's alibi. Though wherever he said he was, and with whom, it would have been a lie. Ralphie had probably been fingering someone's washing line. Or, of course, he could have been busy murdering his half-sister because she'd put out for every man in Saltern apart from him.

Carter smiled. Now there was a thought.

CHAPTER TWENTY-FIVE

Max entered Jackman's office just before the shift was ending. 'Charlie called, sir, so I spoke to the Humberside boys. They caught the hit-and-run car on CCTV earlier today, and they've pulled the driver. Turns out it was the father of a kid that Ponytail has been getting up close and personal with. The dad had warned him off, but later found him in the garden of their bungalow with a hi-spec camera. Since it was two in the morning and he was outside his daughter's bedroom, he didn't react too well. Ralphie ran for it, but Dad took him out, using a pretty heavy SUV crossover. So, nothing to do with us, sir.'

Jackman had expected something along those lines. A degenerate like that rarely got away with it for too long, even if the punishment was meted out by someone outside the law.

'And his alibi?'

'His friend seems to have gone AWOL, sir. Can't track him down at all. I'm wondering if he ever existed, or if Ralph was just giving us the runaround to keep us busy.'

'Most likely. So, how did it go? Did he give you any reason to suspect that he had been at Suzanne's that night?'

'Well, I'd checked the PNC and his profile was not on the National DNA Database, so I took a sample while we were there. He tried to object, told me I needed his written permission, but I explained really nicely that we have every right to take a non-intimate sample because it was necessary for investigating a serious crime. And that was that. At least we can see if he's on Prof Wilkinson's list from the crime scene.'

'Long list, unfortunately. And he'll most likely be there because he's family, sort of.'

'Yeah, I guess, but at least we've got him on the database now, so if he ever tries anything pervy again, we can tie him in.' Max sniffed. 'He's a rum one, sir. But Rosie and I decided that we can't see him killing Suzanne. He seemed genuinely cut up about her death, and to be honest, I don't think he'd have the bottle to go up against a woman like his sister.'

'Did Charlie tell you that we suspect her of being a domestic abuser?'

'Yes, sir. I just feel for that poor sod of a husband. Looks like that crash took him out of a world of pain.'

'Bit of an extreme way to leave her, Max.' He grimaced. 'Still, get off home, and thanks for what you've done.'

'No probs, sir. I was sad there was no sangria, but Scunthorpe isn't famous for it.'

'And you did get a few hours out for a drive with Rosie.' Jackman grinned.

'Has to be *some* perks to this job, sir. See you tomorrow.'

As Max left, Carter walked in. 'Can I request a few hours off tomorrow, sir? The marina have rung and said that they want to bring the lifting gear in tomorrow to put the Eva May back on the water.'

Jackman saw the light in Carter's eyes, and immediately agreed. This was a very big day for Carter, and he'd want to be there to see the process through. Then it struck him that it would be a very traumatic occasion too. He'd be alone, instead of with the lads who had worked alongside him. 'Ask Marie if she'd like to go with you. She's a good friend, isn't she? I think she'd appreciate being there for such a special event.'

Carter gave him an odd look.

211

'I'll ask her, and thank you. I appreciate it.'

'Get home, Carter. No late night tonight.'

He nodded. 'Yes, I've got a few last-minute jobs to do on the old girl, so I'll take you up on that. Good night, sir.'

Jackman sighed. He really must remember to tell the super that the directive about relaxing formalities was a definite no-no in Saltern-le-Fen.

* * *

Robbie was certainly going to have a late night. He had spent two hours at the cottage, and was only halfway through all the things he wanted to check. He'd already skimmed the reports, so he wasn't interested in what was in the evidence store. He was looking for different stuff. Things that told him about their everyday lives. He had always believed that Suzanne would tell him what really happened, and if he couldn't see her body, then he'd look through her home and see if he could hear any echoes from her time there.

Robbie took the old place room by room, carefully looking at anything that told him how the Hollands had lived. To begin with it had felt strange, almost ghoulish, peeking into the home of two dead people. Then it felt immoral, as if he had no right to be there. Then it felt eerie, being in a house full of ghosts. Finally he pushed all those thoughts away, and went back to being a detective simply checking out a crime scene.

He opened cupboards, pulled out drawers, read post-it notes stuck on the fridge, noted what book titles were on the shelves and looked in the bathroom cabinet to see what tablets and medicines they took.

He checked the pockets of Tom's jackets and he looked at the kind of jewellery that Suzanne wore. Then he sat down on the bed and wondered if he had learned anything useful at all. Maybe he would have to go the evidence storage route after all. At least there he would find all the basic stuff, laptops, phones, address books and so on.

He stretched and decided to call it a day. He was already losing the light. He looked at Tom's side of the king-size bed with a feeling of real sadness. Tom's bedside cabinet looked very much like his own, with a clock, a coaster, a phone and a book.

He picked up the book, a cold war spy adventure. He turned it over and read the blurb. It sounded good. There was a bookmark three-quarters of the way through, and it made Robbie even sadder to think that Tom Holland would never know the ending.

He placed the book back on the cabinet. Then he saw something glint on the shelf beneath. He leant down, moved a pile of magazines that were obscuring it, and pulled out a digital photo frame.

'Oh, someone really missed this on the first sweep,' he murmured.

He stared at it for a moment, and excitement sent ripples down his back. This was what he had come here for! He just knew it.

It was a good one, and not cheap. When he checked the port, it already contained a memory card. All he needed was the mains adaptor.

Robbie scrabbled around in the bottom of the cabinet and pulled out a box of tissues, a heat pad and several catalogues. Then he found it, and a remote control as well. 'Bingo!'

He stood up, looked around for a socket, and plugged it in.

He made a few adjustments and a slideshow began to unroll. He took a deep breath, switched it off, unplugged it and took it with him. There could be hundreds, maybe thousands of images, and he wanted to look at every one very carefully indeed.

At the door he whispered his thanks to the deceased owners of Holland Cottage. Then he glanced down at the photo frame and said, 'If you can't talk to me, Suzanne, maybe you can show me . . . why you died.'

CHAPTER TWENTY-SIX

When Jackman arrived early the next morning, he found Robbie sitting on the edge of his desk. At his side were two coffees and two Danish pastries in an open white box.

'Big breakfast? Or are you expecting a guest?' Jackman asked.

'Well, you're here now, so . . .' Robbie held out a cup.

Jackman took it. 'My office? It's comfier.'

'You can say that again,' laughed Robbie, picking up the box. 'Apple and blueberry or cinnamon pinwheel?'

'You choose. I like them both.' He sat down and took the top off his coffee. 'Is this some sort of celebration?'

'It depends how you look at it. But it is another step forward, in a kind of convoluted way.' He reached down to a bag at his feet and took out what appeared to be a tablet. Then he looked around and located a socket.

'Take a look at this, sir.' He pushed some buttons on a small remote control and scrolled through a stream of brightly coloured photographs. 'It belonged to Tom Holland. The memory card in it is definitely his. You'll see why in a moment.'

Pictures blended into new pictures. Robbie slowed them down and flicked through them, one by one.

Jackman stared at fragments of Tom Holland's short life.

Tom on the Eva May, polishing a brass plaque and grinning inanely at the camera. Tom with a beer bottle in one hand and an electric saw in the other, trying to look dangerous but just looking idiotic. Then there were the other dead men, all behaving like big kids and being — Jackman swallowed — being so happy. He tried not to think how far away it was from their death. Months? Maybe only weeks? He could almost see the Grim Reaper sitting on the prow of the old boat.

'This is difficult to watch.'

'I know, sir. I've watched them all. Hundreds of them. He liked his camera, did our Tom.'

'Are there any in particular you wanted me to see?' By now, Jackman just wanted it to end.

'Here. It's in this selection. They are at a party. It wasn't at Holland Cottage, but all the gang are there, and it's in a kind of sequence.'

Jackman squinted. Everyone was either having a very good time, or pissed. Probably both. Glasses were raised, food was being eaten, women danced provocatively, men danced badly, and there were a lot of rude gestures to the photographer.

Robbie stopped on one image. 'Look, sir! The guy watching Suzanne.'

Jackman didn't recognise him.

Robbie moved to a shot taken from a different angle, and Jackman saw the ash-blond ponytail. 'Ralph Doolan?'

'Mmm. I've checked it. It's him. And look at his expression.'

'Lecherous.' Jackman snorted.

'Doolan doesn't appear again, but wait for the next ones, sir. They must have been taken just before the party ended. It's a kind of finale.' He clicked the remote.

'I thought you said Doolan had left. He's there.' Jackman pointed to a ponytailed man entering the room, a glass in his hand.

'Keep looking.'

Jackman did. First there was one bespectacled Ponytail, then two, then three, and finally four.

'They were taking the piss out of Ralph Doolan. Wigs and horn-rimmed glasses. I checked against pictures I downloaded from the Internet. We are looking at Ray Barratt, Jack Corby, Matt Blake and Carter McLean, all dressed up as Ralph. Then someone takes the camera from Tom, and you see all the five friends together in the next picture.'

Jackman stared at five "Ralphs" lined up, all making lascivious faces, licking their lips and gripping their crotches.

'They really liked him, didn't they?' Robbie switched off the picture frame.

Jackman took a long swallow of his coffee. His Danish sat on the table, untouched. He realised the implications immediately, and sat back feeling as if the air had been knocked from his lungs.

'It could be any one of them that Alan Pitt saw that night at the cottage. A wig and dark-rimmed glasses. Tom? Ray? Jack? Matt? Or . . .'

'Carter?' Robbie spoke softly. 'I don't believe that, sir. Not for one moment. And don't forget, anyone could know about those wigs. The lads could have dined out on that little party caper for months afterwards.'

But it wasn't someone else, was it? thought Jackman. It was one of those five friends. He had no proof, but he was sure he was right. Marie had asked what it would do to Carter, should the killer turn out to be someone close to him. How would he take this news? Or should it be kept from him? Because, like it or not, Carter had just entered the frame for killing Suzanne Holland.

'Leave that digital thing with me, Robbie, and don't say anything just yet. I have to take this upstairs.'

216

Jackman caught Ruth just as she was closing her office door.

'Only if it's urgent, Rowan. I need to get to a commissioner's meeting.'

'Five minutes, ma'am, and it really is important.'

Inside, he closed the door and immediately told her what they had seen on the digital photo frame. Her expression darkened.

'I am going to have to remove him from his post, you realise that, don't you?'

'Ma'am, normally I'd agree. But he's the only person left alive who has first-hand knowledge of the people involved. And no matter how bad this looks, I *cannot* believe he killed or even accidentally injured his best friend's wife.'

Ruth did not look convinced. 'I, on the other hand, believe that Carter McLean is capable of anything if he thinks it fits in with his own very special moral code.'

'This is that old feud, isn't it, ma'am?'

'Let's just say that I try very hard not to make the same mistake twice. I allowed Carter to do things his way once before, a long time ago, and I regretted it. Someone close to me suffered, and I have never forgotten it.' Her voice softened. 'I've never spoken about it either, Rowan. I just made it my business to hold Carter back whenever I could. I've always thought he was damaged goods and not the kind of man to hold a position of trust.' She paused, clearly wondering how much to tell him, then she seemed to make her decision.

'We were working together on a very sensitive case involving some vulnerable youngsters. Carter has always had a number of informants on tap, and using these he worked out who the abuser was. Unfortunately he had no proof, but he took this man down by anonymously leaking information to the press, and they did the job for us. Trouble was, the media blamed our chief superintendent.

They slated the way the police handled the investigation and he lost his job. Rowan, he was a dear friend of mine.'

'Did you know that Carter was the leak?'

'Oh no, not until the whole affair was over and done with, and even then I couldn't believe he would do such a thing. It was only later that I realised he would stop at nothing to get criminals behind bars.'

'Did you confront him?'

'Not directly. I made suggestions and he flatly denied it. I don't think he ever meant it to go as far as it did. I certainly don't think he meant the chief super to get it in the neck, but that's what happened, and Carter was to blame.' She shrugged. 'He's not a bent copper, he never was, but he is driven to succeed by any means, fair or foul, and that can lead to casualties.' She sighed and seemed to deflate in front of him. 'I have never told a soul about what I suspected. Now, I know that what I am about to say sounds hard *and* hypocritical. I am eternally indebted to him for getting my Leah back in the way that he did, but he *cannot* be allowed to work this case. End of.'

'Give me until the end of the week, please, Ruth?' Jackman looked into her eyes, pleading with her. 'Three days, that's all. And if at any point I think he was involved, he'll be upstairs and inside this office, and his feet won't touch the ground.'

Ruth stared back, and for a moment Jackman thought she was going to hold fast.

Then she let out a painful sigh. 'I just pray I don't regret this. Three days, Rowan. Not a second more.'

* * *

Back in the CID room, Jackman called Robbie and Max. 'I want searches made of the three other friends' homes, and I want Holland Cottage turned upside down. I know it's a long shot. It was over a year ago, but I want to know if those wigs still exist.' He looked around. 'Carter and Marie are out this morning, so do it quick. I don't want Carter to know about this just yet, understood?'

'What about warrants, sir?'

'Ask the relatives nicely. Explain that we believe the premises may contain evidence or material that will be of importance in any subsequent trial. But if all else fails, I'll find a lenient magistrate.'

Robbie and Max hurried off.

'Sir?' Gary Pritchard approached him. 'Since Marie and Carter are off making a rerun of *Pirates of the Caribbean*, is there anything I can do to help?'

'Stick with me, Gary,' said Jackman. 'I could do with a sensible head at the moment. My brain is full of plausible theories and utter fantasies, and I'm not sure which is which.'

* * *

Marie and Carter got to Stone Quay not long before the men from the marina. They found Silas and Klink waiting for them.

Carter introduced them. Klink immediately made a beeline for Marie.

'Hey! You're gorgeous!' Marie ruffled the dog's ears, and squatted down to make a fuss of him. Klink responded by rolling on his back, legs waving in the air.

Silas's mouth dropped open. 'Well, I'll be damned! Ain't never seen him do that since he were a pup!'

'This can't be the ferocious guard dog you told me about?' Marie looked up and grinned.

Carter shook his head. 'He must have eaten something.'

'Dog always did have a mind of his own, and he certainly knows what he thinks about you, miss.' He looked at Carter. 'So. Reckon it'll float, young'un? Or go straight back where it came from?'

'Oh, it'll float, old timer. Just you watch.'

'Sure's 'ell will.' Silas sat down on a block of stone. 'This day's been a long time a'coming.'

'Too right.' Carter looked at the Eva May. 'Time to feel the tide beneath your keel again, my friend.' He gently touched the side of his beloved boat.

Marie felt a lump in her throat. She knew he must be heartbroken that his friends were not here with him.

And indeed, he turned to her and said, 'This was going to be such a big day. Loads to drink, a barbecue on the quay, a photographer from the local rag, loud music . . . The party would have gone on all night.'

He looked around sadly. Marie wondered if he was looking for his dead friends. 'It's still a big day, Carter. It's a massive achievement, and it's a wonderful tribute to your friends that you went ahead and finished what you all started.'

He squeezed her arm. 'Thanks, I appreciate that. And maybe it's better that it's just us today. A quiet tribute, huh?'

Marie nodded.

'Think yer marine mates is 'ere.' Silas nodded in the direction of the lane where two big trucks, one with a crane attached, were making their way towards them.

'Time to shine, Eva May!'

Carter's eyes were misty, and Marie fought back tears.

Once the crane was safely positioned and levelled, they all watched with bated breath. The procedure didn't take nearly as long as Marie had thought it would.

Lifting tackle, webbing slings and a four-part chain sling were attached to the crane hook, and the webbing slings passed under the boat. The Eva May was hoisted up.

The crane slewed towards the quayside carrying the old lifeboat out over the river. Once it had cleared the quay, they waited for Carter to give the signal to lower away.

Everyone cheered when she touched the water.

'What's happening now?' asked Marie, trying to hide the catch in her voice.

Two men in hard hats, protective gloves and steel toe-capped boots had stepped aboard.

'They are the slingers. They release the webbing slings from the chains, then direct the crane driver which way to bring the chains out of the water and round and back onto the quay. Then we'll secure her by the hand lines.'

Carter was watching closely. He had once told Marie that when he was a kid, his father often left him playing by himself in his boatyard. He was completely at home in this environment.

Soon the crane and all the equipment had been packed up ready to return to the marina. Carter paid the man in charge and handed him a gold box that Marie knew contained a very good malt whisky.

Marie looked at Carter. 'And now?'

'I will have to test the engine, and possibly make a few adjustments, then she'll be good to go.' He smiled. 'But right now, I'd like to propose a toast.' He walked to the car and came back carrying a cool box and three folding seats.

He set the box down on the quay and opened it. Inside were three glasses, a bottle of Laurent Perrier champagne and an assortment of expensive snacks and nibbles. 'We can't put the old girl in the water without wetting her head, can we?'

So Marie spent the next hour sitting on Stone Quay drinking champagne with a poacher, a detective and a mad dog, surrounded by water, marshland, acres of fields and a sky that went on forever. The whole thing was quite bizarre.

When they had finished, Carter said, 'I think I'll stay here for a bit, Marie. I know you need to get back, but would you cover for me?'

'Sure, no problem.' Marie knew that Jackman would be quite happy for Carter to be away for a little longer.

'Just don't get stopped on the way!'

'And don't you drink any more either, Carter McLean. Remember you've got to get home too.'

'Promise.' He handed the bottle to Silas. 'Si will give this a good home, don't worry.'

Marie gave Klink a final cuddle, shook hands with Silas and walked back to her car. 'Thanks, Carter, for letting me share today!' she called back.

'There's no one I'd rather have shared it with. Drive carefully.'

Marie knew this wasn't true. He would much rather have shared it with Tom, Matt, Jack and Ray.

CHAPTER TWENTY-SEVEN

After the hush of the quay, the CID room was a buzz of noise and activity when Marie returned.

'Glad you are back. Where's Carter?' Jackman looked behind her.

'I left him on the boat. I guessed you wouldn't mind. I think he wanted a bit of time to himself. It was all pretty emotional.'

'Best thing all round. We've had some developments.' He lowered his voice. 'Max and Robbie, along with some uniforms, have gutted the Holland Cottage, and they found a box containing five ponytail wigs and a bag of cheap horn-rimmed glasses. We have had further confirmation from Harvey Cash in Spain that Suzanne was indeed abusive, and he's prepared to swear to it. So it all puts Tom Holland very much in the frame for his wife's death.'

'The kind and gentle giant?' Marie whispered.

'Looks that way. Even the gentlest people can be pushed too far.' Jackman scratched his head. 'Let's get a coffee. I want to tell you something else.'

They walked along the corridor to the vending machine. For once, the area was quiet.

'That website demanding we do something to find Suzanne's killer has reared its ugly head again.' Jackman gave her an exasperated look. 'It appears they want our cooperation to, as they say, *put our side of things*. The super told them that it's an ongoing investigation so we are not at liberty to join in their bunfight. I don't think it went down too well.'

'It'll go down even better if they find that we are looking at the dear departed and much loved Tom Holland for her killer.'

'Tell me about it.' He passed her a coffee. 'My worry is, if it is Tom, or one of the other friends for that matter, how on earth are we going to find her body when all of them but Carter are dead?'

'And he certainly won't help if we tell him we suspect his best mate, Tom. He honestly believes that Tom will haunt him until he finds Suzanne's killer. This is not good!'

'And worse, that creep Ralph Doolan is definitely off the hook. His friend, well, his alibi, has surfaced, and swears they were in a Peterborough club that night.'

'Proof?'

'True to form, our Ralphie made a pass at a barmaid. He was thrown out and barred. Apparently it's on record.'

'Wonderful. Just wonderful.'

They walked back to the CID room. Rosie told Jackman he had a call, and he hurried off to take it.

Marie sat down at her desk, wondering where all this was going. Her phone ringing broke into her thoughts.

'Thanks for being there today, Marie.'

'No, thank *you*, Carter. I felt privileged. And I met a new friend, so that was nice.'

'Silas?'

'Oh, him too. It was Klink I was thinking of.'

Carter laughed. 'That really was a first. You have no idea how honoured you are. He can be a devil with strangers.'

'Silas?'

'No! Klink!'

They both laughed again. For the first time in ages, Carter sounded easy and natural. Getting the Eva May back where she belonged seemed to have calmed him. Before she could say anything more, Rosie hurried over and pushed a scribbled note in front of her.

She nodded at Rosie and told Carter she'd ring him back.

'Something going down?' asked Carter.

'Alan Pitt has just rung the DI. He says he's on his way in to see us. He's remembered something else.'

There was a short silence before Carter spoke. 'Then let's hope it's something that will get things moving at last. Keep me up to speed, won't you? Speak later.'

Marie hurried over to Jackman. 'Did he say any more than that?'

Jackman shook his head. 'He wants to speak to us privately.'

'Now we know that Ponytail wasn't Ralph, this could be very interesting.'

Jackman looked worried. 'Actually I'm terrified. Aren't you?'

* * *

Sam could not settle. The afternoon was hot, and even an hour in his favourite bird hide failed to hold his attention.

Sam had retired willingly from a life of research. He had had enough of the academic world, and had chosen instead to become a simple birdwatcher, a lover of wildlife and a gardener. He spent hours watching the visitors to his wild garden feeding, pollinating or simply resting in the shade.

But now he was back in his office, surrounded once more by books and papers. He had been reluctant to return to the dusty room and the dustier tomes it held. But Sam wanted to be there for Laura Archer.

She had been his best student, his shining star. Sam had never had children, but if he had, he would have wanted a daughter like Laura. Gradually, he had become a father figure for her, especially since he'd retired and she had embarked on her own career.

Sam smiled, rather smugly. He was proud to have put her on the right path. She was a very good psychologist, and her work on trauma was already well respected.

His own field had been memory, in all its different forms. It had fascinated him since his schooldays, and although he was now more involved with social communication among starlings, it still did.

Sam thought about his meeting with the infamous Carter. It had left him confused.

He now understood a little of Laura's problem. Without a doubt, Carter was a very charismatic man, even in his agitated state. He exhibited both strength and weakness at the same time. The look in his eyes pleaded for your help, and then he withdrew and locked you out.

Sam Page, Professor of Psychology at University College, London, Fellow of the British Psychological Society, and highly respected author of over 600 scientific papers found himself totally at a loss.

Laura had said she was missing something, and now he knew exactly what she meant.

He was also pretty sure that it would be up to him to find out what that something was. With a grunt of annoyance, he went back to his studies.

* * *

Jackman and Marie tried hard to appear calm, but the interview room almost crackled with nervous tension.

'I woke up very early, around four, and found myself thinking back to the night that woman went missing.'

Jackman knew they shouldn't hurry Alan, but he desperately wanted him to get to the point.

'I remember walking along the towpath worrying about my dog. If I were to die, I mean. I knew my wife would look after him, but I do all the walking, and he needs his walks.' He paused. 'That was when I realised I wasn't alone.'

'The man with the ponytail and another man,' Marie prompted.

'Yes, and then I remembered what one of them said — well, some of it anyway.'

Jackman leaned forward.

'I heard him mention a name. Not a person's name . . .'

Jackman stifled a curse.

'It was a place name. Amsterdam.'

Jackman straightened in his chair. He felt Marie tense beside him. 'What about Amsterdam?'

'One of them said, "And we *must* still go to Amsterdam." Then the other seemed to remonstrate with him, hence the heated conversation. That was when I decided to slope off.' He looked at them apologetically. 'I'm sorry it's no more than that, but I suppose it might help?'

Jackman wasn't sure if help was the right word, but it certainly pointed in a very definite direction. The five friends were going to Amsterdam.

'I'm sure I didn't dream it,' Alan went on. 'Does it mean anything to you?'

'Thank you, Alan. We can't say anything at this time, as I'm sure you will understand, but you have certainly helped us narrow down the field.'

After Alan Pitt left, Jackman and Marie sat on in the interview room, each worrying over what they had just heard.

'What do we do now?' Marie asked.

Jackman looked hard at her. 'Do what we should have done a long time ago. Stop trying to be kind, and interview Carter.'

* * *

227

'His phone is not picking up, sir.' Marie stared at her own phone for a moment before ending the failed call. 'Maybe he's working on the boat.'

'Is there a signal out there?' asked Jackman.

'Fairly good one, considering where it is.' She looked at him anxiously. 'Shall I go and look for him?'

Jackman shook his head. 'Now I think about it, maybe tomorrow will be better. It will give me time to work out what to ask him, instead of wading in, all guns blazing. We'll talk to him first thing in the morning.'

Marie had to make do with that, although she was very worried about Carter being out of contact. She returned to her desk and began, yet again, to go over the sequence of events.

'Robbie, got a moment?'

'Sure, what's the problem?'

'You know more than me about what happens in an abusive relationship. We know that Tom Holland left the marital home to stay with Ray, but if Suzanne had contacted him, would he have gone back, even after he had made the break?'

'Like a shot, Sarge. I can't tell you how many times my friend went running back when she called him. It was horrible. From the outside you could see exactly what she was doing, but all he could say was, "She's sorry for what she's done. She swears it will never happen again."

'But it did.'

'Every time. And it got worse.'

'Why do they go back?' Marie could not get her head around it.

Robbie leaned against her desk. 'It's like Stockholm Syndrome. The victim identifies with the aggressor and even goes so far as to defend her behaviour.' He shrugged. 'My mate was totally controlled by his girlfriend.'

'So, even though Tom was supposedly out of the picture when Suzanne went missing, in fact she could have called him, and he'd have gone back.'

'I would swear that if she said she wanted to talk, said she missed him, she loved him and all that, he would have gone.'

'But he never talked to Carter about his problems,' she mused. 'I find that odd.'

'Shame, guilt — and would *you* confide in a copper?'

'I would confide in Carter. I mean, they were so close, more like brothers.' She thought for a moment. 'So why ring Ray?'

'Because Carter was working a case. Tom couldn't have gone to him. Something about being on obo, I think. He just wasn't there.'

Marie didn't like what was going through her mind. She would have to check it out. Where exactly was Carter when Tom ran away from home? There would be an incident log of whatever case he was on, and it would also be in his detective's diary. He would have to hand it over if requested, but she wondered if she could look at it without his knowing. Even if she couldn't, Jackman might be able to check what cases were running at the time. 'Thanks, Rob, and by the way, what happened to your friend?'

'He died of an overdose.'

'Oh my God! I'm so sorry.' Marie felt terrible. 'I didn't mean to pry.'

'It was ten years ago now, Sarge. It was recorded as an accidental death, but she killed him alright. Slowly. Until he couldn't take any more.' He looked at her intently. 'If you ever come across one of these women, Marie, don't be fooled. They don't want help — they don't think they need it. Abusive personality types are bullies, narcissists and psychopaths. Believe me, I know.'

'And Suzanne fitted that definition?'

'Read Harvey Cash's statement. There's little doubt.'

Marie thanked Robbie and went off to find Jackman.

She told him what Robbie had said to her. Jackman said, 'I know exactly what case Carter was on, and so do you. At the time, he was with the drug squad on the Heron Bank job.'

Marie threw up her hands, 'Of course! The big cocaine haul from that fishing boat!'

'Carter worked mainly with DC Rusty Gates on that. It did entail hours of surveillance.' Jackman pursed his lips. 'I could get hold of Rusty. He's working as a civilian now out of Peterborough. His diary could tell us where Carter was.'

'I hate to be doing this, sir. I really just want to be sure in my own mind that Carter is telling the truth. In my heart, I don't believe for one minute that Carter is lying, but . . .' Marie sighed deeply.

Jackman's voice was full of compassion. 'I know, Marie. This is hell for you, isn't it?'

'It isn't good, sir.' She swallowed. 'God, I know he's been a chancer and at times he's bent the rules out of all recognition, but he's always been on the right side, if you know what I mean. He's made some staggering arrests and cleaned some serious shit off our streets. He's not *bad*, he's just . . .'

Jackman gave her a rueful smile. 'He's just unconventional. Sadly, that does not always go down well with our senior officers, or the hierarchy that we now have to operate under.' He glanced at his watch. 'It's getting late. Get off home, Marie. We'll tackle this in the morning, okay?'

Marie decided that for once, she wasn't going to argue.

CHAPTER TWENTY-EIGHT

At around two thirty in the morning, Sam Page heard a hedgehog grunting. He got up, pushed his feet into his slippers and padded to the bathroom.

The hedgehog wake-up call was becoming a nightly occurrence. He was pretty sure they had set up home under some garden trimmings that he had set aside for a bonfire.

Halfway along the hall, Sam froze.

Bonfire! Burning!

He hurried back to his room and found his dressing gown. Then he went to his office.

An hour later he had a list of questions and several bulletpoint references scribbled on a sheet of paper. He was pretty sure he would not be able to sleep again. His brain was firing on all cylinders and he couldn't slow it down. He went to the kitchen, made a hot drink and sat in his favourite chair looking out over the garden, and waited for the dawn. He had a feeling that no matter how early he rang her, Laura would be pleased to hear from him. Especially as he believed he had made that vital connection, the one that had evaded her for so long. That thing she said was missing.

Marie's phone rang at 3 a.m., and for the first time ever, she decided not to answer it. Then her conscience kicked in. 'Marie Evans.'

'Hi. I know I promised not to do this to you again, but . . .'

'Carter? You *do* know what time it is?'

'Mmm, but this time I really need to talk to you.'

Marie caught something in his voice. She sat up and pushed the duvet back. 'What's wrong?'

She heard an intake of breath. 'I have to tell you something, Marie, and then I have to ask you a favour.'

'Well, at least I know you can't be asking for money, so go ahead.' She meant to sound upbeat, but she was anything but.

'I'm not proud of what I'm going to tell you, but I need to tell someone, and who else would I talk to?'

'Me, but I'm not sure I want to hear it.'

Carter was silent for a moment. 'I've done something terrible.'

Marie felt the tension build inside her.

'I'm going to tell you what I've done, and try and explain why, then ask you the favour. And, Marie, I won't ask anything of you that isn't strictly above board. I want to tell you the truth. Then you must tell the authorities.'

'You're scaring me.'

'I scare myself sometimes.' He gave a humourless laugh. 'But here goes. You know that as soon as I got back to full duties, I desperately wanted to get onto the Holland case. Then we had the trouble with Leah, so that put paid to that for a while.' He took a breath. 'What I have to tell you is that it was me who paid Danny Hurley to take the flowers, the chocolates, and the cards and all that shit.'

'What?' Marie yelped.

'I wanted to cause a furore, so that the team would be overstretched and I would be brought onto the Holland case. But it totally backfired on me. I never dreamed in a million years that Ruth Crooke would ask *me* to help her!'

'I don't understand, Carter. You put her through hell!'

'Which is exactly what she's done to me for most of my working life! She's held me back and made sure that I never get promotion. After the accident, she almost had me pensioned off. I wanted to get my own back and make her suffer. But never, never once did I think Leah was in danger. I swear I never knew that Danny was obsessive.'

'That's why you were so bloody sure it was a storm in a tea cup! And . . .' The penny dropped. 'That's how you caught him out!'

'It was touch and go, Marie. I nearly shat myself when I found out what he was up to.'

'So it wasn't Cannon family retribution?'

'Sorry, it was just me.'

'And your old headmaster? Sidney?'

'Paid him to cover up for me.'

Marie saw Carter leaning over the older man, whispering in his ear, and handing him a bundle of notes. A lot of notes, too many for a simple bit of info from the streets.

Marie exploded. 'You lying bastard! Do you know, I can almost appreciate your twisted thinking. But you've spent days lying your head off and playing me like a bloody violin! That's the bit that fucking hurts, Carter!'

'I'm sorry. Truly I am.'

'Oh good! That makes it all better, doesn't it?' Marie didn't think she'd ever been so angry.

'I wanted to tell you, but then it went so badly wrong. I was shocked to the core, and scared stiff.'

'That kid could have finished up dead, all because of your bloody games,' she snarled.

'Don't you think I know that? I've thought of nothing else.'

'How could you be so *stupid*?' Already, the fire was dying. 'And lie to me that way?'

'That's what I hated most. It was unforgivable.'

'Yes, it was.' She exhaled. 'And now you have the gall to say you want a favour? I don't think so. I've had it with you, Carter. I thought I knew you. Well, I certainly don't know what's going on inside your head.'

'Believe me, I don't either. Sometimes I don't even know what is real and what is fantasy. I see things, I hear things, I smell things, and I know they aren't there. I'm a mess, Marie, and I don't blame you for hating me.' His voice was low. 'But I'm still going to ask you that favour.'

Marie felt drained. The fight had gone out of her. 'I don't hate you. I couldn't. What do you want?'

'I want you to tell Jackman everything, and also Ruth Crooke. I know I'm for the high jump, so will you just allow me a few hours? Go to see them later this afternoon? Then I'll throw up my hands and come quietly.'

Marie's head throbbed. 'But why?'

'The Eva May. For the sake of the others, I want to take her out on her maiden voyage. I've got to make sure the tides are right, so I'll leave Stone Quay around eleven. It won't take long, two hours max. It's something I really need to do. Then I swear I'll face the consequences.'

Marie thought about that wonderful hour on the quayside. She would let him have this last break, because after that, his career would be over, and Tom Holland would probably haunt him for the rest of his life. 'I'll give you until two this afternoon. And, Carter? Never ever lie to me again.'

'Thank you, Marie. For everything.'

'I'm a fool,' she whispered, but there was no one to hear.

CHAPTER TWENTY-NINE

Carter drove onto Stone Quay at around four in the morning. He parked the Land Rover close to where the Eva May bobbed proudly in the water.

The silence was overwhelming.

He sat without moving, watching the clouds scud over the river.

For once, the voices were silent.

He got out of the vehicle and stood for a moment in the familiar spot, listening to the birds call and the river lap against the Eva May's hull.

He turned and saw Silas walking towards him, Klink ambling close to his heels. He had a flat package under his arm.

'So it's today, is it, young'un?'

Carter nodded.

'Then I guess you'll be wantin' a bit o' company?'

Carter drew in a deep breath, then exhaled. 'No, Silas, not this time. But I am going to ask you to do something for me, and I swear it will be the last time I do.' He rubbed his hand through his windblown hair. 'This favour. It's not exactly above board.'

The old man gave a snort. 'Since when have I cared a jot about that?'

Carter smiled. 'I know, you old rogue, but still, it goes against the grain to ask you.'

'Then don't ask. But you know I'll help you, no matter what.'

'Remember the old Causley Eau pumping station?'

'Aye, on the Saltern Drain. Been falling to bits for years since they stopped usin' it.' Silas thought for a while. 'They say it's dangerous, so no one goes there anymore.'

'I know.'

'Then we better get off, hadn't we? I'm supposing you want to be back to catch the tide?'

Carter opened up the side door of the Land Rover, and called to Klink. 'In you get, lad.'

'Boot's good enough for him, grubby little tyke.'

Carter shook his head. 'Not this time. I need the space.'

Silas shrugged. He slid the flat, badly wrapped package behind the passenger seat.

They drove for a few minutes, then turned down a slip road and bumped along the drain edge for about a quarter of a mile.

The old pumping station had been empty for years. The steam engine that had helped feed water from the reclaimed saltmarsh fields had been moved off to a museum, and now a new station did all the pumping and drainage.

Carter backed up the Land Rover close to the building and got out. He produced a key from his pocket and opened the padlocked doors.

Klink refused to get out, even when Silas ordered him to. Carter decided that he was better off where he was, so they left the dog in the vehicle.

With Silas a few steps behind him, Carter walked slowly and deliberately towards the back of the building, where he used a second key to open a small storeroom. If Silas was shocked by the smell, he didn't show it. And Carter made no comment.

The bundle was tightly wrapped in layers of extra thick black plastic sheeting, taped tightly with gaffer tape, and carefully concealed behind some old rotting wooden shelving units.

Between them they half dragged and half carried the cumbersome bundle to the Land Rover. Carter opened up the back and they pushed it into the boot.

Klink gave a low growl. Silas spoke to him quietly, but his hackles were raised.

They said nothing on the trip back to Stone Quay, but it wasn't an uncomfortable silence. Carter felt like a boy again, back where he ought to be, sitting next to Silas Breeze, the only man he really trusted.

It took them no time at all to get Suzanne's body off the quay and into the Eva May. He tried hard not to imagine what she looked like after eighteen months, but he had seen too many rotting corpses in his time on the force not to know. Even so, he felt no compassion for her. She had been a cruel, heartless bitch. Whenever things didn't go exactly her way, she turned on Tom. She physically battered and abused him, and the gentle giant never raised a hand or said a word against her.

'Tide's about right, young'un.' Silas was making his way slowly down the ladder from the quay.

'Go back, Silas. I have to do this alone. For my fourth friend. For Tom.'

'Go back up and fetch Klink, would you?'

Carter frowned.

'Go get my dog . . . please?'

'Oh Silas, no . . .'

'He bit a kid last night, boy. There'll be a knock on my door later today, and we don't want to be there when they come for him.'

Carter felt a lump in his throat. He climbed back up the ladder and carefully lifted the old dog down into the Eva May.

Silas nodded. 'Everything in order?'

'Shipshape and Bristol fashion, Cap'n.' He saluted smartly.

'I don't mean the boat.'

'Nor do I.'

With a long look at his two unexpected crew members, Carter started the engine.

'Sweet as a nut,' Silas crooned. 'That lad knew his engines, didn't he?'

Carter turned the Eva May out into the river and felt the wind tug at his hair. Oh, it felt so good! He breathed in the salty ozone and let out a whoop of delight. 'We've done it, Si! The Eva May is back where she belongs!'

'Should be horns and sirens and bunting! An escort out into the Wash!' Silas's old eyes sparkled.

'Then raise the flag, old timer, and let's drink a toast to the Eva May and the men who put her back together again.' He pulled a bottle from under one of the seats and passed it to Silas. 'Will this do you?'

'Single Highland malt! Twenty-five years old — and a Speyside. That would have made a big hole in your pocket, boy. Three figures?'

'It's a special occasion. And as we are underway, the Ensign is waiting to be attached.' He grinned at Silas, 'And I've not brought metal clips either.'

Silas happily launched into a speech about flag etiquette and halyards, and Carter felt a rush of affection for him. He was glad after all that his oldest friend and his crazy dog were with him.

They poured the whisky into plastic tumblers and drank toast after toast. They did not drink to Suzanne Holland.

'I've been thinking for a while about making a will.' Silas suddenly became serious.

Carter stared at him. He thought of the ramshackle hovel of a cottage and its contents, and began to laugh.

'Tek the proverbial, if you will, but there's "The Poacher" to consider.'

Carter stopped laughing, and considered what the old man was asking of him. 'Ah, right.' He took out his mobile phone, sent a brief text message and switched it off. 'Sorted.' He then looked long and hard at his old friend. 'Why are you here, Si?'

'Saw the doc last week, not that I got too much faith in them and their new-fangled machines. Still, there weren't much point arguing with the results of my tests.' He shrugged and sipped his drink. 'A trip on the Eva May is my whole bucket list rolled into one.' He looked around contentedly. 'And we picked a great day for it, didn't we?'

The only sounds were the thrum of the engine and the occasional call of a water bird. Around them, the water, the marshes and the big Lincolnshire sky. Carter breathed again. He was free of enclosed spaces, the smell of burning. And there were no voices other than his own, and that of Silas.

'He killed her, didn't he? Your friend Tom?' He looked intently at Carter, and then his eyes narrowed. 'Or did he?'

Carter sipped his whisky. He saw everything clearly now. All along, his night-time chats with the boys had been nothing but memories, old conversations and old secrets. His "dead" friends had told him nothing that he didn't already know. And that included what had happened to Suzanne.

'He'd finally found the courage to walk out on her. Then, after a while she rang him, and said she wanted him to go back. She said she loved him. He was going to go, but Ray stopped him, and then it all came out. He broke down and told Ray everything, all the things she'd done and the terrible ordeals she'd put him through. He was distraught. Ray called me, but I was on a stakeout and didn't get the message. So he rang Jack and Matt and they decided to go and confront Suzanne.' Carter sighed. 'They found another man there. She had set it up so that Tom would walk in and find them, then she would tell him that he was such a loser she'd had to go out and find a real man. The guy did a runner, so she tried it on with Jack. He was utterly disgusted and pushed her away, roughly. She fell heavily and hit her head on the stone mantelpiece above the fireplace.' Carter pointed to their drinks, and the old man poured readily.

'When they realised she was dead, Ray, Jack and Matt panicked. They did everything wrong.'

'And the daft buggers made it look like murder?' Silas asked.

'They didn't call an ambulance. They didn't even dial 999. And they tampered with the scene.'

Silas shook his head. 'Surely if they'd just . . .'

'I know, I know. Then Ray finally saw sense. When I got off duty he called me and told me things I'd never known about Tom's beautiful wife. She told people that Tom hit her, that he cheated on her and even stole from her.' He gritted his teeth. 'When in reality it was all the other way around.'

'And Tom couldn't have proved otherwise?'

'No. She was far too cunning for my lovely brain-washed mate, Tom.' Carter took a long drink of his malt. 'So I told Ray to tell the others to get out without being seen, and I raced over there and helped Ray. I used all my copper's know-how to make it look like she had been attacked and abducted.'

Silas looked at him. 'Wasn't there blood?'

'Oh yes, a lot, but there was no use touching it. No matter how hard you try to get rid of it you always leave traces that luminol will pick up. Better to let it look like a violent attack.' He lifted his glass in the direction of the black plastic bundle, now bound round with lengths of weighty chains. 'Then I brought her down here while I decided where to hide her. Luckily no one knew that she had had visitors that night. Their cottage had no near neighbours and there was no CCTV for miles. Even so, I put on a ponytail wig and glasses. We had worn them once, a piss-take of Suzanne's pervert of a brother. I reck-oned if anyone saw me while I was there, they would think

I was him. I didn't know until this week that Ray and I had been seen by a dog walker.' He stared into his drink. 'I got all the guys together and we worked out watertight alibis, and finally, to make it all seem really kosher, we decided to carry on with the arranged stag trip to Amsterdam. Tom never knew a thing about what happened. Suzanne's blood wasn't discovered for several days, and by that time they were all dead.'

Silas grunted, took another mouthful of whisky and fondled his dog's ears. 'I'm guessing Tom was never suspected, even though she had been spreading lies about him.'

'It turned out that very few people believed a word she said. Most thought she was someone it was best not to get involved with. No, Tom Holland was never a suspect. Until now. Things have taken a turn for the worse, Si, and I've had to sort it out, once and for all.'

'Life. I'll never fathom it, young'un.'

'Me neither.'

'But, it's a lovely morning to be going to sea with good friends.' Silas bent down and drew his dog a little closer to him.

'That it is.'

* * *

'Run that past me again, Sam. Now that I'm awake.' Laura sat up in bed and ran a hand through her sleep tousled hair.

Sam started again, this time more slowly. 'We've been looking at Carter McLean's problem all wrong. We've assumed that what he told us about his friends manifesting themselves, and then him experiencing the terrible smell of burning flesh, was correct. But that's incorrect.'

'But he swears that's the case.'

'He's wrong. He gets the smell of burning *first*, and then the imaginary friends appear.'

Laura scratched her head. 'There's a difference?'

'Phantosmia.'

Laura frowned and dredged up some of her medical knowledge, 'Olfactory hallucinations?'

'Phantom smells. Smelling something that isn't there. Do you have his medical record with you?'

'In the office, yes. I have it in a secure file.'

'Go down and check something for me, will you? It's important.'

Laura pulled on a dressing gown, grabbed the office door key and ran downstairs. She had never heard Sam so intense.

'Okay, it's accessing it now, what do you want to know?'

'After the accident, what does it say in his injury assessment?'

Laura scrolled back to the first report. 'He sustained a fracture to the right humerus at the surgical neck. Three broken ribs and a hairline crack to the sternum. This was attributed to the crash itself. Then there were minor topical burns, temporary deafness and concussion, all sustained from the blast when the plane exploded.'

Sam groaned. 'That's what I wanted to hear, Laura. Concussion. And what causes olfactory hallucinations?'

'Tumours, epilepsy . . . oh, brain damage.' She let out a long sigh. 'This isn't simply post-traumatic stress at all, or panic attacks. He has suffered a brain trauma.'

'Or maybe a tumour that has manifested itself since the accident. He's not suffering a psychological reaction at all. He has a very real, physical symptom of a brain injury.'

Laura was horrified. 'I've been treating him for the wrong thing! And I never saw the truth. What have I done?'

'Don't worry, Laura. If I'm right, and we have no proof yet, his psychological condition masked his illness. What we need to do now is tell him.'

242

Laura ended the call, found Carter's home number but got the answerphone. 'Carter, it's Laura. I have to speak to you, it's urgent. Ring me as soon as you get this.'

She tried his mobile, but it was switched off. She had never felt so frustrated. Wait! Marie! He could be with her, or she might know where he was.

Marie answered on the second ring, and in a rush Laura told her what Sam had said.

There was a long pause, and then Marie said, 'He's taking the Eva May out later this morning for her maiden voyage. We might be able to catch him before he sets off. Shall I come and get you?'

'Yes, please, Marie, and hurry. I need to tell him this. It will make such a difference to his life.' She stopped abruptly. 'When did you say he was going?'

'Elevenish, I think.'

'No, that can't be right. He'll need the high tide to get over the sand bars and out into the Wash. High tide is just about now.'

'I'm on my way.'

* * *

Marie had the blue light flashing all the way to Stone Quay. Beside her, Laura drummed her fingers on her knees.

They jumped from the car and ran over to Carter's Land Rover, parked next to the empty stand that had once supported the Eva May. The engine was cold.

Marie's heart sank. She turned to Laura. 'She's gone! The Eva May! He's already taken her out. Laura, he lied to me for a reason — about the tides I mean. He didn't want me here. And he told me things. What he told me means he will lose his job, the job he lives for!'

Laura bit her lip. 'Then he'll have nothing left at all. We have to catch him.'

Marie stared down the river towards the estuary, but the expanse of water was a ribbon of steel. Unmoving.

243

And there was no boat in sight. She took a deep breath and ran back to the car. 'If we go back to the main road and take the Wash lanes to Arun Point, we can see where the river joins the Wash. We might be able to get ahead of him.'

The two women sat in silence. Marie concentrated on driving as fast as she dared along the narrow winding lanes.

When they reached the Point, Marie brought the car to a screaming halt and grabbed a pair of binoculars from the back seat. She and Laura hurried from the car park and up the steep sea bank, to where they could look out across the grey waters of the Wash.

'There!' Laura pointed.

Marie trained her glasses on the small vessel. Yes! It was Carter! She grabbed her mobile and rang him again, but it went straight to voice mail.

Laura was waving frantically. 'What about the coast-guard?'

'And tell them what?' Marie groaned.

'I don't know, but surely . . .'

Looking again through the binoculars, Marie realised that Carter was not alone on the Eva May. Another figure sat close to him. 'Crazy Silas?' she whispered, '*And* his dog?'

Suddenly hope coursed through her.

Carter had taken Silas with him for the rebuilt life-boat's maiden voyage! He'd wanted it that way, but rather than upset her again, he left early. No more than that! They had caught the early tide and were celebrating together. She said as much to Laura, then exhaled. 'Of course he didn't want anyone else along! This is a very personal thing, to mark his friends passing. And Silas looked out for him when he was a little boy and when his mother died, so they've made this trip together.' Her smile widened. 'He's letting them go. At last, he's letting his dead friends go!'

Laura said nothing. She stood and gazed at the old wooden boat heading bravely out into the North Sea.

Marie continued to stare through the powerful binoculars. Then her euphoria faded. She squinted and tried to adjust the focus to make it clearer. It seemed as though they had jettisoned something heavy into the water. She blinked a few times, but now she wasn't sure what she had seen.

She trained the glasses on Carter. He was staring directly at her.

'He's waving! He's seen us!'

She passed the binoculars to Laura.

After a moment Laura passed them back. 'Look again.' There was a catch in her voice.

Marie did.

Carter stood, with his arm raised, as if he were stretching towards the two women on the far shore.

'He's not waving, Marie. He's saying goodbye.'

Marie went cold. Oh no, please, no.

She felt Laura's hand grip hers. 'Oh God! The Eva May. She's sinking.'

Marie swallowed. She could not move or take her eyes off the wooden lifeboat. It was still moving away from them at a steady speed, but something was terribly wrong.

Laura was right.

Marie lifted the glasses for the last time. She could hardly bear to look. They were low in the water now, but neither man made any attempt to save themselves. They sat close together, the dog beside them, and a shaft of early sunlight reflected off something in Carter's hand. A bottle?

Marie lowered the glasses. She could have sworn they were laughing.

EPILOGUE

Marie sat down and sighed. 'Gary's found himself a nice little bungalow out on the edge of my village. He's going to be moving on, Jackman. I'll miss him.'

'More to the point, you are going to miss his cooking.' Jackman grinned at her.

'Don't worry, we've already arranged a regular weekly get-together, and he's going to rustle up whatever I want.'

'Spoilt woman.'

'Spoilt in more ways than one. Did you hear that Robbie is going back to Spain to see Harvey Cash?'

'Really?'

'He's talked to him on the phone, and he thinks Harvey's changed since he admitted what Suzanne did to him. Robbie reckons it was a cathartic experience. He thinks that Harvey deserves a proper explanation, and maybe some help to get on top of his drinking. So, he's taking a short holiday in Sanxenxo.' Her smile widened. 'And he's asked me to go with him.'

'That's the best news I've heard in ages. Good for you.'

'You'll cope without us?'

'I'll try.'

She looked around the office. There was something different about it. She looked again and saw that the picture of Glory, Jackman's old horse, had been moved to the wall behind the desk, and in its place hung an old and rather faded watercolour.

Intrigued, Marie went to look at it. It showed an old man, his dog beside him, pulling a salmon from a landing net in a river. 'He looks just like Silas Breeze.' She looked at Jackman, her head tilted slightly to one side.

'It's called "The Poacher," so no wonder you made the connection.'

Three bodies had been recovered by the Underwater Search and Recovery Diving Unit. Carter McLean, Silas Breeze, and Klink the dog. The Eva May had broken up, and since she was no danger to other vessels, she had been left to lie where she was.

'Where did the picture come from?'

Jackman took out his phone and scrolled through the received messages. He passed it to Marie.

"Please collect parcel behind seat of Land Rover. Take care of it for us."

'Carter?'

'Yes. I'll probably never find out why it was so important to him. I'm certain there is a story attached to it, but it's a kind of bequest, so . . .'

'Have you received the Marine Accident Investigation report yet?'

Jackman evidently didn't want to say. 'You won't hurt me, you know,' said Marie. 'The facts will help me put this whole horrible affair into perspective, then I can file it away and move on.'

'They discovered several places in the hull that had recently been "doctored."' Jackman looked thoroughly miserable. 'He rigged it so that a series of bungs could be removed. It was a deliberate sinking.'

Marie nodded. 'I thought I'd imagined it. So what I saw was true. They were drinking together when she went down.'

'Confirmed by the bottle they found floating in the wreckage.' Jackman pointed to a file that was lying on his desk. 'Are you sure you are ready for this, Marie? It doesn't have to be dealt with now.'

'I think it does. Let's put it to rest, shall we?'

'The post-mortem confirmed that Professor Sam Page was absolutely correct. Carter did have a lesion in the temporal lobe of his brain. It may have been there for a very long time, or it could have been a result of the concussion. Whatever, it was probably inoperable. If he'd known, or if any of us had guessed, maybe . . .'

'We can't turn the clock back, sir. Carter made his choice. I don't think the tumour would have affected his decision in the end.'

'Probably not.' Jackman looked up. 'The authorities have disregarded the letter that he left. He confessed to killing Suzanne Holland because she was an emotional and abusive bully. He was on duty when she died, and the diaries prove it. The ACC suspects it was an attempt to protect one of his friends, probably Tom Holland.'

Marie wondered. Carter had lied so much that she was no longer sure what the truth was.

'In the light of what has happened, the investigation has been scaled right down. It has been decided that the witness statement about the two men arguing gives credence to the fact that someone attacked her and took her body away. Rory's re-examination of the blood evidence also indicates that she died in the house. It's also likely that her body was disposed of by person or persons unknown. As everyone who might have been a suspect is now dead, the super says we don't have the resources to take it further at this time.'

Marie nodded. 'I think she's right, don't you? Time to call it a day.' After a moment she asked, 'How is the super?

How did she take the revelation that Carter was behind Leah's stalking?'

Jackman pulled a face. 'Non-committal. She told me that it was in nobody's interest to make anything of it since Carter has died. She saw no reason to do any further damage to his reputation. And then she told me not to mention it again. Case closed.'

In the ensuing silence, Marie found herself wondering what she thought she'd seen, moments before the old life-boat sunk. Had they been lowering something over the side, or had they simply been adjusting something on the Eva May herself? Maybe even preparing to sink her? She looked across the desk. 'Can I ask you a question, Jackman?'

He looked at her intently. 'Of course.'

'Have you ever, how can I put it . . . ? Let sleeping dogs lie?' He thought for a while. Marie suspected he was thinking of a particular occasion.

'Yes, I have.' He raised one eyebrow. 'Is there anything you'd like to share?'

Marie smiled back. 'No, nothing. Absolutely nothing.'

THE END

ALSO BY JOY ELLIS

JACKMAN & EVANS

NIKKI GALENA SERIES

DETECTIVE MATT BALLARD

STANDALONES

Join our mailing list to be the first to hear about Joy Ellis's next mystery, coming soon!

www.joffebooks.com

Thank you for reading this book. If you enjoyed it please leave feedback on Amazon or Goodreads, and if there is anything we missed or you have a question about then please get in touch. The author and publishing team appreciate your feedback and time reading this book.